D0523898

Also by Rick Moody

Garden State
The Ice Storm

THE RING

of BRIGHTEST

ANGELS Around

HEAVEN

A Novella and Stories

RICK MOODY

07463125

An *Abacus* Book

First published in the United States of America
by Little, Brown and Company 1995
First published in Great Britain by Abacus 1996
This edition published by Abacus 1998

A CIP catalogue record for this book is
available from the British Library.

'Twister' and 'The Ring of Brightest Angels Around Heaven' first
appeared in *The Paris Review*; 'The James Dean Garage Band' first
appeared in *Esquire*; 'Pip Adrift' first appeared in *Story*; 'The Grid'
first appeared in *Harper's*; and 'Phrase Book' first appeared in
Mississippi Mud.

ISBN 0 349 10835 8

Printed and bound in Great Britain by Clays Ltd, St Ives plc

Abacus
A Division of
Little, Brown and Company (UK)
Brettenham House
Lancaster Place
London WC2E 7EN

For John Hawkes

CONTENTS

THE RING
of BRIGHTEST
ANGELS Around
HEAVEN

THE
PRELIMINARY
NOTES

1   I began recording my wife's telephone calls without
her knowledge the Monday after the third weekend in April
1993.

1.1   I used twin Panasonic SP-77 dual-cassette answering
machine systems that were nestled on a wooden filing cabinet
(cherry, with a dark finish) here in my office. There was one
machine for my line and one machine for my wife's line. They
were each resting there on the filing cabinet, an antique that I
bought in Chester one Sunday after we were married — during
the first intoxicating month of our union. The filing cabinet
was flush against the wall by my desk. The office was, and is
now, situated just down the hall from the kitchen, on the first
floor. Its decorations were simple and unobtrusive and included a pair of cheap, imitation African masks and a poster for
an exhibition by an artist I once met playing squash (a misty
New England harbor dotted with seacraft). That morning, in
my office, there was robust sunlight from two sides: north and
east.

1.11   When her telephone rang I simply engaged her answering machine — the one that collected *her* messages — in the usual fashion. Normally I kept the volume on the machines turned down to a murmur so as not to distract me from my professional responsibilities. This habit had the coincident value, that morning, of concealing my activities. There was the cloak of silence. I was therefore able to accomplish three objectives: 1) to record my wife's conversations; 2) to conceal this recording from my wife; and 3) to leave myself free to make a living. It was simple. If we are considering the technology involved, it was simple. In one instant the machine was off and in the next it was on.

1.12   Later, with similar calls, I found that if I was busy I kept the volume on her machine turned down entirely. I simply depressed the "record" button on a small remote-control device whenever her line rang. I studied the contents of the first call, as I did with others, when I had quality time — usually in the evenings, with a glass of wine (I'm a collector) when my wife was out and our child was asleep. Then I would engage the CD player on repeat mode with a stack of baroque anthems while I drank California chardonnays and played the incoming message cassette from my wife's answering machine. I had an inexpensive "box"-style tape player for the "playback" of these low-fidelity recordings.

1.121   Certain passages from these tapes I repeated, certain important moments from important conversations — just as I repeated the CDs of baroque music (*Die Kunst der Fuge,* the *Water Music*) — relentlessly, until the meters and stresses of my wife's conversations, her assonances and dissonances, her melodies and harmonies, her euphorias and dysphorias, her inhalations and exhalations, her strophes and antistrophes, her caesurae and enjambments, her melancholies and exuberances, her appointments and disappointments were as complex and enthralling as the finest love lyrics. When I had reached this critical moment with these passages, I went on to play them still more until I had exhausted all meaning in them, until I, too, was depleted and confused. My feelings had a tortuous progress. At the completion of each such evening, I made an observation to myself. Aloud, I said, *I'm going to fix her ass in court.*

1.2   As I have made clear, I was working that morning. I was in fact composing a report about a woman from Parsippany who had fallen in the lobby of a local department store. The tilework in the lobby had been slick from a late winter storm. The customers had tracked in some portion of the slush — as they could not help but do. The success of department stores depends on this kind of traffic, and only the most vigilant maintenance could have prevented the fateful accumulation of moisture. The woman, who was carrying home a teal bathroom throw rug (high pile) in a bright blue department store plastic shopping bag (large size), a bag emblazoned with the store logo, went into a skid in the lobby, on the aforementioned precipitation, within the purview of onlookers, the bag spilling its contents out onto the muddy entryway, befouling her brand new purchase, humiliating the woman in question, tearing a ragged seven-inch rip in her puce housedress and multiply fracturing her hip. It must have been really painful.

1.21   My work in the case consisted of studying the surface of the tiles in that lobby, their tendency to promote pedestrian hydroplaning in inclement weather and their converse relative safety when covered in high-density anti-skid textured rubber matting. (No matting was present on the day in question.) This kind of technical reasoning I then rigorously organized into an opinion, given orally or in deposition, such that my client — the firm of D'Antonio, Frost, and Berkoff — could bring a negligence suit against Caldor, the department store in question, on behalf of Mrs. Hilda Rodale of Parsippany, N.J., the woman with the bad hip. From a professional point of view, I was interested in questions like viscosity and drag and the melting points of sleet and freezing rain. Which is to say that my vocation was and is the vocation of *engineer as expert witness* in cases of negligence and/or personal injury.

1.3   I was attempting to write the report about the Parsippany case when the telephone rang. It was April 19, a Monday. Maybe 7:45 A.M. The technological possibilities of dual-cassette answering machines presented themselves to me that morning with a crystalline simplicity. The only surprise, really, was that I hadn't thought of these possibilities sooner. I heard my wife pick up the telephone. In the kitchen. Just down the hall. Her machine was usually on — she left it on in order to *give me space* — but that morning for some reason just the opposite was true. The cat had walked across the machine, possibly, padded across its keypad in one of its evening strolls. Or perhaps my boy — who was prohibited from entering my office under any circumstances except by verbal invitation *extended by me* — had been exploring.

1.31   Whichever the cause, I simply turned on my wife's machine. Though she was down the hall. That is, I heard her voice. I glanced at the lowboy. I scrambled for the remote control, which was in my pen drawer next to my supply of high polymer erasers.

1.32   The "record" button on the answering machine lit up promptly. Whereas the machine would not otherwise have recorded the call — since my wife had lifted the receiver, theoretically disengaging the recording head — it now recorded this conversation in full. My feeling is that Panasonic often manufactures reliable and sturdy electronic products. Their warranties are good. In this instance, the recording indicator lit up as it was designed to do and the recording head met the surface of the metallic tape as it was designed to do and the tape collected the call, regardless of the ethics entailed in my recording it. I turned up the volume a bit so that I could hear more than the sleepy burbling of her voice from the kitchen. I turned it up loud enough *so that I could hear.*

1.321   It goes without saying that the calls I was able to tape were those calls that took place during hours when my wife and I were together on the premises. That is, in all the instances herein described I was present to engage the telephone answering system. I had to be at home. I wouldn't have been able to engage it, for example, from the Radio Shack in Chester. Therefore, any conversations in which my wife was totally alone are absent from this description of my activities.

1.33   It was a man's voice. On Monday. The voice of her interlocutor. It was the voice of a particular friend whom I knew well enough. A man. An acquaintance. You will think this was the reason for my concern. You will suppose that some suspicion of her *infidelity,* of her betrayal, of her expending somewhere the finite morsel of understanding she had been given to parcel out to me, her helpmeet, would be a cause for alarm, as would the way her voice dwindled down — as I was listening — to a hoarse whisper, but this was not the case at all. Evidence of an infidelity might certainly have *fixed her ass in court,* but from a personal point of view this unfaithfulness was a mushroom already affixed to an enduring rot. Still, I decided to prepare a label for this cassette that indicated time, date, name of caller, and (briefly) contents.

1.331   I could tell from his voice, however, that this person, this man, was a heavy smoker. I had met him at barbecues and cocktail parties and yet I hadn't noticed this particular quality before, his addiction. It was early in the morning — as mentioned above — and already he evinced the muffled, cottony baritone of a seasoned nicotine addict. There was also the hacking cough. It wouldn't be long now before he had his own portable oxygen tank and a yellowed plastic feeder line to clamp onto his nose. I could see him dragging this oxygen tank (and feeder line and nose clamp) around on metal casters; lugging it upstairs, down escalators, through subway doors; believing a lie about his diminishing vigor. His death would be slow and uncomfortable. With the right lawyer, he could represent a fine product liability case.

1.4   However, at that moment I was mainly transfixed by the sudden fact of surveillance and by the sound of my wife's voice. My wife's voice when she did not know I was listening. My wife's voice at the moment when, with a sigh of relief, she announced to this man I have just described that I, her husband, was locked in my office *probably making rubber cement balls or jerking off or something.* I could hear her voice both in the kitchen (down the hall) and here in the office. At the same moment. There was a doubling of voices, a voice and its technological identical. These two wives of mine were in lockstep. They were in perfect unison though they represented entirely different motives: A) my wife in the kitchen was discreet about her troubles; B) my wife on the black, plastic Panasonic answering machine speaker was voluble, even melodramatic.

1.41   And, I should say, she was speaking on a cordless remote telephone, a Sony product (not at all as reliable as the AT&T model of similar design, but my wife had selected it herself). She could easily have walked down the hall into the office — while talking — and happened on the fact that I was recording her call, because the thrall, the swoon, the *cryogenic rigidity* of my eavesdropping prevented me from doing anything initially but noticing the situation and immersing myself in it. She would have known something was amiss, because I wasn't working, as I almost always was; she would have known because I couldn't even glance up at the color enlargements of our boy upon the corner of my desk. She would have known. It was only eleven feet six inches down that corridor.

1.42   Her voice on the line was *sad and lost.* The way you would expect a voice to sound while it is being surreptitiously recorded. Sadness, however, is part of the interpretive signal error of surveillance, and this interpretive effect should be alluded to and then discounted. Beneath my wife's superficial, technological melancholy, then, was a much clearer waveform, one I had never heard before. A sound beyond contempt, beyond frustration, a sound as new as the particularly singular call of the first emergency car alarm I ever heard (I was an early proponent of these alarms, because of my interest in security); as new as the overtones of a church choir ricocheting along chapel transverses. It was right after she said, *If I have to listen to him lecture me one more time — about anything — about how you shouldn't use more than one pillow or how you should always dry your feet thoroughly — or the importance of dental floss, just one more lecture, and I think I'll take the fucking extra pillow and stuff it over his face while he's sleeping.* Right after that, she began to weep.

1.421 Or to put it another way, she was, in the first moments of the tape, as I experienced her generally in the later years of our marriage — passionless, wan, older than she had once been, in sweatpants and lavender Converse All Stars and a turtleneck with little blue flowers on it, arrayed in mediocrities, in signs of a giving up that had taken place in her, displaying the slack of middle age, of ambitions dispensed with. These qualities permeated her enervated whisper at first. I recognized there also insoluble problems, insoluble domestic problems, problems so entrenched and implying such rueful options that *people were certain to get hurt.* But then she began to sob, and this anguished sound was far in excess of these other examples of hopelessness I've just catalogued. This was the passage I played over and over again. Gosh, it was really something.

1.5 While her boyfriend prattled on tautologically about how *marriage, well, is marriage, and it does pretty much what marriage is supposed to do* and *children, you know, they're children, and uh, well, they bounce back* in a way he must have imagined was supportive, my wife sobbed with such abandon that it was difficult for her to continue the conversation. Yet she managed not only to stay on the line but to *continue preparing breakfast.* I could hear the saucepans clanging and the refrigerator doors opening and closing. I could hear an egg timer. I could hear my child watching educational programming — as he was constrained to do according to a written contract he had signed. I could hear these things both through that tiny speaker and down the corridor that connected my office to the kitchen. Then, as the egg timer neared its bell, as the microwave finished bombarding the instant coffee, as breakfast, in fact, reached liftoff time, my wife gathered up her resolve. Her snuffling diminished. There was a pause, a breathless silence. Then my wife told her lover. *She had to leave me.*

2   I had become preoccupied with the Parsippany case.

2.1   I had been asked to look into the matter in late March by the firm of D'Antonio, Frost, and Berkoff. On the first weekend of April I drove to the Bergen Mall (taking Route 287 to I-80), with my boy, ostensibly to look at *weapons simulations systems* for his approaching birthday. I also intended to examine the foyer at Caldor. The day was wet and cool, but there were intervals of sunshine. We were driving a beige Oldsmobile Cutlass Supreme ('87) with sixty-eight thousand miles on it. To my boy I had said, *Son, come with your dad to Caldor and I will explain to you a few things about surface mechanics.* I dislike the emphasis on stockpiling loot at contemporary birthday parties and so I did not want to overindulge him with the promise of glittering prizes. It was to be a working holiday, but there would perhaps be a reward. My boy was obliging.

2.2   Technically, the situation with Mrs. Hilda Rodale was
no different from those complaints for which I had given testi-
mony in the past. My clients, the law firms themselves, often opposed large corporations, because — as Leonard D'Antonio had
explained it to me — these corporations had the resources. A
settlement of one or two hundred thousand dollars could impact
greatly on the lives of our injured parties, while, to a corporation
like Caldor, this money was — and here I use Mike Frost's
term — *chicken feed.* The lawyers themselves were paid by plain-
tiff contingent upon a favorable settlement. However, I was paid
regardless of the outcome. For some years, in spite of a declining
client base, the difficulty in obtaining payment, and bad fiscal
times in general, I had supported my family in this way.

2.21   However, there was something different about the Parsippany case. I tried to explain it to my wife. One night, before
bed, as I folded my chinos and rugby shirt and set them on the
armchair next to our uncomfortably narrow mattress, I began
telling her about the last case, the prior case, the one before
Parsippany, the case in which the man had had his arm crushed
by a crane in Passaic, and then I told her about the two boys who
were electrocuted by the video game at the arcade in Nutley and
about the cancer clusters around the particularly large satellite
dish outside the school in Peapack and about the Legionnaires'
disease outbreak that had killed seven at the Cape May Ramada
and about the red tide, the nuclear effluents, the ultra-high-
frequency wave emissions. I was telling her about my work. I
was trying to tell her. I was trying to make conversation.

2.22   And then I began to describe Mrs. Rodale's case. I told
my wife how Mrs. Rodale ·had made her purchase at Caldor

after seeing, in all likelihood, an advertising circular in her Sunday paper (the *North Jersey Herald and Tribune*), how Mrs. Rodale had braved threatening weather to go to Caldor that day, and how this evidence suggested she *really needed* her teal bathroom throw rug. Mrs. Rodale had parked (I'd learned) at some distance from the entrance to the store itself, and was intent upon hurrying back to her car after her purchase. Perhaps she had met someone in the store, someone she knew, who had described the size, scale, and menace of the blizzard, which was just then heading our way from the Great Lakes region. Whatever the case (I told my wife), Mrs. Rodale, with bathroom rug in hand, was simply hoping to make it home *in one piece* when she began her passage across the lobby of Caldor. She believed at that moment that her interests as a good-faith patron of Caldor were identical with the interests of store management. She believed the premises were safe or at least not gauntlets of danger. And then, I told my wife, just as the wet and really heavy snow had begun to fall (eventually there would be an accumulation of fifteen inches), and thus just as it was beginning to be tracked in the west wing entrance of Caldor, just then, as onlookers *like stunned livestock* gazed abstractly upon her, Mrs. Rodale, in a puce housedress, beige raincoat, and practical but slightly elevated pumps, went into her epic skid.

2.23   When Hilda came to rest (I told my wife), with her possessions scattered in a semicircle around her, with her dress torn, with her car parked *on the open-air level of the parking facility,* when Hilda arrived at that moment — disoriented, injured, and alone — she tried to stand. Imagine. She was *in shock.* She was confused. Her children had no idea where she was; *she* had no idea where she was. There was just this feeling in her of a primitive and urgent *tardiness*. She had to get home. She had to make things right. She stood. And in this way she learned that her femur and her hip were severely compromised by the fall. In fact, a young boy alerted her to the situation, pointing and crying aloud as she struggled upward and then collapsed, *Her bone's sticking out!* — this according to Mrs. Rodale's deposition. There was her ear-piercing cry of pain. A stretcher arrived.

2.24   But just as I was describing the arrival of the stretcher, the sound of sirens, my wife announced that she would hear no more. Abruptly she informed me, *No more tragedies before bed, sweetheart,* she said, and there was an exhaustion to her voice, *I mean I know things haven't been going well with us, let's be honest, you know and I know things haven't been going well, I feel like I haven't talked to you in months, but I just can't listen to this, I just can't. You have to try to think about my feelings once in a while — for a change — I just don't want to hear about it. You've got to try.*

2.241   And her language was remarkably similar in her call of 4.24.93, 6:15 P.M., again to her nameless and chain-smoking paramour: *I used to think he was funny. I mean I used to think the way he thought about things was funny, like he would tell me about some guy whose leg got crushed by a steel girder and I would think it was funny, but I just can't listen to it anymore. I don't know it's not funny like it used to be. We used all of that up . . .*

2.3   Three days after the bedside heart-to-heart with my wife, I stood in the mall entrance with my boy. The following were my instructions to him: *Son, on a straight line from that circular door to this glass one by the perfume department how many steps do you think it is? How many steps do you think Mrs. Rodale had to undertake to safely reach the department store? Go ahead, go count them out. Go ahead.*

2.4   In the foyer, he looked up at me hesitantly. (It happened that at this time my son's feet were exactly eight inches long, at least when armored in his light-up, pump-style basketball sneakers. I had measured.) A throng of shoppers rushed past, in pursuit of advertised specials for anti-freeze and self-lighting charcoal briquettes. In the midst of this throng, my son held his ground. One mustachioed shopper, however, actually shoved my boy. By being stationary, I could now see, he had emerged as a foyer hazard, and with his lost and plaintive countenance he *could* eventually create a disturbance and thereby draw the attention of Caldor plainclothes security squads. I had to intervene — though I had intended just then to use the beaker I was holding to collect a sample of precipitation from just inside the revolving doors. I also had on my person a Minolta fully automatic 35-millimeter camera and a Dictaphone (Sony). However, it was obvious that I needed to exercise some leadership where my boy was concerned. *Go on!* I cajoled. *Go on, Son! It's all right.* And then, thoughtfully, ungracefully, he began to count the steps, heel to toe, heel to toe, heel to toe. Twenty-one feet eight inches, roughly, or thirty-two and a half sneaker lengths.

2.5   When he had completed his measurements, I exhorted my son to make a return trip to the revolving door — where I was standing — *in a sprint*. On the slickest portion of the floor, in front of Caldor. Perhaps it seems unwise now. Nevertheless,

I will say that my boy seemed intrigued by this part of the investigation. Like a real trooper, he set up at the revolving door, grimaced impressively, made fists of his slender hands, and dashed headlong into the crowd. My arms were outstretched. I was grateful for his devotion to me. I was grateful to have a son.

2.6   *When I saw him too begin to go down,* therefore, when I saw it in the sort of stop-motion footage with which it would have appeared in court, on quarter-inch videotape, as the plaintiffs and defendants processed and recessed, when I saw his feet begin to go out from under him, when I saw that his far-too-baggy denim jeans were caught under one sneaker, when I saw that he was tumbling into the shins of a large woman in seamed stockings carrying a basketball in a hexagonal box, when I saw this woman also beginning to fall, taking with her her wailing daughter, as though they were leashed one to the other, when I saw the two of them land fully upon my boy, when I saw his glasses fall from his face and skitter end over end, when I saw his hand reaching in my direction, and I heard his muted voice cry out, calling *Daddy, Daddy,* I knew at once that I had made a mistake. I was a dangerous man.

2.61   From the tape of 5.16.93, 7:13 P.M., containing, among other things, a conversation between my wife and her mother (I have slightly digested this excerpt): . . . *and you wouldn't believe the shit he does, you wouldn't believe it! Takes the kids out to go to the zoo or so he says and then he's taking them to some scrap metal dump or something that he's supposed to be working on for money, like one time he took Cassidy to the Bergen Mall for some stupid case and made him run through the uh through the entranceway so that he could see how easily his own son slipped, which Cassidy did, he slipped and banged up his* *knee pretty badly and afterwards, get this, he feels repentant so he offers* *to give Cassidy a Dictaphone! Can you believe it? And not a new one* *either! His* own *goddamned Dictaphone!*

2.611   When a tape was filled with recorded calls, I stored it in a nondescript Banana Republic bag and locked it in my wine cellar in the basement. My wife was not in the habit of drinking wine unless I offered to select a bottle for her. Her palate, in this area, was not developed, especially as to aroma and flavor. The key to the wine cellar was on a nondescript key ring of useless, dummy keys that I kept in the top right-hand drawer of my desk. I believed that this was a secure location. I believed that my wife respected this as my private domain. At least until Memorial Day Weekend of 1993, that is, when I, attempting to stem the course of my lassitude (my inability to progress beyond anything more than preliminary notes in the case of Rodale vs. Caldor, my compulsion to take *power walks* up Birch Lane, in which I listened to selected conversations — greatest hits — of my wife on a compilation tape inserted into a Sports Walkman), decided to go to a barbecue at my neighbor's. My wife then apparently located the keys in my desk, found the correct key among the dummies, unlocked the wine cellar cabinet, and searched the cabinet for a handgun she believed that I was still keeping in that formerly secure location. I had disposed of this gun years ago. Instead of locating my .45, however, and my stockpile of ammunition, she found the tapes. After which, she left me.

2.6111   Just as I listened to her voice, then, to the melody of its hardships, to the way it praised my absences, *so then did my wife listen to her own voice.* As I reconstruct it, she selected a tape from the overfilled Banana Republic bag in the basement, carried this tape to the inexpensive "box"-style tape player that was usually stored on a shelf by the upstairs bath, fitted it into the left-hand "playback" deck, depressed the red "play" button, waited for the leader tape to play through, and then *heard her own voice* emerge from the tape. (In all likelihood, it was the May 14th, 2:45 P.M., conversation between my wife and her friend Debby, which filled an entire sixty-minute cassette. Later I found the case for this tape by the tub.) *I thought I knew the guy when we got married but I don't think I know him at all, you know? I don't know what he does in there in his office or where he goes half the time and I don't care anymore. I just feel like puking all the time. I never figured you could live with someone and know so little about them and the more you know the more it's a mystery. It's enough to make you sick to your stomach . . .*

2.6112 She never mentioned finding the tapes to me. One morning, on a leisurely reconnaissance mission, I simply found that the Banana Republic bag was gone. Along with my bullets.

2.7   After the first trip to the mall, I began to look for biographical correlations between my life and the life of Mrs. Rodale of Parsippany. I found, for example, that Mrs. Hilda Rodale was a drinking woman. (She admits as much in her deposition to Leonard D'Antonio of April 1, 1993.) With this information, it would be possible, inductively, to formulate some likely ancillary symptoms of her illness. Tax evasion, e.g., check kiting, frequent lateness, abject culinary failure, credit card abuse, preoccupation with Smarties and other disagreeable candies, impulsive indulgence of her boy and girl, late nights with friends, late mornings with headaches, and sullen moods. After which she would drink again. I imagined her drinking on the nights she was paid, and on the days before payday. I imagined her drinking when praising her children and drinking when beating them. She was a woman who drank. The evidence was everywhere. In fact I could posit her drinking simply based on the pattern of her regular audits by the Internal Revenue Service — five years running.

2.71   My wife was a drinking woman too. I do not have a complete chart of my wife's alcohol consumption over the month in which I tape-recorded her telephone calls. But I can do a thumbnail analysis here. She drank between one and three vodka and tonics some nights after the children were in bed. And, since she is just over five feet and weighs about one hundred pounds except in the third week of her menstrual cycle, this is more than enough to intoxicate her on a regular basis — taking as a bottom line for argument a one-jigger-of-hard-alcohol-per-hour intoxication model, derived from my vigilant observations of levels of bottles and numbers of empties.

2.711   On nights when I have been out with her at her bars, inns, public houses, taverns, etc., where I refused to accompany my wife on her vapid missions of fellowship with her vapid friends, and their vapid folk music and vapid covers of songs from the god-awful nineteen-sixties and nineteen-seventies, she could often drink much more. On one occasion, I had to carry her from a bar. This was when we were courting and her eyes were lively and I was willing to try new things. In the flush of love, I was perhaps more flexible than later on. In general, however, in a bar setting my wife drank between three and five drinks, between two and four nights a week. I would need a good algorithm to exactly describe the curve of her increased tolerance. Later, I was no longer invited on these journeys, and I would wait up for my wife. Later still, I slept through her evenings out. I had been drinking myself.

2.7111 I hoped, with the tape recordings of my calls, to better chart the pattern of my wife's intoxication and thus to *fix her ass in court*. I was looking not only for conversations in which she said, *Ohmygod I'm so hungover*, or *You wouldn't believe what I drank last night*, or *Have you seen my purse?* or *What was it I said? I can't believe what I said!* or even the heartbreaking *If you lived with him you'd drink too*, but also conversations in which she alluded to dabblings in controlled substances such as marijuana, cocaine, and so forth. I was looking for evidence of crimes I hadn't even considered, such as fraud, child abuse, sex crimes, orgies; I was looking for all conversation that took place exclusive of me, for the moment when I had been erased from my wife's conversations, and in this pursuit I scoured the tapes, hustling from one to another with the cassette boxes scattered around me on the floor of the living room (had my son been sleepless for any reason he would certainly have wondered why *Mommy's voice was coming from the stereo*), but I never found this moment, this moment of my absence, because, after all, it was missing.

2.7112 Ultimately, through this system of uncanny parallels, we arrive at the most important question about the Parsippany case, a question which came to me on Wednesday, April 21, three days before my son's birthday, two days after I had begun taping my wife's calls. I had spent the morning reshelving and realphabetizing my books, the books here in my office. I had done no work on the Parsippany case. I had avoided returning the calls from the firm of D'Antonio, Frost, and Berkoff. I remember that the shadows of afternoon sun through the trees were oppressive to me. When my wife's line rang, again, with the dreadful consistency with which it was ringing at that time, I simply unpocketed the remote control, which I kept on me at all times. However, the accumulation of tapes no longer satisfied me. Not really. My shelves had an insidious layer of dust. I had neglected to make use of the small maize-colored whisk broom with which I kept my office spotless. Still, I was working my way through the science section, through some books on basic circuitry, which I had clearly shelved haphazardly (unless there had been a visitor unknown to me going through my library), when the question came to me. *Where was Mr. Rodale?*

2.8   I am a crack researcher. I am attentive to details. I can draw a straight line with a free hand that diverges no more than a sixteenth of an inch. I can read a circuit diagram. Within minutes, I was poring over Mrs. Rodale's deposition (Express Mailed to me on the first day of April), all seventy-five pages of it, glancing here at a description of her bathroom throw rug, here at a description of her car. I was so engrossed in the deposition that when my wife called down the hall to say that she was going to the shopping center to look for a new baseball glove for our son, I didn't even grunt from beyond my closed door. Mrs. Rodale had a boy, Peter, 13, with Hodgkin's disease, and she had a daughter, Marilynne, 11, and she had a cat, Pussywillow, but there was no mention of a husband, of a wedding ceremony, of a day in May when blossoms had blossomed and vows had seemed like poetry. Perhaps Mr. Rodale was just a retiring sort. But I knew better. There was a pattern to loss, I knew, as there was a pattern in fractals, as there was a pattern to the way city planners designed public spaces, as there was a pattern to the orbit of heavenly bodies, to the distribution of stars rushing outwards from a first infinitely dense singularity, there was a pattern to loss. Losses came in threes. Losses were inexplicable. Losses could be contained and controlled in the elegance of equations.

3   At my son's birthday, I was a dutiful and attentive parent.

3.1   Two days prior to this natal anniversary, the day of celebration, I journeyed again to Caldor, at the Bergen Mall. It was late afternoon. We were there, my son and I, to finish selecting a gift, or a series of gifts if appropriate, for my son's birthday, a process that had remained incomplete since our last outing. I remained committed to something relatively wholesome, something without too many moving parts — like a pump-action BB gun, or a G.I. Joe action figure. That was what I told Cassidy, at least, but my passage across that foyer, my passage into Caldor, my passage into the main arcade of the mall and then into Toys Я Us, into the throbbing corpus of capitalism, was impossibly slow, as though Mrs. Rodale's own meaty hands held me back. It was clear that shopping, again, would have to take a backseat to my professional obligations. I found myself pacing restlessly back and forth in front of the stuccoed foyer mural of American ethnicities pushing, as one, a gigantic shopping cart. I had believed that my burden had been lightened by the understanding that Mrs. Rodale and my wife were one and the same character, and yet I was still haunted by the question of Mr. Rodale, in the way that Heisenberg must have been haunted in the instants before formulating his renowned Uncertainty Principle, and so I decided to *call* Mrs. Rodale, (908) 588-6235, *evenings and weekends best.*

3.11   This was contrary to all the guidelines that had been established for me as an independent contractor (expert witness) in the employ of D'Antonio, Frost, and Berkoff. I was to have no truck with the plaintiffs whatsoever; I was to route my opinion through Leonard D'Antonio's assistant; I was to keep my investigations brief and to the point; I was to incur a minimum of expenses. It was likewise contrary to my own view of my profession. I considered myself to be a man of the law — detached, rigorous, incisive. I suppose, however, that I was moving into a transitional period. I had become an annoyance to my family (to my son standing absently at my side sucking on a curl from his far too long strawberry-blond mop) and to the society of the Bergen Mall, and to the ethical bodies of the legal community. I had become unsure of myself. So I decided to act. I dialed the twenty-five digits necessary to charge the call to my MCI credit card. And then I waited. And then I drummed on the side of the AT&T model pay phone with a Magic Marker emblazoned with my own name. I had bought four hundred such pens ten years ago to give away to clients. I had bought them in the first flush of my marriage, when my wife was rosy-cheeked and carrying our boy. By my current estimates, I still had more than three hundred and twenty pens.

3.12   Mrs. Rodale was not at home. Her answering machine, an antiquated dual-cassette recording model with heavy distortion on the out-going message, featured a voice gruff, ill-tempered, and clipped — (908) 588-6235, *leave a message . . .* I learned much just from the sound of that voice. I could hear the reverberations of difficulty there, I could hear the bitterness of fiscal hardship. There was a certain way her voice trailed off at the end like a violin plummeting down through the melody of some baroque canon, there was the trauma of her accident and the difficulty of a life in which all is amortization; it was a life without a mate; it was a life of single parenthood, with its impossible list of chores and appointments. Just as I was doing a thumbnail sketch of her hospital charges (emergency admission, prelim. examination, semi-priv. room, anesthesia, surgery, artificial ball socket, cast, phys. therapy), I heard the apocalyptic beep.

3.13   *Son,* I said to my son, because he was tugging on the hem of my khaki trousers, *go look at the Sega display. Go look at the Gulf War simulation game if you want. Pick the finest game. Be a good comparison shopper. Whatever you want, Son, I love you.* And then I uncupped the mouthpiece and to the machine I said (as fast as possible, in case it was a model with a maximum-response time), *Mrs. Rodale, you don't know me, but I am the expert witness in the case being prepared by the firm of D'Antonio, Frost, and Berkoff, pursuant to your action against the department store called Caldor, pursuant to your fall and injury on March 13, 1993, and I have followed the details of your case very closely, I mean that I have been out to the Bergen Mall several times, in fact I am here now, and I just have a couple of questions I'd like to ask you, Mrs. Rodale, on the subject of the deposition which you have filed concerning the case, on the report which you deposed, Mrs. Rodale, I just have a few questions I would like to ask you . . . about the nature of your fall, Mrs. Rodale, and, for example, about your recovery? Has your recovery been difficult and which parts of it exactly have been difficult? Physically which parts of your body have been longest in healing? And emotionally speaking, have you found that your family has been there for you? And where was your husband at the time, Mrs. Rodale, at the time of your fall? Was your husband no longer at home? And what would have induced him to be with you at the time? What would have induced him to traverse the locations of separation which I assume have come to characterize your marriage, Mrs. Rodale? What would have made it impossible for him to avoid coming to your side, Mrs. Rodale? What language, what sequence of words, might you have used to per-suade him? Couldn't you have asked him to come, Mrs. Rodale? Can't you enlighten me on this, Mrs. Rodale? How alone were you at the time? Couldn't you have asked him? Couldn't you have made it clearer? Mrs. Rodale, don't tell me you couldn't have made it work. Don't tell me.* Or this is close to the text of my message, though, as you can imagine I am not in possession of this tape and never was. As a historical footnote, it is worth adding here that Mrs. Rodale did not return my call.

3.2   I bought my son a wealth of high-technology video game products, for example, a Sega Genesis game system bundled with the popular role-playing game *Mortal Kombat,* as well as a CD-ROM player with a copy of *Fall of the House of Usher.* I charged such a wealth of digital goods for my boy, all of them involving the evisceration, murder, and/or imprisonment for life of wanton criminals. He couldn't believe his good fortune. He was trembling with excitement. He didn't notice, for example, that I was completely silent on the ride home, a ride that took place at dusk, in the cover of enveloping darkness, and that, beside the Morristown Historic State Park, in deeper night, at exactly 55 miles per hour, in perfect silence, I experienced the realization that very soon I was to live alone.

3.3   The cake was a vanilla-with–chocolate swirl interior (Duncan Hines), iced with chocolate, decorated with pink and lavender roses and white hand-lettering — *Happy B'day, Cassidy, Ten Yrs Old!* I lettered it myself. I actually used a stencil system as well as a straight edge to make sure that the penmanship was exemplary. And I had held my wife around the waist as she took the cake pans from the oven (using two potholders in the shape of lobster claws) and I said, *Honey, those look fantastic!* and her waist was small, as I remembered it from when we were closer, and her hair, which was tied back in a kerchief, was the color of honey in morning sun and I made her give me the knife to lick the frosting from it and the sweetness in my mouth was like flowers on fresh landfill and we watched from the couch as our boy opened his gifts and turned on the Zenith wide-screen television or plugged in the CD-ROM player and I could tell that my wife was uncomfortable, or at least I had an idea that she was. It was almost eleven years now we had been married and I knew her finally, better than I had ever known her before, and in the future I would know her even better, I would know all 360 degrees of her, because I would know at last her contempt, the contempt that comes with giving up. I leaned over to put my arms around her. Gently, decisively, silently, with one palm in the center of my chest, she resisted.

4   The next morning, a Monday, I resolved to *fix her ass in court. A week had passed.* It was April 26; the notes for the Parsippany report were in disarray on my desk, two weeks

overdue, probably always to be unfinished. Having snacked at 6:00 A.M., on canteloupe, in a solitude that was quaintly predictive, I was stunned out of an unpleasant revery about my estimated quarterly income taxes. The phone had rung. Her line. I reached without hesitation for the remote control recording device in my desk. Next to the erasers. The "record" light. My loss. The music of her voice.

THE
GRID

Inside, in the warm light of contemporary domesticity, her roommate is talking long-distance to the first boy she ever kissed. She's talking while vengefully chasing their cats, the cordless phone cradled like a papoose at an interstice of ear and hand and shoulder. We can just make out the melody of her joy. We are standing outside under the window, on the front step. There's not much more to the tableau than this. The screen in the window above us is frayed; the paint on the sill is peeling. Crumbling masonry. A taxi eases by, prowling. There's a profusion of couples and dog walkers on the block — dog walkers with those little rodents that pass here for *canis familiaris*. A siren passes — Doppler-style — down Seventh Avenue.

And it's late and we have to work tomorrow and we are in our twenties and *we too* are about to kiss. We are going to kiss one another for the first time. The arrangement of our faces and noses, whether there is a complete mutuality to our kiss, whether particles are trapped between our teeth, whether she will action-paint me with lipstick — these are some of the variables of the instant. Do I let my palm rest lightly on her shoulder, on the right angle of her black pullover sweater? Do I pull her to me, gently? Do I let her pull me closer? It seems easy enough to do, to kiss her, as I have kissed others, but even so, the implications of the practice expand around us, like the spirits of our baptized ancestors, like airborne pollutants. There are legislative issues surrounding us, there are sociological and aesthetic issues, there are issues of fashion. And then there's this awkward personal stuff.

Later, for example, she will believe that her lips yielded too easily during this kiss, that she didn't react with an equal and opposite *frontal lip force coefficient*. A kiss, she thinks, has to be entirely balanced — it has to have a little conflict, a little dialectic, a little revolution. And since in her view this particular kiss didn't have these things she will worry that she doesn't know how to kiss a boy, really, or anyone else, that her mouth is unaccustomed to the proximity of other mouths, and this worry will trouble her on the afternoons when she should be working on her dissertation. During a period in which we are again briefly dating she will ask me to teach her how to kiss. I will spend a number of evenings with my mouth open trying to instruct and be kissed at the same time, my lips painfully chapped as a result. *No, it's better if you move really slowly at first. Slower, even. Right, good.* Initially, during these lessons, her tongue will just swab at my lips, as if she's taking a tissue sample from me, but then she will learn to dart with it, to dart lustfully. It will be late on a Saturday night when the meaning of lust will come to her and at the same time the couple in the next apartment will be fucking. Through the wall: *yes, oh, faster, oh yes, oh God, oh, yes, yes, deeper, oh yes.* She will learn to kiss and she will take these lessons in kissing and put them to good use with someone else.

The frayed screen in the window above where we are standing will be the weak link later when her apartment, this very apartment, is robbed. By then, however, this woman I am about to kiss will have moved elsewhere with her new girlfriend, her girl lover. A different tenant will have undergone the ritual initiation of looking at the space and signing the lease and repainting. This new inhabitant will be different in every way, blond and completely heterosexual, or so she will say, and successful, at least in the accumulation of things. A professional woman, a financial analyst downtown. Her specialty: the energy industry. At work she will have an aged bumper sticker on her Quotron machine that says *More people died in Ted Kennedy's car than at Three Mile Island.* One night while this analyst, Nina, is in a bar on the Upper East Side with a guy wearing a Jerry Garcia tie, a guy who mousses his hair and drives a Jeep Wrangler, her apartment — frayed screen and open window serving as the method of ingress — will be robbed.

In the bar, in fact, she will be having a first kiss with this trader, and the lighting will be low, and she will be playing with the wax on the table candle, and then they will reach for one another — their hands crawling across the table, fingers meshing; their faces falling together; their lips colliding — and she will feel a ripple of contentment for a second that will spike through her like 220 volts of household current. This electromagnetic pulse will come to rest in her spine, and it will feel great, even if she's had too many margaritas. At the same moment her CD player (but not her Joan Armatrading and

Shawn Colvin albums) and her personal computer (but not her Quicken software and Microsoft Works) and her jewelry (but not her Vermont teddy bear) will all be carried out the front door of her apartment and sold on the street. Other people, with their own indelibly memorable tales of first kisses, will then enjoy these fine personal effects.

The perpetrator of this felony will be Joe, who no longer makes love with his girlfriend, no longer disrobes in bed with her, no longer becomes aroused, no longer feels this high-pressure system of consolation, no longer recognizes that there is an equation in him that is balanced only by the presence of a certain kind of companionship, but who can, in the recesses of his semiconsciousness, *recall a first kiss on a really dark night in the Bronx when he was a little bit drunk and she was too and this kiss was so easy like slotting a diamond stylus into the grooves of an old LP.* This is the guy who will manhandle the dangerous cross-hatching of screen in the window of Nina's apartment. His first kiss with Joanne — who still lives with him — is always distant, always lost, always something from which he has lapsed or fallen. It is a hollow in him. To fill this abscess, he steals and then he cops and then, temporarily, the hollow is plugged — with an amber oblivion. Or at least this is the pattern until he gets clean and goes to *Narcotics Anonymous* and *Drugs Anonymous* and *Assholes Anonymous* as he calls it and relapses and relapses and relapses and causes the woman he loves a lot of heartache, so much that she eventually leaves, after which he goes to a halfway house and finds religion. But that's much later. On the night in question, the window in the apartment will be open and the early autumn breeze will be blowing through it and then Joe will empty out the premises.

One of the couples passing on the street that night — it's

almost one in the morning and Joe is standing on Sixteenth Street prying up the frayed and unwinding grid of the screen, crowbarring the window grating — will be Eleanor and Max. They will be walking home from a dinner party arguing vehemently about whether to have children now or later. At the party Eleanor will have loudly remarked to a friend that children were no more than *bloodthirsty dwarves* and this glib lie will have set Max off. As their arguments usually take place *sotto voce,* restrained to the point of whispering, Joe (looking for a good handhold just inside the windowsill) won't notice Max and Eleanor coming up the block. And anyway they will have become impenetrably quiet and regretful. Max would prefer to have children *now,* because his job is going badly. Eleanor totally disagrees. She will be holding his arm. They will proceed very slowly, both through the narrative of their argument and up the street, as if one of the burdens of disagreement were sluggishness.

And neither of them will know that they are each recollecting their first kiss, which took place in Baltimore seven years ago. They were students at Hopkins. At a pitcher party. All you can drink for five dollars. A number of the carousers there became sick. One woman, Nina, visiting a frat boy for the weekend, had to have her stomach pumped. Eleanor and Max didn't get sick, however. They just kissed. It was a sloppy kiss — it tasted of beer and pizza and cigarettes and there was a platoon of wasted school chums egging them on — but when they were through with it, when Max let go of the back of her head, let go of that handful of her blond hair, when their lips parted, when the music on the sound system unaccountably lapsed, they *laughed.* It was the most incredible laugh — for both of them — it contained all the tonal shades of laughter, the sputtering of wonder, the chuckle of discovery, the guffaw at the idea of not being a kid and not being alone, of being part of some larger migratory pattern, some history of lovers. They decided to go home with one another on the spot. They dropped everything. Left behind their cronies. And they stayed together after that.

On the night of the robbery, Max will look up from the wow and flutter of this recollection — and from the cyclical and endless heart-to-heart about whether or not to have a baby — to see a pair of legs disappear into a ground-floor window up the block. *Holy shit,* he will say. *Did you see that?*

Eleanor will reply flatly: *See what?*

I think that apartment is being robbed. Look at that! Really!

Other first kisses will be taking place at this very moment. At a phenomenal rate. All across the city. If there were a light-up map showing the pattern of the dispersal of these kisses it would put to shame any of the other light-up maps used to oversimplify the scale and range of our decaying metropolis. Ginny and Steve. Mark and Dan. Ramon and Samantha. Miles and Kay. Lola and Kim and Pete. Bernard and Elisheva. Eliza and Katie. Innumerable others. The first kisses of this day alone, if harnessed, could realize a city-wide savings on the power grid; solar cells or a Mars shot could be developed with the money that would result as savings. These first kisses could wipe away the tendency in the five boroughs toward spontaneous street violence, except in the cases of first kisses that would actually cause street violence (adulterous or unfaithful first kisses). These first kisses could cushion financial hardships and class differences. They could bring the ethnicities closer together — except when they would drive them farther apart (unfaithful multiracial kisses). These kisses would result in millions of dollars in lost productivity due to excessive happiness and on-the-job ennui. And it's this way because first kisses preceded the discovery of atoms by tens of thousands of years and preceded the wheel and preceded the lever and the screw and the arrowhead and the papoose and the paving of, say, Sixteenth Street, where according to archives kept by the Church of Latter Day Saints, 14,131 first kisses have taken place since the first humanoid amphibian crawled from the East River and gasped a breath before beginning its desperate search for a mate.

I will be crossing Sixteenth Street myself that night. The night of the robbery. While Joe is liberating the apartment of Nina's CD player and ugly Tiffany jewelry, etc., I will be coming from the East Side. While Max and Eleanor are coming from Chelsea. I will be looking at my feet, dragging my heels disconsolately as I occasionally do on this block because it is a gauntlet of memories, but I will look up for a second because I cannot pass that window without thinking about this woman (the woman whom, at the beginning of this account, I was about to kiss) and I will see these black jeans and Converse All Stars slipping in through the half-opened window, the screen wrenched out of its frame. This will stop me, draw me up short, and I will simply stare.

I'll realize then that I will pass this window even in years in which she is a part of my life and she lives elsewhere, in SoHo, and I will be sad on these occasions just as I am sad in the years when I am not involved with her. On a variety of missions, both aimless and purposeful, I will pass this spot — 131 West Sixteenth — and when I pass I will remember and be sad and the only thing worse than that, the only thing sadder, will be when I forget, and am sad for forgetting. Sadness will mark the period with her and the period after and the time in between and it will even mark — a little bit — my next first kiss — which will perhaps be with Eleanor, who is soon to be divorced.

Meanwhile, the drama of the robbery will begin. I will meet Eleanor's eyes as we pass. Joe will fall into Nina's apartment through the open window. Banging his knee. Seizing the stereo. And right then the Allstate representative who sold Nina her renter's policy will be kissing his wife, and his daughter will be kissing her boyfriend (in a Mustang in the parking lot at the Roosevelt Mall), and her best friend Alene will be kissing a boy Nick whose cousin Tony will be benevolently kissing his dog, the father of which dog (a husky) is owned by the First Councilman of Roslyn, Long Island, a radical Republican and sexual asphyxiatist, who will be kissing a seventeen-year-old boy in a motel in the next town, the father of which boy will be kissing his mistress, Cairo, whose boyfriend is back in her apartment in Bay Ridge actually kissing Cairo's sister, whose boyfriend has gone off on scholarship to the state school in New Paltz, where he is kissing his academic adviser (consensually but even so inadvisably), Katherine Miller, Ph.D., who has kissed several of her students as she herself was kissed by Leonard Blandings, the novelist, who was fired from one appointment for kissing a female student who was herself just discovering that she was a lesbian, who was discovering that nothing was fixed in her life, that all was drift and erosion and that the road to her identity would be littered with broken hearts and unfulfilled crushes until at last she found this girl at the Clit Club and they went back to this girl's place on Sixteenth Street in the middle of a blizzard and kissed.

But before all that, before all these things happen in this

order and this way, before I go on to kiss others and you do too (and perhaps in this way you and I have something close to a kiss), *I have to kiss Susan.* The woman to whom I have pledged myself for this brief instant. And so I do. Her face is small and round, but she has enormous blue eyes that seem to say that *all the stuff you are thinking is true,* melancholy eyes, eyes with a sorrowful determination, and she has lips made for kissing, made for the sympathetic gesture, made for declarations of affection. I am close to her face now, and lacing my fingers around her back, the better to make the instant irrevocable, and then I am grazing her lips with mine, measuring their pitch and arc and force, and then we are falling into the lassitude of kisses where I am going to dwell. *We are together.* Everything, even the busted lamp above us on the step, and the job I'm going to lose, and her brother who is going to die, and the way she will leave me later, and the apartment that will be robbed, and the people spinning out around us, all this doesn't matter for the moment and that's the way I prefer to remember it, before our lips part, with her roommate cackling in the background on the phone with the boy who first made her dance. Her roommate dancing in that low wattage as she talks to him, that first boy, pressing the light-up buttons on the sentimental jukebox of human affiliations, singing, knowing, remembering.

PHRASE BOOK

This one's about the stuff that Lucy said. Lucy, a woman I knew once. Lucy who took seventy hits of acid *in one day* and, in a way, lived to tell. She'd been living in a squat in Burlington, Vermont, when she did it. Living like a runaway. The source of the drugs is unimportant. They were available. Lucy took the poison and meandered along the streets, meandering until it kicked in, until its contingency was her contingency. Maybe she thought she would die of it. In some register of her worried and confused mind she thought this would be a lethal prescription, but she didn't count on how much her husk would resist the effort. Or maybe she knew exactly what would happen to her, that it was pretty hard to poison yourself with that carnival drug. Maybe she knew that she would hallucinate the rest of her life, the next fifty or sixty years of her life, ceaseless hallucinations, hallucinations cut with strychnine and PCP and other corruptions, hallucinations of complete contingency. Maybe she had a dim sense that *they,* the doctors, would dose her with Thorazine in the emergency ward in Burlington and then, pronouncing her incurable, ship her off to a succession of psychiatric hospitals. Where she knew what she was in for at least. Private first and then public hospitals. The kids she knew, the street rats who clustered in Burlington, had carried her to the emergency ward — in an unusual display of compassion — and abandoned her there, like a foundling. She was rudderless in her panic. The doctors tried Thorazine. Lucy was disrupting the E.R., she was scattering her seeds of panic around the premises. Time hardly passed. Then they gave her the injection. Lucy stumbled around like anyone else on antipsychotics — her chin seemed to be fused to her breast — but her head didn't clear. Maybe she knew that if she swallowed that *philter,* that preparation, that the lowest part of her, the part that was already slipping its mooring, would vanish in the process. Maybe that was what she was after. She would be a free thing, a spirit unattached to the rigors of personality. Or a spirit unattached to the security of language. Whichever way you looked at it. There were implications in her choice. She knew this. She knew that she had made some kind of decision and that loss was attendant upon it. She was dressed in this loss when I met her. It was her fashion. She had regrets, even if she couldn't articulate them. She was as sad as you could be. I met her in the locked ward, see. I was there, too. She was sad even though she tried to appear happy sometimes, happy during games of volleyball when she would crouch under the net looking to spike that motherfucker. It's a good thing, watching a woman spike a volleyball. Crouching under the net in basketball shoes somebody must have given her, ready to leap. It helped me, just seeing her. But mostly Lucy didn't get out of bed. She lost track of herself, misplaced herself in the corridors of Wingdale. She didn't make sense. She was a loose constellation of habits associated with her past — a faint lisp and a certain way of brushing back her dirty blond bangs and of balling up her fists when she was frustrated. So her past was mine to derive. Because the seventy hits of acid had pried apart her syntax. Word salad. That's all she could manage. That was one term for it. Word salad. Alliteration and poetry and falsely matched non-sense, mismatched nouns bristling against one another like she was transliterating ideograms — *tattooed brains* and *rugs with eyes* and *towns inhabited by hands* — all the trippy shit. That's how Lucy talked. That's how she talked when I was talking with her. Before I got out. Before they patched me up.

Glass Fires

Way back, seven or eight or ten years ago, there was a girl Lucy whose dad left when she was a child. Just left. No long and exhausting drama. Nothing to pin the blame on partic-ularly. He was there and then he wasn't there. His motives were obscure to her, even after. She was twelve. There was no whispered or tearful conversations on the phone, no china sailing across their tiny apartment in Bridgeport, Conn., no confrontations, just the long, slow dissipation of respect. None of the legal stuff, either, the proposals and counterproposals that might have given the illusion of explicating the situation. Love had come to its conclusion in Lucy's house. All the rooms were gloomy and poorly lit. Her mom was working a secre-tarial job. Lucy and her brother went to public school. She had a little brother, a couple of years behind her. She was a homely little kid — long and lanky with stringy hair she didn't wash all that much, taller than everybody else but without any lips or breasts or hips to distinguish her. Only her skeptical gaze,

that gaze that understood her father's disappearance long before it happened, that understood how time was telescoped
because time was no respecter of human dignity. Her brother
was homely too. Scrawny. They walked to school by themselves. Her dad had gone. It was a year later or eighteen
months later — she had lost count — and her mom was going
to be fired because, she said, she was unable to perform certain
tasks. Her mom couldn't photocopy, for example, and she
wouldn't take dictation and a little sorrow wasn't enough of an
excuse for these lapses. And her mom was seeing a married
guy — it was a rebound situation — and was trying to pass
him off as Lucy's dad, out of desperation. Or trying at least to
slot him into the space recently exited by the other guy, Lucy's
dad, who had vanished after the long, slow dissipation of
respect. Plugging this guy into those battery terminals. What
was his name? Willard. *Like the rat in the movie.* Willard was
intended to fill in on those afternoons when he could steal
away from the other woman who loved him, his wife. *Oh shit,*
Willard was on the phone and her mom would give Lucy a
smack across the face, smack her one, and tell her to *get the hell
out of the way, please.* Willard was on the phone. She was on the
phone so please get the hell out of the way. Where was the
brother? Where was Steve? And how troubled was he? The
brother was shut down, drydocked like an old, leaky boat.
Never a word passed from his lips. He stumbled around in the
world as though he had an awful inner-ear problem. Lucy's
brother was in the other room with that narcotizer. *Go in there
and watch television with your brother. I'm on the phone.* Then
suddenly the married guy was in the house, visiting, with an
expression of forced joviality on his mug. Their father was
gone and no one could explain it to them. *Kids,* her mother

would say with irrepressible glee, *Willard is going to take us out to the movies.* Or: *Willard thinks it would be nice if we all watched the ball game together.* Or: *Guess what, kids? We are going to have a picnic lunch with Willard.* The day of the picnic actually arrived. In spite of all the evidence, Lucy was hopeful for a minute. The married guy showed up to take them out to a picnic. He had a hunted look. He feigned a paternal expression, a mail-order paternal expression. They were going to Sherwood Island, in Westport, to park, to barbecue. Willard was in charge of purchasing for this adventure, or that's what Lucy's mom said. Her mom was so desperate for Willard to be adventuring with them, so desperate for him to carry Lucy's brother under his arm, so desperate for him not to be checking his watch or searching the horizon for the acquaintance who would encounter him in the middle of this extramarital imbroglio and give the story up, so desperate that she attributed stuff to him that he didn't do and had no intention of doing. Lucy packed the picnic basket herself. No, wait a second. Willard did indeed seem to have a wicker basket with little plastic dishes in it and some bug repellent and some Cokes, a thermos full of crushed ice, a thermos full of vodka. He was going back to his wife after this but he was trying to be a good sport for the afternoon. He was a pharmaceutical sales representative and he was married, but he had borrowed his wife's picnic basket and had come out here with this hunted look this expression of devotion mixed with an awful lot of anxiety, to picnic with the truculent secretary he had met somewhere. They were in the battered green station wagon driving into Sherwood Island Park. At dusk. Lucy felt like a kite whose string had just been released. She felt like adults were speaking backwards to her. She wanted to push her brother's head under the water and hold it down for a while. She wanted to sprinkle ants in Willard's ears. She and her brother were awkwardly hitting a shuttlecock back and forth on the rocks while her mother pulled down the tailgate. They had parked the battered green station wagon right at the edge of the sand. Her mother and Willard were moving imperceptibly, carrying the ritualistic picnic basket to the ritualistic blanket and laying out the chalices and stuff on the blanket. Her mother and this married guy had carved out an area where they knew exactly how to act, exactly how to march around each other, an area where all they had to do was unpack this picnic basket and arrange this blanket. Because this was going to be the end of their unsatisfying sexual association, although her mom didn't know this yet. Lucy's mom unpacked carrots and celery sticks and then set out the chicken. She arranged a circle of rocks in which to barbecue. Willard poured the charcoal briquettes from the bag into the campfire circle. Lucy couldn't figure out whether to love her mother or love that sunset, whether love was even relevant to where she found herself now, whether love was just a certain kind of sound and nothing more, whether a barbecue could unscramble her feelings. She couldn't figure out what to feel because she couldn't think straight long enough to enumerate the options. She couldn't explain what her feelings were, why it was that a picnic with its Tupperware assortments of feelings and satisfactions could be the thing that instead of comforting made a hole in her big enough to drive a Mustang through. This was what it felt like anyway. She was twelve. She was sitting in the sand and crying and her brother was calling her stupid names and Willard and her mother were kneeling in silence in front of the chicken. *C'mon*, her brother was saying, dancing in front of her, *C'mon*. Willard and her mother were kneeling in front of the fire. Condiments. There was coleslaw. Lucy had collapsed in front of the sign — SHERWOOD ISLAND PARK CLOSED 7 PM NO CAMPING NO GLASS FIRES RADIOS MOTORCYCLES NO EXCEPTIONS. No glass fires? Kids were always crying — it was just a disguise she liked to wear. No problem. Her tears fell. Later the fire was going and she was still crying and her brother was calling her stupid names and there was sand in the food and ants in the sand and ants in the food and that was when the police came. No glass fires? The police came just as she was biting into a carrot stick covered with sand. No, she was sitting apart from her family and not eating. She was ravenous but prideful. Driving along the beach, the police cruiser approached. And arrived. One policeman flipped through his pad — full of citations — searching for a free page. Pointing to the sign with his Flair pen. Had they read the sign? Lucy was biting into a carrot stick and it was just after the police had come and given them some kind of ticket for barbecuing and Willard was packing stuff up. It was the summer solstice, yes, the summer solstice, and it would have been all right to dance until dawn, to celebrate the languor of summer days, but Lucy's mother was wailing now, it was always one of them wailing, some long plaint about how she couldn't stand it, blah, blah, she couldn't stand it if Willard went back to his wife that night, she couldn't stand it and she was going to do something she was going to do something if Willard was going back to his wife that night she couldn't stand it he had to stay and she couldn't stand it and Lucy believed she was going to do something and Willard was chasing after her brother who was running down the beach *naked* having doffed his cutoff shorts running naked down the beach. Lucy cried out the words exploding from her like fingernails from a nail gun *glass fires glass fires glass fires what's a glass fire anyway?*

Advanced Transvestism

Lucy's brother, in an entirely different sequence of events, was older than she was. Thirteen or fourteen. Just past puberty. It was not her father who had left them this time. It was their mom. Her mom had left and her dad was seeing a married woman. Coming home from work late, a few drinks in him, heating up some food in pouches and drinking more. Dad waited for the married woman to show up once in a while, waited for her to cook for the kids. Lucy's brother was named Steve. Lucy and Steve. Steve's dad dated this married woman and Steve was home early from school padding around the little apartment in Trenton, N.J. He found a dress belonging to this married woman in the front hall, and Steve put it on. Steve put on this silk gown. Steve was rummaging around the house and he found this silk gown and he removed his jeans and his T-shirt and socks and jockey shorts and put on the silk gown belonging to his dad's married girlfriend and he went to a full-length mirror — relic of the time when his mother still lived there — on the back of the door in the bathroom. Wait, let me go back a bit. Steve and Lucy's dad was drinking heavily and working some factory job in Trenton, N.J. at the 3M tape factory, in fact, making double-sided tape. He was coming home late and seeing this married woman who was a secretary, but not a very good one, a secretary about to be fired and he was raising his voice about how it was the *same goddamned one percent, the same rich fuckers, and they controlled the whole population and all the breaks, and if you didn't get a break you died in the same hospital you were born in, and those rich fuckers laughed at the quarter-inch obit that was all that was left of you. You went nuts and you died and you worked for the same one percent and then you died.* Sometimes the married woman showed Steve a little affection, a little mothering — his story isn't all monochrome. She showed him a little affection, chucked him under the chin and whispered to him, because she had no kids of her own and she always told Steve's father she just loved kids. This married woman spent time one day showing Steve how to do a word search puzzle and for a year after that word search puzzles were his only pleasure. So one afternoon Steve was rifling other people's closets, because he wanted to know everybody's secret. He wanted to know the one thing everybody was trying to hide or the several things if there happened to be several things and so he found the silk dress belonging to this married woman. What was she doing with a silk dress there? (Was it really silk?) It was to impress Steve's dad, he thought, to bring him home from the 3M tape company on time, to bring him home from the manufacture of double-sided tape. That's why the dress was in there, in the closet. Steve found suddenly that he couldn't resist trying on the dress. He was alone and he rubbed the silk on his face, first rubbed the hem of it on his dispirited face and then he felt that he had to try it on. He wanted to know if the dress itself conferred on a person the ability to communicate with his father, if the dress had some specific characteristic that softened his father; or he wanted to know if, wearing the dress, he would suddenly understand his mother's departure. But he didn't know he was thinking these things. He didn't know he had motives at all. He didn't know what a bad idea this was going to be. The silk felt pretty good on him. Was there a woman in his future who would wear this dress for him? Steve got an erection, then, not only for his dad's married girlfriend, but for the idea that his dad just might love somebody on the planet. He got an erection simply out of the existence of this dress, the message it implied, the current that passed through it from one lost family member to another. He wanted to be both lover and love object, he wanted to close the whole circuit so that no contact was required for the act. Steve had on bare feet and he was standing on the rug, looking himself over in the mirror — in the gown. There was a little standing water on the bathroom floor. He realized that he had an erection. He had this hard on and he wasn't going to give up on it easily. Then he had the thing on the floor around him — the dress was crumpled beside him on the floor — and he was tugging on himself and banging the back of his head, the primitive, back brain part of his head on the tiles. Like an autistic jerking off, hoping to really stun the part of his brain that controlled his breathing and his heartbeat. Hating himself and hating the inevitability of what he had come to. Saying, *You're going to live like this. You're going to live like this. This is the way you're gonna live from now on.* Then Lucy came home from school — her dad was still at the 3M plant making that double-sided tape — and she found her brother in the front hall wearing a silk gown. He was stoned, she thought; his eyes were stitched up tight. He had been smoking pot. Where did he get a silk gown? They didn't have any money for that kind of stuff. Steve was supposed to be in school but instead he was home. His skin looked awful. His face was red and disturbed. Lucy came home from school after fighting on the school bus with her friend Louisa and in the front hall she stumbled over her brother, lying on the floor in the front hall wearing a dress, a light green gown of some description, with the thing hiked

up around his waist. He was masturbating. Steve was too close
to the crest of this wave to stop. No, he wanted to stop, but he
was actually overflowing right then. When he had spunked on
the gown, in front of his sister, his motionless sister, his immo-
bile sister, he covered himself daintily. *Advanced transvestism,* he
said nervously, guiltily, *advanced transvestism,* he said, or did the
words seem to issue from him against his will, or did they
come from some inanimate source in her? Were they words
embodied or disembodied? Too late to hide it from her now,
the long arc of his peculiar taste. The dress just a rag around
him now. Steve got up on his feet, weaving a little bit, in many
ways his father's son, dripping on the mangled dress. He
reached out for Lucy. Her first idea was to run. He chased her.
He gave chase. He wanted to explain. Lucy was out of breath at
the top of the stairs. She was out of breath locking the door just
ahead of his imploring hands which, for the moment, were
bejeweled or bangled or accessorized. She was slumped at the
foot of the door, the bathroom door, slumped in reflection, too,
in the mirror, her school books scattered around her. There was
a noise in her head like a mining accident. Steve was calling
her, calling her name. Lucy was not the gender she was and her
brother was not the gender he was or her father was not the
gender he was and her mother's vagina had teeth. Her own
mother had carnal designs on her or on her brother and that was
why her mother had left. All these possibilities in solution, in
memory. Her mother hadn't left, hadn't thrown off the burden of
family. Her mother was pursuing her or her brother was pursuing her. Somebody must have left. Must have. There was the hole
to prove it, the hole and the ache. And everybody was trying to
get Lucy's mom to come back because she had left, trying to get
these ghosts to come back or else they were just trying to avenge

themselves, she and her brother and her father trying to avenge themselves on themselves on their family on all those who had somehow escaped family had somehow escaped all that inadvertent harm. Somewhere between these orienting points between this last marker and the next.

International Bull Dyke Conspiracy

Now, Jeff comes into it. Jeff had done a little bit of time (1⅓ years) in the state penitentiary. Convicted of armed robbery. Otherwise he was like most of the people I know. He was no desperate criminal. He wasn't desperate at all. But Jeff was the first guy in his family, the first guy on his street, the first guy in his whole voting district to commit armed robbery and to go to the state penitentiary as a result. How did Jeff wind up on the wrong side of a liquor store cash register pointing a little pop gun at the head of a trembling family man? Guys like Jeff, middle-class fellas, weren't supposed to commit this sort of crime. Not in Albany. One bad idea, though, led to another and another. The scale of bad ideas grew. Jeff's plans changed. He had been at the state school, a frat brother, a guy who would jump from the highest tree branch over the quarry pond, a guy who worked hard to pass his classes so he could *keep on partying!* And then through the slipperiness of his inert stupidity he was stealing a dozen pairs of skis out of the back of a sporting goods store and loading them into a rented panel truck. Selling them. Forging tickets to scalp at some stadium show. The scams were getting more baroque. Dealing Novocain cut with powdered milk. Spending long nights sweating in the bathroom with the blinds drawn and the television turned up loud. Never had a girlfriend to speak of, a girlfriend who might have disabused him of some of these really dumb notions. Never had anyone to tell him not to do it, not to walk into the liquor store alone with the pop gun. Alone. He did it alone. There was a liquidity problem and suddenly if he didn't hold up somebody he was going to get held up himself, or kneecapped or something. Never wanted to talk about it either, the long slide, but then he was going off to the state penitentiary. Suddenly he wanted to come clean. Then he wanted to talk. He was as scared as you can get. A middle-class guy in the pen? His *people* weren't in there. In prison it didn't matter that Jeff had been the frat brother, that at one time he'd had a lot of friends, that he had organized big parties with spiked punch, didn't matter. His 1⅓ years had changed him. The day he got out, before he even went to see his probation officer, he was out driving around Burlington, Vermont — he had taken the ferry across the lake to do it — to celebrate with an old friend there. Not much of a celebration, a sad celebration, really. They drove around Burlington violating open-container laws. Green mountains rising in the east. Mist in the valleys. Sharp cheddar cheese and a knife and pint bottles in the car. This was when Lucy crossed paths with Jeff. This was when Lucy met Jeff the middle-class felon. It wasn't an auspicious meeting. Lucy had been sitting in front of an old hotel downtown, the Arcadia, because she hadn't gone to class like she was supposed to, because she had skipped the entire second half of her freshman year in fact, had just cleared out of school, out of the large freshman warehouse that had been her dormitory, taking some of her stuff but not all of it. She couldn't explain her reasons. School seemed like the biggest scam around. She just didn't want to stay. Jeff and his friend Steve saw Lucy sitting on the stone wall in front of the Arcadia, Lucy dressed in black rags, her hair dyed a silly color, and they circled around a second time in the rented car. Jeff parked and then he and Steve stood in front of Lucy, beer cans wrapped in small brown paper bags, talking to her. The stalemate with her parents had gone on for months and then she just left the dorm and didn't tell anyone where she was going. She saw people in town from school sometimes and she just looked the other way. They left her alone. She looked down or looked away, observed an awkward and distracted silence. She moved into a squat outside of town with a guy who actually called himself Mike Coercion. Mike didn't even know it was a stupid name. Mike the skinhead. Or not a skinhead exactly, but some kind of nomadic thrash guy. Mike lived in this squat with a few other kids. Lucy couldn't have said what her plan was exactly. She didn't know when she'd be going back to Bridgeport or to Trenton or wherever her family lived, but she imagined it would be pretty soon. The connective tissue in her logic was thick with some plaque. She didn't think she would do anything about her predicament, but she thought it would get figured out somehow. And it would. A weak flashlight shone on her decisions, and its batteries were just about exhausted. When Jeff and Steve asked if she didn't want to take a drive around the lake, if she didn't want to violate open-container laws with them, if she didn't want to confess her, uh, innermost feelings, she told them yes. Right away. Because she had been on some of these drives before. She had been on the drive to the Cascades, halfway down the state, where these waterfalls tumbled down through splintering rocks, and she had smoked dope and skinny-dipped in the blue pool where the water collected. And she too had gone off the rope swing at the quarry ponds in Dorset. Lucy said yes to all day trips, to all junkets, to all hasty escapades. There were certain kinds of stories that went with these journeys and these were the sorts of stories that fastened Lucy down. She said yes to Jeff the middle-class felon because the loose confraternity of day-trippers made what was going through her mind — or the way it was going — less troubling. She said yes to Jeff the middle-class felon as she had said yes to Mike Coercion the middle-class thrash guy. He had a ten-point program of some kind. So they were driving around this lake at sunset, drinking, passing beers and a pint bottle of scotch back and forth, radio up so loud that they couldn't have confessed their innermost feelings if they had wanted to, Steve yelling out hideous jokes — something about a whore who had never been *hauled in by the fuzz though she had been sucked on the tits once* — and then laughing sadly. There were some long silences during which Lucy might have worried about the company if she hadn't been drinking so much. Jeff didn't seem to care that he was already in violation of his probation. Then they got to a certain point where the drinking wasn't doing much anymore, wasn't contributing. It was that point where all the scotch and all the radio songs in the world weren't going to keep them from being just *people,* with all the poison dreams and sadness and even *hope* that being young in Vermont entailed right then. Suddenly the story came from Jeff in torrents, the story about the moment when he held the pop gun to the head of a trembling family man. He was getting a little choked up himself, as if the heart of his punishment, the very center of it, would be to tremble ever afterwards, to tremble and know the feelings of that cashier whose life he had threatened. Yep, in the 1⅓ years he had grown to resemble that man. Getting a little choked up. Steve tried to tell another joke in the silence after Jeff had finished what he had to say, a joke about a mule that would only move if you blew on its ass, but the time for jokes was gone. Darkness fell. The whitecaps on the lake were evidence, to Lucy, of a vengeful undersea force. She needed to wash her face. She would count to ten three times. Lucy was telling them about leaving school. The story came out all sideways. It was getting dark and Lucy was telling Jeff and Steve that she didn't know what she was going to do, she didn't know where she was going to go. Jeff leaned back from the passenger seat to brush back her bangs, thinking about laying down with her in an open field full of pine needles. They were exposed in their sadness now but other feelings were part of the moment, too. Jeff was thinking that he *loved* Lucy, that's how much he remembered about relations between the sexes. He was a long way from remembering how violent love could be. Jeff leaned back to touch the crest of Lucy's head, and she was crying. He and Steve hadn't properly thought through this part of the evening. They didn't know in what configuration this seduction — if that's what it was going to be — was going to take place. Jeff and Steve each had an idea about sleeping with Lucy in a bed of pine needles. They each regretted this fantasy, regretted the sentimentality of it, and they each thought about how they might get over on her without the other. Jeff knew he didn't want Steve to be around when he did it, and Steve was having the same idea. Although it was possible they could *do her* together. Lucy knew, but she didn't want to know. She wasn't thinking too clearly. She was hoping the problem would take care of itself. They stopped the car by the lake and the breeze was insistent. No boats disturbed the surface of the water. Steve and Jeff were as composed as stickup guys now, as famished as reptiles. The stars bore an urgent message in an incomprehensible code. Jeff and

Lucy and probably even Steve wanted to talk, wanted to let some easy affection pass between them in words, like ripples on the lake, but they had lost the warp of that fabric. The men fell back on posturing. So the brittle sympathies of that escapade splintered. When Jeff said it, launched into the sort of dizzy monologue that you can only learn from frat brothers or in the military or in prison, a monologue of acute loneliness, the whole drive fell apart. He just snapped. He began to yell. *Women,* he said to Steve, *they're all part of an International Bull Dyke Conspiracy. It's managed in Washington by girls with mustaches,* he said to Steve. *Hey, he said, did you know that the whole globe spins to a conspiracy? Watch out where you put your dick,* he said. *Watch out. The whole world spins to it.* To which Lucy said, *Stop the car, stop the car, you guys. Please stop.* Though the car was already stopped. Standing by the lake, screaming to stop the car. She ran out onto the road, Route 9N, running as she mumbled, flagged down the next driver, already speaking in the haste that would characterize her later. Mumbling desperately, alliteratively. Into the road. Screaming. Mumbling. Crying. Repeating herself. Out into the road. Lucy screamed and bolted from Jeff and Steve. They drove the car after her for a while, pissed off and worried, but there was the matter of *probation* and the fact was that Lucy was nuts and they took a right turn and then slept in the woods that's all I know of them. Lucy made it back to town, though she scared the shit out of the guy who gave her a ride — she sounded like she was speaking in Chinese — but her squat, the squat where she lived, wasn't the best place to go. Mike the skinhead only needed a little push to come up with the same virulent sort of hatred that spilled from Jeff's mouth. Mike called all his girlfriends, of whom Lucy was occasionally one, *spoor cunt.* It was his pet name. And right before he made love he would ask, *What dis-eases you got in that swamp?* They were shooting crystal meth that night, but Lucy didn't do any. And Mike was claiming that Allen Ginsberg had tried to fuck him once, after a poetry reading. And then he started talking about the International Bull Dyke Conspiracy. Right in front of Lucy, only a couple of hours later, he began talking about the International Bull Dyke Conspiracy. It was a shady and inchoate organization. Its tendrils reached into the Skinhead Nomadic Movement (S.N.M.), into the thrash community, and into the state uni-versity system where millions of research dollars were being spent on the feasibility of the permanent isolation of the male gender. The symbol of this virulent underground was an eye with a tear falling from it, an eye ringed with copious makeup, a vaginal eye, a vortex, a vacuum; its mission was the obliter-ation of patriarchy. And this symbol was tattooed on the breast of every woman in Burlington. No, wait, the mission of the conspiracy was the elimination of dads. Wait. Lucy couldn't make much sense of the words, but she dreamed of Mike Coer-cion, while she was listening, dreamed though awake, had a hal-lucination of unimpeachable lucidity, dreamed of Mike in a devastated life that included management of a Jiffy Lube or a 7-Eleven, Mike with an artificial tan, reverting to his last name, Metzger, Mike crushed to death in some scrap-metal compacting facility. Mike's voice rose above the fire they had going in the squat, calling all women, calling all women, all carriers of disease. Lucy slept fitfully, pursued by nightmares she couldn't shake off when she woke. And the next day was the day when she managed at last to get some time alone. The next day was the day when Mike and the rest of his bereaved posse lit out for the mall, for a day stalking teenagers in the mall, the day when Lucy stayed home alone. In this time, in this brief interval of solitude, she managed to purchase her plastic bag full of oblivion. It took a long time to get all those crudely rendered pills down; it took a long time to swallow them with that wine cooler (it was all she could find). She had to remake the decision again and again. Unsure of the outcome, but doing it anyway. Alone. With the first wave of the drug, a lid closed over her.

TREATMENT

sound over of restaurant noise melody of plates falling into the sink and keys on the register and the ebb and flow of conversation the rich moments for eavesdropping the urgent patches of gossip conversation rising up like an exaltation of larks to mean nothing at all but voluminosity of words the awkward and obscure silences restaurant noise and then *fade in* on the table where I'm sitting with poet Dee Murdoch self-proclaimed high priestess of the erotic underground self-proclaimed in the East Village small waifish with shoulder-length black hair unruly falling over her eyes raw silk black blouse dozens of silver bracelets she stands to search out the crucial ashtray from the chrome service station the rest of the outfit visible the black tights and black cutoff shorts yes shorts in late October homely and lovely at the same time not a high priestess at all unless a cut-rate New York priestess of disappointment and bitterness and publicity unless these are the stuff of erotics no desire on her at all and no superficial affectation nor blush nor fragrance will give her this impression still you'd like to hug her really hard and sway her with fabulously exaggerated language about her rich ornamented future how all the world even the East Village pulses with energy of human kindness this if nothing else would make me a bad date Dee Murdoch all synthetics titanium joints and bottled blue-black hair and lip pencil and underneath the silk blouse the fluvial course of the faded blue-black scars every vein callused and leathery yet *the camera sees in her as I do* a barely concealed courage she moved once too often growing up the brisk lessons of love could catalyze this she might let slip this armature so carefully calculated in love her eyeliner would run her mascara a gray wash upon her cheeks she'd tell you four stories of loss as all New Yorkers would four stories of aspirations squandered of hopes vanquished a story of her dad and his drink and the oppression of the countryside and the almost constant rain *after introducing us in space at the table the shot takes a long slow pirouette around the room* catching a guy three tables away reading phone sex ads in the *New York Press* a couple talking about movies and another couple eating a gray lamb dish that looks like an industrial R&D failure one of these patrons points at Dee surreptitiously a crooked finger cable television recognition and then *the camera wheels violently in our direction the third character this camera inconstant jittery* we have been sitting at this table seems like ten minutes but on screen much abbreviated not a word between us Dee the high priestess awkward and bored and me mute uncertain studying the menu and its arcane Moroccan specials couscous couscous couscous to delay the moment what the fuck are we going to talk about *the excruciating duration of this shot* the lingering of it and *then swollen period titles like the kind from the bad romantic comedies of the early seventies scroll down and linger over our worried faces with the name of this movie Mystery Date* just as quickly the titles disappear surly and frowning with black nail polish and lace bodice the waitress appears in her posture-evident disdain I defer to Dee and her regular patronage and have the same thing please waitress snaps up our menus as though again we have ordered brutishly the wrong entrées or broken some implicit East Village dress code Dee lights the candle scorches her thumb briefly the appalling moment arrives no choice plunge into that grim canyon of talk I ask Dee haltingly is her agent any good is it someone she trusts her agent and she tells me that actually like uh she has a number of agents there's the ICM film guy who handles movie interest and stuff and then he hands off her literary interests to someone else at ICM and then she has this manager does her music stuff and a booking agent to handle the performance touring but not the music touring which the manager does and she can hardly deal with all the calls uh the phone is really a drag really ringing off the hook um she can hardly sit still to get anything done but she returns the film guy's calls anyway and well she went on this audition for a movie the film guy set it up and next week she has this MTV thing with this band um Smashing Pumpkins and the lead singer from like the Chili Peppers *yes the camera circles slowly around Dee as she names the names getting tighter on her* he's really a good guy actually although he has these women around him all the time these incredible women and then Dee says she's booked through next September and there's the record deal and the problem with the guitar player or the drummer uh who's supposed to be on the record and Dee's paying her so what's the problem and then I say oh that's cool and there's another silence and a voice-over in which I admit that my professional life has been going pretty well too never get to say this though Dee doesn't ask in fact she's still talking voice completely devoid of affect as though reading straight from a

TelePrompTer or just making it up *jump cut more or less the same angle bad continuity Dee's hair suddenly parted differently* and she's smoking waiting for couscous out of desperation close-up of rivulets of sweat coursing down my neck near tangles of my longish uncombed hair I lurch into another topic health insurance what kind of premium does she pay is the deductible high and did she have trouble getting it you know because of hospitalization because of treatment for you know because we have both been treated for that did she have to sign anything or conceal anything *yes untrained actors we are untrained actors* and in a burst of candor actually using these words burst of candor I say I am really awkward you know and that it's going to be a long night and she laughs screen laugh *the camera has edged in on our faces* Dee's makeup imperfectly conceals her askew smile ribbons her face strangely a certain amount of anxiety and concern in its disarray close-up of me entirely dominated by my nose I look like I have just waked grains of couscous entrapped in the chapped fold at the corner of my mouth *camera could pull back here off-camera* there is a P.A. working for nothing holding up the cue cards Dee is unable to memorize doesn't matter because of the manner in which the director an N.Y.U. film student maybe a U.C.I. semiotician views our performances *she really wants to get close to the actual first date experience to the comedy the tragicomedy the folly that's at the heart of the first date with all its implications political cultural sociological* and so has arranged this actual first date actual and fictional and so we are talking about movies now a movie about movies featuring a movie within a movie if you will talking about movies on this date because Dee doesn't read interrupting each other the language coming a little easier to us now over the first hurdle through the first act the larger pool of restaurant sounds and sights just decora-

tion now we both like *Nightmare on Elm Street, 3* I'm describing
the shot where the kids are having the party and this guy um is
finally getting the opportunity to spider his bumbling teenage
hands across the breasts of his cheerleader girlfriend the two of
them behind a system of shrubs and he's going to french kiss
her a kiss of novelty and possibility except that just as he's
about to do it his pink suburban tongue venturing forth between teeth perfected by orthodontia just then his teenage
tongue gives way to the Freddy Kruger protrusion a long gray
slick penile tongue that wriggles from his mouth eight or ten
inches long the color of decay this sequence now cut into the
movie our movie he sees the tongue his own tongue his and not
his serpentine wriggling out of him though the cheerleader
with eyes closed does not see it coming he gasps tries to fit the
thing back in his mouth squashes it back in with his palm
before she sees and Dee laughs avuncularly at my description
but she doesn't remember the sequence or maybe she's trying
to repulse my own kiss my own gray tongue something not
genuine in her laugh like Kruger himself laughing I blush
slightly for the camera *it registers only dimly in this candlelight
nonetheless augmented by the thousand-watt Klieg lamps borrowed
from the Tisch School of the Arts* acting's really easy I say we both
should be doing it for fun and glory because it's so easy because
the money is fabulous but she says uh actually what I'd really
like to do is direct and she's the one with the film agent and
I'm just a guy on a date the flat monotonous line readings that
prove this may be my one and only film performance no longer
like the twenty-one-year-old P.A.'s do I have on my side effortless good looks in my thirties fighting a losing battle against
the riptide of middle age which I say to Dee fighting a losing
battle against the riptide of middle age surly and frowning

waitress ambles grimly to a rheostat on the wall and spins the dial so that the ambient light is even lower now cinematic obscurity *just our faces coming up out of the candlelight the Caravaggio light* in fact Dee the self-proclaimed high priestess of the erotic underground looks for a second like she could live up to the name but the fabulous ennui of independent features precludes anything but disaffection and miscommunication and failed opportunities as the first date itself the institution precludes anything but miscommunication in the dim light the dim sense of a pointlessness in this meal pointlessness in this neighborhood on this avenue in this town in these lives an emptiness but Dee doesn't see goes all sweet and voluble on David Cronenberg on how everything in the world has to do with David Cronenberg a monologue she wrote about David Cronenberg and some guy lead singer of King Missile who wrote a song or maybe a monologue too about Scorsese Marty Scorsese calling him Marty and we laugh and load the remaining dunes of couscous into our mouths *cut to* later on the street on the way to see this movie about food movie within movie directed by Marty Scorsese Marty a movie about food I paid the bill on our first date I settled it up because Dee admitted that she was having kind of a cash flow shortfall kinda thing then *a slow-motion shot intercut with footage of us walking toward Loew's Village Theater VII slow-motion shot of surly waitress back at the Moroccan joint* picking up an order at the kitchen counter the chef sliding over one bill setting down another then waitress ringing up our bill and shoving the 20 percent into the pockets of her black jeans the Moroccan restaurant emptying out now slowing down the last rattle of the last plates circulated through the hot spray of the dishwasher the circularity of this spray like the circularity of the *360-degree pan of St. Mark's*

Place and then v.o. of the guy from King Missile intoning Martin Scorsese I fuckin' love that guy Scorsese Marty Scorsese Marty Marty Marty Scorsese these words containing the secrets of all lost religious sects and *then v.o. of Dee laughing wryly* reciting her monologue about David Cronenberg to a partisan crowd at the Nuyorican Poets Café and the keen surprise of this audience this Bridgeport Film Festival audience as distinct from the partisan already converted Nuyorican audience the audience seeing the film of our first date discovering that the sweetly confused self-centered homely sex goddess shouts stuff like get off my dick or who are the lesbian bitch rock critics from hell intercut now with a moment from a Cronenberg film where a woman is extruding a dozen alien babies from her birth canal babies packaged in some B-film red Jell-O this woman alone in a cabin with the savage cannibal newborns crawling out of her and also a shot of us walking across First Avenue Dee almost killed by cab running a red light pedestrians everywhere nimbly leaping out of the swath of these murderous immigrants the film of our first date as sad as our actual first date as sad as this treatment of the film of our first date as characterized by miscommunication lurching and falling *kitschy ironic slow-motion close-up of our faces* I nervously zip and unzip my leather jacket thinking in voice-over hey I wonder what monologue or song or story I would write about a film director what contribution can I make to this most celebrated American medium thinking it because Dee doesn't ask me because some linear communication which takes prior communications as its field some back-and-forth is not part of this first date of this silence *dutch angle of us walking up the street* more cabs swerving flipping them the bird I can think only of the directors I used to admire like Godard and Hitchcock and

Woody Allen and Scorsese and Bergman and Douglas Sirk but I don't really like any of them anymore and besides don't want to sound like I have advanced degrees *in v.o. long tedious voice-over* because Dee Murdoch is a high school dropout all I want to do um is hug Dee for a really long time but I am busy uh pretending to be a sullen downtown painter or a rock promoter or a drummer *the camera dollies back across St. Mark's across Third Avenue in front of us* picking up the thrift-store plaids and leather jackets with bondage decoration the commotion and the mild desperation of Saturday night suddenly the audience of the Bridgeport Film Festival realizes that this dull and excessively realistic film is actually a yuppie costume drama nonetheless taking a decaying urban milieu as its setting indeed a sort of *Age of Innocence* in fact *Age of Innocence* is the film we have come to see but the film is sold out all movies are sold out on Saturday and the streets are crowded first dates all trying to see films every film in America sold out and in this way our first date stumbles to its dismal close in which we discuss the last installment of *Friday the 13th* Jason's hockey mask the struggle to find commonalities between us I walk her back to her place what else can I do and it's a long walk but we walk for a while like people who want to be in one another's company or in some company at any rate *the camera following us at a discrete distance citing in the process the lockstep of amorous couples throughout film history* this last effort to make the film of our first date an art house hit this treatment now shifts gears Hollywood romance boy meets girl meets cute screen chemistry suddenly Dee Murdoch played by nineteen-year-old girl with incurable bulimia and breast implants and my part handled by Johnny Depp during his sensitive period music coming up behind us now not the thrash of the first two-thirds of the film but instead cheap ambient trance stuff the end of the date that didn't work the end two sensitive but troubled souls trying to make a connection in an ever more complicated world not a dry eye in the house that's right the huffing in the row behind you is the middle-aged woman with the artificially orange hair leaking into her third monogrammed hanky and *v.o. in which I say that I expected nothing to happen* I had no expectations but then I said to her hey I know you have this guy coming into town I know you're in love and you have this guy this crush with the right kind of credentials and I know that among the good feelings you have there won't be room for me and that's okay I want you to be happy I want you to know the happiness out there where the air is brisk where there's a feeling like everything is new but I gotta say Dee there's a feeling between us and I think you ought to take this chance because in this bleak neighborhood the crosstown bus of chance doesn't always stop not on your street and that's the moment when I hug her and in the film my arms fit around her just so and the camera catches this hug like it is happening at some great height a hug as sudden and spontaneous as religious conversion a hug as sudden as fifteen minutes of fame and then I say Dee I'm not living my life the way it's supposed to be lived and *cut to* tangled on her couch yes on her couch with its worn and missing cushions beside us there are stacks of rack-sized mystery novels her leg in its black tights thrown over my hip my arms encircling her the tensile strength of her ribs I can't tell you how much I love the cheap sense of possibility in these moments how like the stop-action nature programming of blossoming flowers I love these moments more than I love the people in them insert epiphany here *third act begins* when I realize the name of the director I would write when I realize the shape of my personal cinematic history not Cronenberg not Marty it's *Andy Warhol* the films of Andy Warhol and I tell her this while I am kissing her lightly on the corners of her mouth while she is wiping the lipstick from my cheeks I tell her Warhol it's Warhol once I had this girlfriend concerned about the civil rights of the women who performed in sexually explicit films were they exploited *and then this tawdry flashback exactly mimicking the style of the films of Andy Warhol* my old girlfriend and I in some completely nondescript room in a four-poster bed myself bored and unclothed and arguing desultorily about sexually explicit films so we decide to rent the films of Andy Warhol art films really they're art films with a lot of fucking in them along with totally improvised dialogue and scenes where people just kind of sit there and the first one we rented was called *Heat* where Little Joe Dallesandro goes out to California to make it big in movies in the process ends up sleeping with Sylvia Miles a formerly glamorous screen legend character there is also Andrea Feldman Sylvia's daughter in the film she also gets involved with Joe in one scene Andrea gives this deaf-mute guy a blow job my girlfriend was getting her Ph.D. in comp lit at Columbia she knew a lot and probably still does about Derrida and Foucault and the various responses to Lacan's Purloined Letter seminar but she was keenly interested in that blow job I do not know which mechanism of identification or analysis the symbolic and the imaginary was involved only that her eyes were like plates she rustled around under the covers my girlfriend as though the blow job itself represented some purloined communication some proscribed contact between desolate hearts some breakthrough in the packaged and celluloid topography of contemporary life in which filmscripts movie dialogue movie ambitions have fully contaminated the spontaneous and

the real have taken for their prey all conversations between
men and women still for a moment *Heat* thawed the ache between us restored us we were in some shiny condition all the
next week we did Andrea Feldman imitations *Mother, gimmme
some of your monaaaaaay* and this was how I started to love the
films of Andy Warhol I told Dee and in Dee's apartment on
the couch flickering neon of a neglected neighborhood bar out
the window the chill of incipient winter in the open window
all the past is with us wrestling together until the bar across
the street closed and *a brief moment intercutting Andrea Feldman*
giving the deaf-mute guy with the blond ringlets a big smile
after she has finished with him a movie within a flashback
within a movie within a treatment and Dee and I tangled in
one another's arms and nine times out of ten the things you
think about another person make it impossible to touch them
but here we are in this treatment in this movie touching *with
these grips and gaffs and P.A.'s and sound people and so forth standing around us drinking complimentary diet sodas checking their
watches* here we are touching regretting and I'm just making
the dialogue up now and I tell Dee that between the two big
premieres of *Heat* in 1972 Andrea Feldman jumped out of a
twelfth-story window on Fifth Avenue at Twelfth Street not far
from here and she had a Coca-Cola and rosary beads with her
when she did it Dee and I met a guy who jumped ten stories
and he broke everything every bone in his body in traction for a
year and he survived except that he came down sick from blood
transfusions but Andrea Feldman is dead and that's where the
movies got her and Andy Warhol is dead and I am single now
and the furniture is gone and all the stuff you do to prop things
up Dee all this stuff won't get you one more day and your name
in the papers will not get you one more day and when you are a

director if that's where you end up will you remember this night when we were on the couch making up this dialogue *as the final credits marched over our faces* and there was no heat in this night no heat and when the credits are done and *the theater is dark* and the theater is empty big question is residuals net points foreign-distribution options videocassette pay-per-view rights digital storage and retrieval novelization television spin-off toy likenesses theatrical licenses electronic rights and they treat writers like shit in that business Dee sequel to come will you remember?

THE
JAMES DEAN
GARAGE BAND

He walked away from the accident, of course. He left the insurance adjusters and the film agents and lawyers to sift through the wreckage for his remains, and he walked away. Ahead, an old Ford sedan making a left turn. On Route 466. Dean had been driving all day. Speeding like a motherfucker. Rolf Wutherich riding shotgun. Wutherich had tuned up the car that morning. It was performing. This much is well known. Dean said, *That guy has to see us. He'll stop.* But the Ford didn't stop. And then Dean seemed to be steering straight for it. *Wait,* said Wutherich. He had a wife and kids. Wutherich panicked. Grabbed for the wheel. Dean held him off. The Ford telescoped. The Porsche did a couple of jetés and came to rest top down in some scrub. Engine already in flames. A stillness. Again: the sound of the skid and of the chassis being reconfigured, sculpted by chance, the explosion, and the quiet. Dean told me later. Quiet. You could pass from one life to the next without a sound.

Besides the tweed jacket, he was wearing khaki pants, a white cotton T, and Jack Purcells. He got out of the car and dusted off his jacket. He kicked the upside-down door of the Porsche. He hustled Wutherich from the passenger side and got him several yards away. Dean had to extinguish Rolf's hair. It was on fire. He worked desperately, shamefully. Wutherich also had a deep head wound. He was losing a lot of blood. But once Dean was satisfied that his friend was out of danger — the guy in the Ford was completely uninjured; he was standing nervously by Dean's side — once the practicalities were settled, the *opportunity* in this calamity became apparent. It was like an opening between cloud banks. It was like the interstices between fact and fiction. This opportunity was about motion. Leaving behind Wutherich and lawsuits and countersuits and the paperwork and the medical bills and the studios and the tabloids. Leaving the scene of the accident. Dean started walking out into the desert. He was crying. The sun was on its way down. He had no water. But he felt impervious to scorpions or rattlers or magic crows or thirst or anything else. He just started walking. And though he was no athlete soon he was running. Running as fast as his skinny cinematic legs could carry him. Into the desert.

Three or four hours later. The only earthly light from a filling station a mile distant. Above, the stars bloomed like the lights on a marquee. With no good idea about the ramifications of his escape, except the good idea of rugged individualism, James Dean was heading up into the hills. And that was how he arrived in *my town*. Lost Hills, that's the name of it, in Kern County. Fifty miles northeast of Bakersfield. Population, eleven hundred. No industry of any kind. Principal activity: drinking.

We were rehearsing that night.

*   *   *

Garage bands are always in the family. My brother and I were rehearsing, as we did a couple of nights a week, with a guy from up the street. We were in a rut, musically speaking. I can admit that now. We knew only a few songs. We had a couple of originals. We had been thinking about getting some horns, a saxophone player. In those days, you had to have a sax; they squawked at all the dances.

We'd been rehearsing in the shed for two years. For my kit, I made do with a snare, a couple of toms, and a cymbal. My brother, Wallace, played standup bass. The third guy, Rocket, could do a passable imitation, on an electric guitar, of the kind of swamp blues that faith-healed, produced spontaneous tears, and conjured devils. Rocket could sort of play actually. Which is more than I can say of Wallace and myself. I couldn't drum, and I still can't.

There was a knock outside, a knock we didn't hear really, a knock that registered only subliminally in us, and the garage door slid up. I remember thinking that the crickets seemed too loud that night. And the light of the moon was grand. There was this guy in a tweed jacket and khakis. Standing there.

My brother, Wallace, has said in a televised interview that Dean was wearing a tattered shirt and that his face and hands were dotted with blood. Wallace has said that Dean asked for first aid. What a lot of horseshit. Dean looked like any other guy from Lost Hills — he had that beleaguered, small-town, jobless look. There was nothing more to it. *You guys could peel paint with that shit,* he said. He meant the way we played. Then he stood there awkwardly, hands deep in his pockets. We didn't say anything. I wasn't terribly interested in making him comfortable. Rocket was fiddling with the knobs on his amplifier. I started adjusting the height of my stool. It happened, though, that there was an extra guitar, a Telecaster, standing against the wall, next to a rusty hoe. You know how coincidences work, these humdrum celestial interventions. It was a '52 Telecaster. First year they made the model, and I had saved up for months to buy it. Drove down to Bakersfield on a pilgrimage. With the garage door open that night there was a portentous moonlight reflecting off the sunburst design of the Telecaster. Really. That's how it was. Dean seemed to be looking at it. We were all looking at it. The guitar, the moonlight, and James Dean.

Can you play that? I asked.

James Dean said, *Can't really play shit, but I can teach you boys a trick or two. You gotta strum that thing like you're using it to harrow graves.*

Sure, you think I knew who he was. You think I read the papers back then, that I kept up with what was playing at the drive-in or on Main Street. But the papers didn't mean anything to me. I was an ugly kid. I wore glasses and was unnaturally thin, like a sickly version of Buddy Holly. Few girls had kissed me, not even my mom that I could remember, and I spent most of my time at the library. And I'll tell you what I *wasn't* reading. I wasn't reading *Drums Made Easy* or *Guitar for Beginners.* No, I was trying to read Kierkegaard and Nietzsche and the translations of the Gnostic gospels (the Jung Codex) — on interlibrary loan from L.A. — and I didn't give a damn about the movies. Wallace was getting ready to do a mortuary sciences degree. None of us went to the movies. Weren't interested. I was twenty-one and Wallace was a couple of years younger. Rocket could have been anywhere from twenty to forty-nine, *and he huffed glue.* Some kind of aeronautical solvent his dad brought back from the assembly line at McDonnell Douglas.

And it wasn't a garage, actually, where we were playing. Over the years people have asked if it was a real garage. It wasn't. It was a shed *with a garage door on it.* In fact, it was a fallout shelter. My parents, forward-thinking survivors of WW II, built the shelter after Eisenhower's "Atoms for Peace" initiative, about the same time that Fender introduced the Telecaster. The shelter was on an empty patch of desert. A couple of miles from my parents' house, on the outskirts of town. There was room there, on this empty stretch, for Lost Hills to get interested in civil defense. There were a half-dozen shelters, like post-industrial burrows, on the land out there. The desert wasn't well irrigated yet. There were a few windmills fluttering around us, though. I loved windmills. I loved electricity.

When we saw that he wasn't going to leave right away, we set aside our equipment and took those old canvas folding chairs from the shed and set them out back. Weather balloons in the evening sky. Experimental aircraft. It was like there were fireworks out there; it was like the goddamned Fourth of July. And it was no coincidence either that we were sitting in that spot, no coincidence at all. That was where we always sat when we were dreaming big.

Dean told us he was James Dean and explained how he'd made a pretty good movie called *Rebel Without a Cause,* and that he was looking for some peace and quiet, and, well, if you wanted to know the truth, he was dodging this reputation, man, he was fighting off the calculation and spiritual impoverishment of fame, yep, and he had gotten into this accident and hurt a guy he cared about, and he was running from it, and thinking he wanted to be a small-town bank teller and to manage his kid's little league franchise, and to be able to cry at Memorial Day parades and cheat on his taxes and get fat if he wanted and leave a bloated and pasty corpse and carry a pistol and sleep with his best friend's wife without a phalanx of photographers and reporters around, because, he said, *fame and remorse, boys, are one and the same thing.*

I thought he was just a handsome guy. Could have been a pansy maybe. Dean wasn't exactly charismatic when you get right down to it. Wallace, for example, was worried that he didn't *drink* enough. We'd been raised not to trust men that didn't drink. I'd read that in Mongolian culture to refuse an offered drink was dangerous — you could be killed for it — and the desert of central California was in those days a lot like Mongolia. In Mongolia, the shepherds and their great herds of yak and mutton just ambled this way and that, wherever the best grazing took them. And that was what we were doing, as adulthood overtook us. We were southwestern tumbleweeds, going end over end, according to the government of the winds.

I didn't know what Dean was talking about where fame was concerned. Sounded like a lot of complaining to me. Wallace knew, though. He could see the writing on the wall; he could *visualize* the quadrilateral shape of the James Dean Garage Band. He could see how Dean needed us, how he'd been brought here to experience the authenticity of our dim, narrow lives. And Wallace could see how we needed Dean. Pretty insightful for a guy whose job it is now to fill dead bodies with formaldehyde. After a few beers, my brother looked Dean right in the eye and put it to him. *Are you going to give us a hand with*

the combo? Because we hadn't gotten out of the fallout shelter
yet. We hadn't even played a church social or at the V.F.W. or
even for our parents. Our great expectations were locked deep
in us. *Hey, why not,* Dean said, without conviction, *until you find
someone else. Sure. But I can't sing at all.*

We nodded *yes.* Emphatically. The shooting stars burst in
multiples over the sere part of the West.

We did it because we knew, even then, that a three-piece
lineup wasn't enough, wasn't going to get to the sound we
were hearing in our heads. We did it because we had some
models, some music we liked, stuff like Edgar Varèse and
Robert Johnson and John Cage, who had just been doing the
pentatonic scales, stuff like the kind of music LaMonte Young
would soon be making. We wanted to make these pieces that
sounded like the wind blowing through a barn, or like a
neglected tea kettle, or like the little cry of pain that escapes
your lips when you are really lonely. At least these were the
sounds in my head, and I was trying to teach Wallace and
Rocket about them, but I didn't really have the terminology
yet. The thing we had in common then, as a band — and it
was the thing that Dean helped us articulate later by applying
Stanislavsky to the garage band format — was that we had
been *forsaken by earthly affection.* That was the only lyric we
needed. Everything else was just a restatement. Everything we
played was just a simple sentence about our loneliness, about
loneliness and the tan from aboveground tests, loneliness and
jobs at filling stations, loneliness and homeliness and grade
school humiliations, loneliness that we were only now digesting into song. Maybe we thought Dean could help us in this
way. And maybe in the calculating lobes of our American
skulls, we figured that having a movie star guitarist would

help us play the dance halls in Bakersfield. So we could quit our day jobs.

See, Wallace and I had bought a trailer out on the edge of Lost Hills with some money we had inherited from our grandmother. That was where we were living. I didn't know where we were going to put Dean, where in the trailer, but the way I saw it, an actor fleeing the studio system didn't need luxury accommodations. He could just sleep on the floor, as Wallace used to do on his way to blacking out. And that was what happened. That night, James Dean slept on the floor of our trailer, with dirty T-shirts as his pillows, with empties scattered around him. He woke with a stiff neck.

Next day, we went back to the fallout shelter, the four of us. We drove out in a dusty, hand-me-down DeSoto that my parents had given me when I turned sixteen. Dean probably never figured that he'd have to spend his time in a working-class vehicle like that. He probably thought he'd left that way of life back with the Hoosiers. We drove at cruising speed, just above the minimum. Windows down. Desert breezes in our crewcuts. We were eminences from a marginal culture.

The garage door creaked mournfully as it slid up. The shelter smelled like a crypt. I made Rocket use his own guitar at that first rehearsal, even though he was always bugging me to play the Telecaster. Instead, Dean strapped it on. We had a single-tube amp that looked like it was going to short out all the time. You could have fried an egg on that thing. No microphones. Tentatively, at first, we decided on one of the faster numbers, a thing by Rocket with lyrics he made up on the spot: "Rocket from the Tombs." I counted it off. And the engine of our success roared to life. Right away, the tempos were sped up. Right away. Because of Dean. As though the automotive ghost of his Porsche were urging us on, into the dusty attic of our small-town memories. In a couple of takes the song started to sound pretty swell. That wasn't all, though. I want to let you know the enormity of what happened, the real miracle of the first rehearsal. We got Rocket's song — the lyric seemed to concern dead people driving convertibles — up to, oh, about 150 beats per minute. That's what they'd say now: B.P.M.'s. And suddenly, instantly, effortlessly Rocket landed on this certain riff, as though his fingers had been rehearsing it for months. It sounded appropriated, it was so right. *It was the Chuck Berry riff.* Like a year or two before Chuck ever committed it to vinyl. Rocket's fingers did it. Dean pushed him into it. The song slotted into that groove. We were tilting at history.

Dean grew a beard. He wouldn't leave the shed after the rehearsal. So we let him stay there. Until his beard grew in. I wondered how, over the long haul, he was going to live in that tiny, airless space. He was used to Beverly Hills or Santa Monica bungalows with their artificial landscaping, air-conditioners, toy dogs, ocean views. But as the days passed we found him cooking canned beef stew over the olive flames of Sterno, sitting on the reinforced concrete, reading and rereading the opening of *Dharma Bums.* He looked, if not happy, at least relieved.

He started to grow his hair out, too, like a beatnik. Or that's what I supposed, though Wallace and Rocket and I didn't exactly know what beatniks looked like. I'd read Ginsberg and I liked the sound of his catalogues, but I was more interested in continental thinking — Camus and Sartre. We hadn't actually seen any beatniks in Lost Hills, so we made up what we thought they were. They were figures of myth, like film actors.

According to our imaginations, the beatniks had borrowed from every pertinent strain of Western thinking — strains both ascetic and decadent — and had thrown off anything they didn't like, anything that constrained the articulation of desire. Something like that. And these ambitions turned out to be Dean's ambitions. He taught them to us. He used sense memory. *He used the Method.*

When Dean finally had the beard he agreed to go out in public. He had put on a little weight, too, he was getting himself one of those country midsections that spills over a turquoise belt buckle. He'd started to drink. No one ever gave him a look in town, though. They just didn't care. And even if they had known this was the guy from *Giant,* even if they'd known he was here among us to slip the noose of Hollywood, well, the people of Lost Hills weren't going to get in his way. No one ever walked up to him and said, *Hey, didn't you die in a car wreck a couple of months ago?* It would have been rude.

It was about this time when we got the gig at the jazz club, Wally's. In the weeks before, Dean led us through a crash course in free jazz. He'd blindfold us or make us play our instruments backwards. He said we had to stop adhering so strictly to the downbeats. It was Wallace who had the first breakthrough in this area. And this breakthrough was truly emblematic of our sound, of what we did later. In fact, Wallace's jazz work is really important to any real critical exegesis of the James Dean Garage Band. If you were going to do a psychoanalytic reading of our dynamics, say, you would have to point to Wallace's relationship with my dad — always stormy, and punctuated by long periods of parental neglect — and to his resultant need for a father figure, or at least an older brother figure, who could make him feel secure enough to provide the bedrock structure — or in this case the *freedom from structure* — that we needed in the lower end of our sound. This need was fulfilled in the appearance of Dean. Through Dean, Wallace suddenly understood the way his bass could wander from the rigors of the blues as they were traditionally played. He ate better after that, too.

Having secured this first convert, Dean started holding me after rehearsals. *He had jammed on bongos with Monk and Coltrane,* he said, *and the thing they knew was how to let go of the time signature, just let go of it,* he said, *and see where the kit takes you after that, plug into the rigors of your feelings, man, and let go of the beat, not worry about it,* he said, *just play what you feel, just play anything, let it happen, feel your breathing, feel your pulse, the way it's faint and insistent, the way it comes and goes, the way it protests and whimpers and then sings, cries out its hortatory cries, just let it go, man, remember, remember.*

Of course we couldn't play jazz fast — Wallace couldn't do those long convoluted bass solos, I couldn't make the brushes work right — but Rocket was doing something wild. His guitar came to some terrible conclusions during our jazz period. He arrived at a system of accidentals and bad fingerings that sounded like infantile bereavement and rage trying, working, and ultimately *failing* to enunciate themselves. Just the way Strasberg talked about it. Later, of course, Hendrix was aiming for the same thing. It sounded as if Rocket was going to overcome the mechanism of his own breathing, as if the whole history of governmental oppression and religious intolerance were being digested and boiled down in his solos, and also the legacy of his uncomfortable childhood. He played melodies with the bittersweet pathos of silences.

*　　*　　*

Wally's was empty. There were maybe three or four guys on the premises the night we played, guys with really long hair, the kind of hair that Dean was growing, and they were all sitting at the bar. Bikers. I'd never seen any of them in Lost Hills. They'd never seen me either. The tables by the stage were completely empty, little red candles flickering weakly on them. Dean looked like James Dean, you know, as we stepped onto the proscenium — he had shaved his beard by now — and we were playing in public — we were entertainers — but these guys at the bar, they looked right through us.

Here was Dean's bind: if he pretended he was nobody, he was condescending, and if he pretended he *was* somebody, he was putting on airs; he was arrogant. As a result, at the inaugural gig of the James Dean Garage Band, *Dean played with his back to the audience.* A couple of times he stepped up to the extra mike, when we were singing backing vocals on a rave-up chorus, but mostly he was turned away. He was shaking so bad that his playing sounded great — the Telecaster was buzzing and warbling with tremolo. The guys in Wally's didn't give a shit. They never noticed a thing.

As a professional, you have so many preconceptions about playing out. You think because you're on stage that somehow you deserve or command respect. But once we got up there, we forgot everything we had learned in six months of rehearsals. We just plunged ahead. I remember looking at a set list — it was crayoned onto a lobster bib and masking-taped onto my drum case — and feeling like I was going to be sick. We were playing all those songs? One ended and another began, though, without nuance or detail, and we didn't have time to worry. Wallace broke a blister and by the end of the night his strings were covered in red cells and pus. And Rocket's throat closed up. Too much whiskey and epoxy. But it was okay. Rocket sounded like one of those eighty-year-old back-porch Delta blues guys whose life has been a sequence of tragedies. Dean, in the meantime — in one of his forays into the recesses of the stage where no one could see what he was doing — had re-tuned his guitar. It was in some ornery sitar tuning. Sounded really lousy. He was trying to get the rhythm guitar to do some drone stuff. He was getting hip, he said, to Armenian duduk music.

At the same time, I was trying to hold down regular time. I was slipping between four/four and six/eight with these little bursts of sevens and fives. I didn't know what I was doing. As the set wore on, the desert rats at the bar got up and left. We cleaned the place out. We emptied it. Wally himself was shaking his head, mopping the floor as we finished the last few songs. The stench of spilled beer. The sound of the swabbing of Wally's mop. The ringing in my ears. Then: the skein of stars out in the desert. The sputtering of the DeSoto. The rasping sleepers beside me. As I made my way, at thirty-five m.p.h., through the desert.

Back to the garage. More rehearsal. Only way you bounce back from those off nights. Rocket was the next one to develop the avant-garde ambitions that were so crucial to our success. He was starting to learn the rudiments of *feedback* on his guitar. It happened like this. The old amp blew out, our single-tube amp. None of us really had the money to get another. Except Dean. Dean still had some residuals that he had secreted away someplace. In some foreign account. In a Swiss bank, or an offshore trust. With these funds, we made a trip to Bakersfield. We got two Fender amplifiers. One for Dean. One for Rocket.

We had the usual band fights about paying for this equipment. Rocket had to borrow money from Dean to kick in his fourth of any group purchase, and then he always tried to rig the repayments so that they favored his fiscal recklessness. I felt sorry for Rocket, so I intervened to arrange a quarterly repayment plan, which Dean, using negotiating experience from Hollywood, insisted would have to include interest. So I was paying Rocket's interest, quarterly, to Dean, while Rocket was borrowing money from Wallace to pay me back monthly, and also borrowing to repay the principal, which monies I would then, acting as middleman, pass on to Dean to hold in escrow until the interest was paid off, when the actual, final payments on the principal would kick in.

It created some real friction among us.

In the meantime, Rocket started playing with the amps. This was 1957, or thereabouts. Fender had finally developed an amplifier that was loud enough for feedback, for that revolutionary noise. One day Dean was mumbling, as he did, about money, and about songwriting credits in the band. (It should have been 80/20 Dean/band, he argued, as opposed to 50/50, like we'd already negotiated it. After all, it was *his name*.) Rocket had simply had enough. Rocket threw down his guitar in front of the amp — already cranked to capacity — and stormed out of the shed. Into the rain, if I remember correctly. A sudden and vehement desert rain. And the feedback from the pickups in the amplifier, in conjunction with the primitive electronics of the amp, commenced to gloriously *wail*. As if the guitar, the circuitry, the tubes, the pickups, as if all of this equipment were falling into lamentation, as if they were doing call and response with the lightning, over the plains, over the hills. It was a lovely, fuzzy overtone, almost aboriginal in its

84

way. Rocket walked around in circles out in the rain, trying to get straight in his head whether or not to punch out Dean, and then I suppose he heard us laughing, heard Wallace and Dean and me laughing at the racket the amp was making. So he came back. Drenched. And he heard it too. *Listen to that,* he said, grinning wildly, *Damn. That is sweet.*

Right away, Rocket perched himself directly in front of the amplifier, sitting on the floor, with the guitar balanced on his knee, and worked with those ringing, bell-shaped electrical tones. He lived in that howl. Just lived in it. He was finally understanding that his body had borders, that he cast a shadow, that he was capable of acting and being acted upon. Rocket had ambitions now. He wanted to be famous. He wanted to be in love.

Feedback changed everything. For our sound, for the band, for the members of the band. It was ritualistic somehow. Feedback foreshortened the great distances between things, and cleared up the mirages in the desert. It made all of the American West seem like a goddamned global village. It was the legend that wired up our thatched huts out in Lost Hills. For example, Wallace and I started stealing. It was a belated conversion to vice. We were catching up on the rock and roll *lifestyle.* We were out stealing cars from the parking lots of repossession operations. Joyriding in the hills, drinking and driving. Driving into the desert, through endless stretches of sage and yucca and Mormon tea. Setting the cars on fire after, leaving them by the side of the road. We'd stay drunk all day. I had even begun propositioning girls. Groupies, you know? I'd see a girl at a diner and I'd say, *Hey, I'm the drummer in the James Dean Garage Band, and I think I need to put an arm around you.* No refusal was possible. The mere name of our band was persuasive. The neighbors started asking questions about us. The local constabulary forces began stopping us on the road.

And my business was going bankrupt. I'd been running a scrap metal operation part-time since high school — it was mostly car parts and space junk or bomb casements. Stuff I found in the desert. At one time I was a canny and ambitious young man. At one time people were glad to make me part of their *scrap metal needs*. Now the business was belly-flopping from inattention. I was broke. We were broke. Just as we were making innovations in popular music that are still being felt today, we were all getting ready to go on public assistance. Dean bailed us out for a while, paid our expenses, but then even he began to get tight. According to his accountants, he was dead.

This all came to an end in '59, I think, when I actually robbed a drive-thru hamburger joint over in Devil's Den. The next town. They all knew me over there — they'd seen us in the DeSoto. I entered the Jiffy Burger franchise with a German service revolver. I demanded the contents of the register. I was never afraid, not even for a moment. They just *gave* me the money. The manager asked politely if I would pay it back later. It was the most forlorn holdup. I did it because we were playing *loud*, because noise was an unstable element, because we were waking up the dormant ghosts of the desert, and there was no way of knowing the effect this sound would have upon us. My dad had to come and give me a good talking to. He slapped me around once and told me if I didn't shape up, if I didn't look after my appearance, if I didn't let go of this childishness and assume my adult responsibilities I was no son of his. There was no way I'd ever inherit the hardware store.

The real point here is that Dean didn't invent feedback, as

the executors of his estate have claimed. The thing you have to remember is that the James Dean Garage Band was a *band*. Four distinct personalities, each with his own contribution and responsibilities. Our advances and experiments took place in a group context. There was a free exchange of ideas. No one person had any more say than anyone else. It was the unique meshing of our personalities, the interlocking of tastes and influences, that led us to excellence.

And Dean was going through a personal crisis. A desert initiation. As I've told you, he cooked his meals out back of the shed. He began using a regular campfire circle, with hot coals — as though he were some kind of Pueblo Indian. He let these coals smolder for days. One afternoon when I turned up to meet him, Dean had taken off his old beat-up Jack Purcells and was trying to walk barefoot over the coals. There was a strait through the middle of the bed where there were fewer hunks of this brimstone. To my amazement, he managed to scoot across with minimal damage. Two or three blisters, nothing more. I didn't believe it, so I asked him to do it again. Maybe he had access to some period hallucinogen. Whatever it was, he seemed to have no pain, and he was yammering the whole time, yammering about a priest from his childhood who had given him a copy of Jung's *Alchemical Studies* and told him, *man, that the search was the thing, and not the destination, that you had a path and it narrowed and it asked sacrifices of you, man, and you were bound to tread upon it, wherever it led.*

Mere spiritual investigation was fine, of course, it was part of the desert palette, except that Dean didn't seem to be able to withstand it. He was crying a lot. Sobbing like a girl. And complaining. And he didn't bathe and his teeth were going bad. A couple of days later, at rehearsal, he had a really horrible toothache. He told me he was going to wait through the three or four days of pain until the tooth died. Then it would just fall out of his head. Which it did.

After two years of living in Lost Hills, the guy looked like shit. He couldn't have secured a part in the monster movies of the period. But he was embarked on some odyssey of personal discovery that didn't require citizenship in this world, an odyssey that was probably activated by and transcending the four formative psychic touchstones of his life, *his mother's death, his father's abandonment of him, the Quakerism of his youth, and the James Dean Garage Band.* It wasn't my place to be his spiritual advisor, but I tried. I tried to let him do whatever he wanted, as long as he showed up for rehearsal.

He had some pretty strange ideas for lyrics, too. Here, for example, never before published, is something he scrawled on a brown paper bag. He intended one day to use it for a song: *It's been two years since I touched a woman / It's been two years / Even back in New York when I was a hustler / I never went this long missing that chemistry / I'm missing brand new refrigerators and lawns / the rich smell of freshly cut lawns / I just want to be held, you know / I don't need a studio contract.*

Nervous collapse was just around the next bend. I don't know what the term would be now. Anxiety-depression disorder. Borderline personality. Loss sensitivity. These days they would put him on a serotonin-enhancer. He would bounce back and repudiate the melancholy of his early performances and become a producer of industrial films. But look at the situation for a moment from our point of view. Was Dean's erratic behavior affecting his personal or business life? *He had no personal life, really.* Was his eccentricity affecting the band?

It was not. We could follow Dean and Rocket wherever their impulsive, shifting, whimsical, malevolent improvisations took us. Dean would teach us a couple of chords one day and the next day the same song would be totally different. He would challenge us to call up the worst incidents from our bumpkin childhoods and to dwell upon them — the accidental deaths of playmates, the sexual explorations of neighborhood girls — and then he would leave us there in the practice room and go down the steps into the shelter to drink by himself. He was erratic like the thunderheads that rolled across the desert were erratic, erratic like the rattlesnakes and the scorpions in the parched crevices of desert, the windmills, the UFO's.

Wallace started doing Sufi spins in the middle of the rehearsal space. He would put down the bass and stretch out his arms and begin dervishing to the riffs around him. The band seemed to be free-falling toward some disorder. There were days we had cases of beer on the floor and we would play "Rocket from the Tombs" twenty-five times, for hours and hours, *actually attempting to summon the American dead from their hellish convertibles.* We played until the rehearsals spilled out onto the empty acreage around the fallout shelter, and we would go sprinting — east and west, north and south — into the night, in search of angels who were never coming for us. In search of the agency that would lift us up and transport us from the lower middle class and from the small town where we'd been raised. Yes, the band had changed us. Dean's fame had contaminated us, and our obscurity had contaminated him. We weren't close, the four of us; we weren't heartfelt *discussers,* men's movement guys, but we gathered out in the sage on these nights and made the campfires of desert mythology and we waited for signs.

It was the last of these nights that Dean gave us the news.

Fellas, he said to us, *I have to tell you something serious. I am sure sorry to bring it up, but I don't see any way around it, and there's no easy way to break the news so I'm just going to have to tell you. . . . I have to go home. Guys. I'm sorry. I'm really sorry. . . . I gotta go home, to California, because I'm . . . Well, I think I'm falling apart. I don't know what's up or down, fellas. I'm all confused. I just can't stay here any longer. I want to. It's something I want to do, but I can't. Look, this has been coming to me in the last few weeks. You know the energy's sort of getting strange out here, I'm feeling like the past is catching up with me. I'm losing it. I gotta admit I don't know why I'm out here. . . . I don't know why I came out here. Because once you're the snack food for this thing, this system, boys, this celebrity, you're snack food for good. You might as well lie back and enjoy it, that's what I'm thinking. So what I'm saying is I don't see any choice, don't see any way around leaving. I hate to do it to you, because you've been like brothers to me. You guys took me in, gave me a place to sleep. But that's just the way it is. . . . It's . . . it's hurting me out here. Hey, listen, fellas, I know, I know, I'm gonna make it up to you. I'm gonna repay this debt I have here. I got a promise for you. I've done a little homework. I've made a few calls. I've booked us into the Café Vertigo. We're gonna play L.A. We're gonna play to the stars.*

It was great news, right? It was the end of our naive ambitions and the beginning of our *total hegemony*. The hegemony of the James Dean Garage Band. It was the kind of good news that makes it hard to sit still. Your body gets a carbonated jumpiness. You can't sleep. You become a compulsive talker. Your posture changes. Your hair inexplicably parts the right way. It was great news! So, to say that Dean's offer *contained the destruction of everything we stood for, to say that going to L.A. to make it big was our biggest mistake* — that would be stupid, would be un-grateful, would be insolent. Well, but listen. There's evidence.

We started having artistic differences.

For example. I was feeling the constraints of the major chords, the major triads. I heard that D-A-G progression in rehearsal and I just about broke out in shingles. I didn't want to play any chords at all. Chords were like the demonic music of radio game shows and political rallies. And they were every-where. Dean would count off and dive into that rut every time. It was a new thing for him — being conservative. That same old Chuck Berry shit. I would be tempted to throw my sticks; I would be tempted to walk out of the shed; I would be tempted to chuck it all and run. If I could have covered my ears and drummed at the same time, I would have. I was trying to get Rocket to tune all six strings to C. I wanted to invent punk rock. I wanted to play unrecognizable chords and shout the most lacerating words. I wanted to bury the popular song in sand, up to its neck. And Wallace was off on his own trip too. He was still into jazz. He wanted to play hard bop. Theme/solo/solo/theme, that kind of stuff. Rocket was doing industrial/thrash/metal crossover noise. It was cacophony.

Dean also decided he should be the drummer. He tried to go behind my back with it, to the other guys. *Behind my back.* Can you believe this? He came over in rehearsal one day and just stuck out his hand, for the sticks, with that smug, passionless expression of his. *If you can't play the darned things, someone else can do it for you, pal,* he said. *I've talked to the boys and they agree. We all agree. This isn't marching band hour. If I have to do it, I will.* I got up off the stool and threw it at him. The stool! And when it missed I rushed at him with my balled fists. Because it wasn't about the band anymore. It was about a way of life! I had become a scrapper — Dean, with his invocations, had converted me himself — and I would stop at nothing now. With a trash can lid I began to beat him over the head. Until he was yelling for help. The little Hollywood fucker curled up like a ball. Protecting his million-dollar cheekbones from the absolutes of drumming, from the unavoidable in this desert life, the unavoidable that he had thought *would not apply to him* when he came to Lost Hills to hide.

Dean was trying to organize us — he was raising his hysterical mumble above the din — as if organizing us was going to be his next great creative comeback. He had become an explainer. *No, listen, guys, listen, we gotta rely on the sound that's going to work for these people in Los Angeles. We have to find a niche and occupy it. Just this once. C'mon guys, don't fuck it up. We have to play to the people this time. You know? That way we'll get more work. You guys want to work, right?* It was a debut for him, he kept saying, it was a debut. And the rest of us were supposed to be happy for the break, happy to accompany him. We were supposed to be happy about any old brush with fame. He tried to make us grateful for a break. But we'd seen now where fame led, we'd seen that no one gave a shit about talent lost or squandered or careers that fireballed to a close, that no one gave a shit about the famous at the moment they put the barrels of automatic weapons into their mouths and their lips tightened around that lavender steel, the famous leaping from highway overpasses or turning blue with needles in their arms, the famous in the state psychiatric hospitals shuffling the lengths of corridors on anti-psychotic medications, the famous running from fame, the famous with night sweats trying to remember why they did what they did, no one gave a shit about them, then or now, except insofar as they could talk about it in public and brighten a conversation with friends who got to be anonymous at the end of the day. Dean was just trying to parlay what Rocket and Wallace and I had been building for four years into another film contract and some paid vacation at a fat farm where he could also have his dead teeth fixed, where he could have some lite cosmetic surgery and get some new clothes and *that would be the end of us.* Right? What about me and Wallace and Rocket? What about the lost souls of Lost Hills? Did *the industry* think it could just pluck us out of the heartland and send us back? What kind of options were left to us?

In fact, there were some options. Maybe we could keep going when Dean left, when Dean sold out. Maybe we could get another rhythm guitarist. We could get one of those really great songwriters, like the guys that wrote "Heartbreak Hotel," one of those Memphis or Nashville guys, one of Elvis's team, and record a cynical and calculating tearjerker that would rocket up the charts. We could put away a little money — after we bought the Cadillacs with the fuzzy dice and souped-up engines. We could invest in pension plans or mutual funds so our children and children's children would attend first-rate private schools and come out at debutante balls and retire wealthy and always have health insurance and full-time nannies.

We went along with Dean. To L.A. We went along.

On January 1st, 1960, we played our first date there, at the Café Vertigo. In a swirling sandstorm, we drove the DeSoto in from Lost Hills. We were tense with excitement. Because we were going to bring these jaded salesmen and women a little of what we knew, which was that life and love were just regret in three dimensions, and that the uplifting ballad, the spirited rocker, the heart-wrenching jazz torch song, these could all be *tools of the mass market.* We could have it all. We could move the hearts of middle America *and* represent the delirium of guitars turned way up, out of tune, played badly.

I would like to tell you, as Wallace has claimed on the television talk-show circuit, that the Café Vertigo was packed, that there was a line around the block for this outfit called the James Dean Garage Band. I would like to tell you that, unlike our first gig at Wally's, our second was standing room only. But as we waited in the front of the café for the audience to trickle in, as we sat at a table sipping drinks, the reality of the situation began to dawn on us. There was no audience. There would be no audience. It was like this: *James Dean was really dead,* as you and I know. His warm body, across the table from us, was an impertinence. No one wanted to know, no one wanted to hear about it. Even Rolf Wutherich, whose life Dean had saved back on the soft shoulder of Route 466, didn't show up that night. He was doing the NASCAR circuit, yanking those tires off in some pit stop. And Clift, Brando, Newman, Martin Landau, those guys? Dean's acquaintances from Strasberg's classes? Forget it. *They had the story of James Dean and that was enough.* Dean had even cut his hair for the occasion. He'd bought a new pair of jeans. He looked like a movie star, relatively speaking. He had a Mona Lisa smile. We were all four squeaky clean pop singers from small-town America. We were going to seduce the daughters of Californians. But this wasn't how it turned out. Instead we were facing the same disenchanted crowd we had faced at Wally's. Alcoholics. Guys with red eyes. Hell's Angels. Guys from flophouses.

In a state of geometrically increasing anxiety, we waited at a table in the back. Dean mumbled about betrayals and favors

unreturned, swivelling desperately each time the door of the
joint swung in. Long stretches of morbid silence. Some love-
lorn country singer warbled on the jukebox. We drank. Then
Dean asked me to write up the set lists. A pre-performance
ritual. We had planned on a program that relied on our most
sanitized, our cheerfullest, our most reverentially pop songs. I
took the four moistened cocktail napkins from beneath our
drinks. I produced a golf pencil I had brought for this purpose.
I licked the tip of it. And then I made *four different set lists.* A
different set for each of us. I took my own initiative. On
Rocket's list, I wrote one song only. "Rocket from the
Tombs." On Wallace's list, I wrote all the jazz songs. On my
own, I listed only some items I needed from the grocery when I
got home. And on Dean's napkin I listed all of our pop
songs — with their perfect pop song structure and their sunny
truths about love. *I did it because I didn't care, or because I did, or
because I couldn't shake the town where I was born, like James Dean
couldn't shake Indiana. I did it because I had to; because it was the
last thing left to do.* When the bartender strode to the mike to
announce us, I handed out these lists. In the commotion of our
decline and fall, the three of them didn't even bother to look.

We climbed the three steps to the stage. Dean didn't greet
the audience and he didn't introduce the song and this is how I
managed to effect my prank. Dean, with his back turned to the
bar, just began to count off. *At a breakneck pace,* because the first
song on Dean's list — in stark contrast to the lilting, Carib-
bean samba Wallace was about to tackle — was one of our
faster numbers. However, the count didn't seem fast. It seemed
interminable. The band knew there was trouble before it even
happened. Wallace looked dumbfounded. He rushed over,
again, to the spot where his set list was taped to the floor of

the stage. Rocket turned entirely away from us and readied a completely ugly minor chord on the upper neck of his guitar. I used a mallet on the Chinese gong behind me. Dean arrived at the middle of the count. Another endlessly sustained gong crash. The feedback in Rocket's amplifier. The buzz of household wattage. The sound of glasses being set upon the bar. A siren outside. Rocket clearing his throat in the mike. And Wallace's simpering, melodious bass tiptoeing into the arrangement.

Dean reached *four*.

It started like a car crash. We fell upon this racket like we had reason to suppose that popular music was trustworthy, that the cardiological regularity of four-four time and verse/chorus/verse/chorus/bridge/verse/chorus structure could in some way forestall our uncertainties. That's what we thought at first. But certainty itself became a delusion in the trajectory of our squall. Nothing was certain. The famous dead didn't even stay dead. The dead walked the street in new jeans exacting their prices, making big Hollywood deals. The living barely registered a pulse. Fame was a sham; the GNP, GOP, the national census, the national debt — it was all the stuff of spooks, the living dead, the body-snatched. We were outside all that. Sensible things seemed ridiculous. We were lumbering through the most awful dissonance. We were playing in different keys. It wasn't going well. But you know what? We didn't stop. We never got to a second song. I kept going. I wouldn't stop. And Rocket was following me. And then Wallace's bass was suddenly strolling along with us. We had become some collective medium, some dictionary of signs and symbols that was wholly unconscious and full of the pitch and shit that no one wanted to think about; we had access to the store of all bad rock and roll riffs past and future and to the encyclopedia of learning that stretched back through the Dark Ages to the Gnostics and beyond to the earliest cave graffiti and suddenly I realized that Dean was leading us again; he was our front man, his face screwed up like a kid whose lollipop has been taken from him, jigsawing these harsh chops on the Telecaster, and we were powerless to stop now and we were doing it because *we just were* and nothing could bring us to a stop. For forty-five minutes, the same two nasty dissonant chords over and over again and then Rocket and Dean had stripped it down to one note they were trading off in call and response, messing with the knobs and the switches on their guitars so that this one droning note with its microtonal variations bent and faltered in the cavelike emptiness of the Café Vertigo and I was riding on the toms now, staying off the snare so that the kit had some prehistoric tribal stuff coming out of it and I hallucinated Pleistocene dancers and hunter/gatherers on the stage on backing vocals and the legion of vision questers renouncing the world doing stage dances among us and then I saw a southwest covered with radioactive glass and computer geeks dancing barefoot in it all night to synthesizer trances. When I woke from this dream Wallace had let go of the bass and he was in the center of the stage, spinning.

The applause was diffident. There was almost no one there. It didn't matter. We had the giddy sense of a failure so complete that it seemed close, as an ideal, to sweetest success. We caught our breath in the men's room. I had my ass in a sink — there were no chairs — and I was smoking a reefer that Dean had passed to me. *Holy shit,* he said. *What was all that?* The joint was laced with some poisonous Middle Eastern hashish or something. Wallace was quietly overtone singing, like he was a Tibetan monk. Rocket was passed out in a stall. And Dean was smiling his winningest Hollywood smile. He never was going to make it in this town again.

We were happy. Happy from the splendid coincidence of noise and space and exhaustion that marks a heartfelt night on stage, irrespective of its reception. We had no illusions about the two inches of press that the L.A. *Times* would devote to us in their rag the next morning. We waited at a motel, we waited for the calls, for the managers, for the booking agents, for the calls that never came. We waited. I remember pushing Wallace into the pool behind the motor lodge. Then Dean pushed me in. Lots of laughs. And then all of us drying out on the new plastic deck furniture they had by that chlorinated puddle. All of us knowing that the phone was never going to ring. Finally, after a couple of days, the money started to get short. In a week we had exhausted all the cash we had. None of us, not even James Dean, the actor, had the money to live in L.A.

Wednesday morning I went to rouse Dean from his coma for the usual half-dozen cups of black coffee. The door was open. His stuff was gone. Of course. The motel room had an antiseptic sadness. The motel room was just a motel room. The motel room was made up as artlessly as if he'd never been there, as though he had never graced our lives in those years after the wreck. In those thin towels and bleached sheets, there was no drama of rebirth or regeneration. There was no drama at all. The light drifting in through the draperies was anemic. My life was a desert highway stretching out in front of me. My life felt irredeemable. My ears were still ringing.

Here's the note he left crumpled on the bed: *Gone to Cleveland. Keep your mouth shut. Use the name if you want. Dean.*

And it was in Cleveland, of course, that he had his second crash.

Anyway, that's how we came by the name. The James Dean Garage Band. And that's how we came to record, in 1963, our one LP with its one hit, "Death Valley Dream Baby." That's the story, all right, and if you have a few more nights to spare I've got a thousand more just like it, because I'm a desperate guy, and like all the anonymous I have the urge to talk. You name it. I've got all kinds of stories, stories based on real stories, stories of the most rigorous truth, stories of legendary couples, stories of their partings, stories of the little guys who live in small towns tucked in back of Air Force test sites. Who's to say? I have time. More than you, probably. This is how I see it: You have your luck as a kid and sooner or later that luck runs out. After that what you have is memories. I run a Hallmark store in Cholame now. Get it? I'm fifty-seven years old. I sold my '52 Telecaster to make car payments. When I was twenty-eight, four or five years after I quit playing music, I married a postmistress. Because she was pretty. Because she was sweet and she loved me. So that we could have two sons who could both be drummers like their dad. For those reasons. But also so that I wouldn't have to wait for my mail. Because there's a letter coming, a letter from the actor James Dean. And here's what it will say: If the life you lead is not the one you dreamed about, *then flee.*

PIP ADRIFT

The longboat was lashed to the side of that struggle, the waves a succession of hardships, the harpoonist with his dart aloft, the others at their oars or bailing furiously. The sturdy planks of the craft were surrendering. Hull groaning, aft end swamped and still the quarry circling them — a multitude of irons in its flank.

Like some bifurcated flag, the way *that tail* shadowed them, like an otherworldly mast with black and gray colors, with its semaphoric message, and Pip aged twelve — his second lowering as after-oarsman in the stern of the longboat — *assembled fearlessness in himself* as he'd been instructed to do. Until the sight of it, that is, the sight of that tail, and then this darkness rose in him. His hands fumbled on the oar, his eyes frozen on the scale of the thing. The sea rushed in through a leak. Pip, quarry himself, prey of watery spirits, *Pip had been born scared.*

Hadn't he once already *proven his cowardice?* Hadn't he already quenched himself on his own shame, found himself *unable to perform his duties?* Yes, he had gone over the side, he had launched himself into that dangerous freedom, that current rushing for *the blade,* as they called it, the blade that separated water and sky, as good as dead that time, except that as he plunged out thoughtlessly, he went *under the lines* as they were uncoiling, the lines spinning out into the drink — harpoonist having just pierced that fish's brow. Yes, Pip went overboard, drenched, sodden, but lashed around chest and neck, lashed improbably against the side of the longboat, strangling, as good as dead, as they inched out toward the mouth of that thing —

Little turd, they had calumniated him. He wriggled there frantically — *you little black turd* — until they cut him free, from that swoon of faintheartedness. Reluctantly. They caught the line just above him, unsheathed their blades, but they'd leave him the next time, they said, *damn right you'll be a piece of driftwood you little turd your skeleton washing up clean that's all*

Still, when he saw it coming again this day, this second time, when he saw the tail, the unnamable digits of that tail, *a black hand* from deepest below, the black hand that *called to all nigger cabin boys,* black calling unto black, when he saw it, the fist in his chest throbbed with its own insistent commands. Commands in the language of the humors in him, in the language of black bile. He was part now of the society of lost causes.

So he leaned out over the gunwale, turning his back to the good men with their pipes and ragged jerseys and their knotted beards, who swatted him in the galley and demanded their seconds — the closest thing to his kin — and as he turned away *he was afraid and crying.* No, no, no, it was spray, just spray, as the hull of their vessel crested another wave, yes, and then that splendid quarry *breached* not ten yards and he saw it for a moment in the air, its perfect mastery of the sea, its illimitable eye fixed upon them, fixed *upon his own eyes* filled with their inadvertent tears. *They will boil me in the try works when they are through with me until I am dead.*

Now the tail came down upon the gunwale, no more than a foot from where he was poised. The stern plunged for a moment beneath the roiling waves. The whitecaps were their company now. The bailers manned their buckets. But Pip *couldn't stay,* couldn't stay. He tarried only a heartbeat once the decision came to a boil in him. The hull's vertebrae groaning, cracking a second time — the tail landing violently upon it. And then the whale, the right whale, the perfect whale, the limitless whale, drove down beneath the rippling surfaces of the sea, the irons piercing him, trailing their several lines. General silence. In an instant, Pip knew. He was unenslaved.

And *dove dove yes dove his ankle catching once* the sound of his splash, the whale breaching again, off to starboard, the longboat behind him, feeling the creeping chill of the depths, the orbit of his exhalations, not knowing which was down or up or *toward the coast of the Hindoos,* not knowing just letting the momentum of currents and the ineluctable ethics of gravity take him. Immersed again.

Until he drifted up at last. The bellows in him recognized where air and sea met. His head bobbed up. He flung off his cap, shook out his curls. His boots, with their own madness,

kicked desperately under him; he reached automatically for
their laces — falling under the surface again — pulling them
from his feet. Free now, coming to the surface, his head above
the surface, blessed particles of wind, blessed particles on his
dark cheek. Was it sky? Was it more undrinkable ocean?
Which was sky? It *was* sky — he could mark the differences —
and the longboat thirty yards off and moving *away*.

They hailed him. *You stupid little fuck I told you you little castaway
fuck I'd throttle you you'll never walk again if you jump one more time,*
but Pip was swamped by the next wave and by the one after
that, gasping when next bobbing to the surface. *Jesus Christ don't
cry stupid fool they'll be around for you hang on just hang on stupid
little fool holy Jesus* And they were off in pursuit, not going to lose
another fish for the witless cabin boy who couldn't keep his arse
in the boat and cleave onto the goddamned oar.

The other two boats having lowered made a slow turn in his
direction. Like enormous swans. He reached to hug the chi-
mera of this rescue, cried out for them, but then, beyond him,
beyond the instance of his terror, there were *spouts,* more
spouts, the civilization of spouts, from each watery acre a
spout. Oh, commerce. These boats, then, turned to pursue the
other longboat, in turn pursuing the quarry, *though Pip was
waving madly.* He bobbed up over some oceanic valley *Hey there,
hey you, fishermen!* But they were off. They were away. Only the
sound of his feet kicking steadily above these fathoms. How
many fathoms? How many below in the long rippled expanse
before him *no ship no boat nor man upon it*

*   *   *

Glittering immensities, *his shallow breaths mounting,* rippled and commingled immensities around him. Ether above. The minutes passed, the sun dipped into the tides. Or the tides into the sun. Or each into each. They were confused somehow, these principalities. His dread, see, not simply of being shredded by daggered jaws or of being sucked into the pillows of some great poisonous squid or of drifting down to the unvisited beaches at the bottom of the ocean, but the dread also, the unquenchable woe, of being somehow suddenly *upside down* head first among phosphorescent plankton or teeming prawns or squawling fishes or the sharks in their restless circles, *upside down* thinking he was moving toward the surface but moving instead down into gray forgetfulness *no air in him* the prey in their glittering dominion or negligent caverns where he didn't belong, the sky below him the sea above and God was airless and Pip had gills had sprouted gills or had his own blowhole in the seventh circle of a kindom of neglect.

Feeling the trousers, the jerkins, strangling him now too, *the fucking coward boy Pip fucking coward,* his black hands wrestled with this garish canvas skin. He pulled them from him until only the white drawers that disguised his cowardly knob remained. And then those off too, until his lower half was exposed in the elements. What was that tickling his toes now? *Oh God let me please see no sharks in this oh my lord Jesus I will not die from this drowning or die from sharks so that my sweet family and their little house will never more know of me please bear me up through all the infinities in your glittering immensity your empty and twinkling permanence in your*

*   *   *

The colorless swells with their colorless manes galloped over Pip and with his free hands he grasped for some chink in the face of the dusk. Clawing now. Was that a boat on that rolling plain? Yes! That *was* a boat. In nautical miles he measured, a nautical mile or more, that spot on the faded charts before him, his acute measurements, his exacting nautical calculations — *my sextant here* — a mile away its oars like the ligaments of beetles *another boat passing this black boy for dead* or just another vision of the pridefulness of longboats at the horizon, the arrogance of them. Not a boat at all. It turned out. His vision.

In the lake where his father first taught him to swim — *his hysteric breaths coming slower now* — the difficulty learning to swim. His father showed him with his enormous palm upon Pip's bellows *see here is how it fills and here is how it empties this part of you breathe in and feel* and held him straight out, knee-deep in the lake. Pip lay out straight, his father holding him, and he locked his eyes upon his father's broad smile *fill the bellows Son* and then his dad began to remove his hands. This miracle, flotation! This miracle of God! Through which we keep the company of fishes, of leviathans! But even at the instant of that magic *No Paps don't take your hands away so that I drift under* afraid even then, afraid to sink helplessly like the boots he once saw on the bottom of the lake on a bright summer's day. Here he was a soldier's boot in the sediment at the bottom of the uncharted lake of the skies.

That hand that teaches us to swim it's as big as a barn, and it keeps us ahead of the first animals ever swum in the sea, their jaws tightening around us *No my Paps don't leave me here* because all domains are the domain of whalers and their folly. They taught us how to drown. Whalers were the first to drown. His father was right there, his father's hands bore him that day from the swimming lesson and carried him home, through the path in the woods, past the horses in the stable in the woods. There was another boy there lofting bales. Sound of mourning doves and horses' hooves. Father carried him from that sweet fresh lake water, used to drink from it when thirsty, until the day his father slept deep in some fever, until Father was home sick, caught it after winter fishing, in the ice, *his Paps,* brought home a dozen stingers he called them and fed the little ones *and then his Paps ashen and silent and sick* and Pip adrift.

Sir please take him to work his father dead and gone His mother came with him to ask for the job. Pip was afraid to speak at first, to make his mark where the man in the waistcoat had asked him to do so. How long had they waited there? And how did that time compare to this measureless instant? *Three quarters of an hour? A whole afternoon?* A minute or less? He couldn't tell the hands of a clock, anyway. His father had made him swim the length of the lake so that he could be sure that Pip would never drown, and Pip did it too one time. He swam a country mile, his father said it was anyway. Pip swam it in his breeches *How long ago was that? How long did it take? How long did he sit in that office and how long languish here?* He was far from there, he was upside down and swimming a thousand miles in the silent kingdom of grief, where the clock ran the other way around. *Could swim* he told the man in the fancy clothes, could carry a crockpot among the men at table, could swim and fetch and carry and earn his keep. His mother held him tight around the waist *No room for a boy of his slight physique and retiring temperament hasn't gone to any proper school why I doubt if he even knows which way this clock runs.* His mother wept. A little rivulet upon her cheek. What was she thinking? And seeing her like that the man relented. He relented. Irritably. *He supposed there might be room for a nigger boy.* What good fortune! Relented so that Pip could drift thus, drift up into the sky and into the heavens where they would name for him a constellation. And his momma held his hand holding the quill making his mark —

Still after all wearing the necklace she had given him for the journey and with one tug he freed himself from it and tossed it back over his shoulder. Each cloud that passed overhead, each with its threat of a tempest, seemed to reflect the face of that whale that was coming up under him now, from dominions underneath, a whale with his henchmen, those famished gullets coming for him to gorge themselves upon him for all his cowardice, or just his mean birth, or his blackness, or maybe this leviathan would simply swallow him and he would be carried off to the limbo of old whale stories. His face would not be his face when he was cut from the insides of that fish it would be the face before he was born, his constellation face *Oh where is the ship Mister Jesus Mister I will never jump again Good Lord Jesus I have no wish to hurt any living thing*

Teeth chattering. His newest worry concerning the fraying hemp in his legs — his legs had reached their limit. His melancholy now like his father's *melancholy of the elements* the circular generations the black men with their quick sad lives and his mother wouldn't sing anymore alone in the Commonwealth of Massachusetts her song *we are all of us adrift in the open seas we are all of us flimsy scarecrow rag doll gunny sack cabin boy bodies diving over the side to drift alone on the seas* as though standing on some strange platform on the head of the right whale *I will sing naked for my death I will sing for my death sing you a song of my woods and my boyhood never gonna see it again* you great black gods of the deep with your fountains where have the fishes taken these fearless white men shucking off the last layer of clothing now his wool blouse one with the lukewarm of Poseidon's fathomless county a tingling in the distant extremities with the coming story with the coming dark with the coming end

could see now the lights on the ship yes it was the ship yes and with it a longboat it was some ship some boat and calling until hoarse oh calling his voice silent or ear-splitting his very heart split with the shrillness of his cries *I didn't mean to jump I didn't mean to oh please sir I will clean your johns and swab your decks and carry your suppers oh please* how far off now how far off? A ship to neglect him a ship of Chinamen or Hindoos who would think him the goblin of this ocean and he *was* a goblin no home but the sea no nation but this brine. The distances all shortened or stretched the very notion of distance unwieldy and fuzzy, shrunk from salt, obliterated from immensity, like the strange reverse timepieces of calamity. He had this tambourine with him, how could he have overlooked it, it was with him now, and there was sweetest music of angels in the lapping of waves, in this disordered rhythm — his threnody across empty expanses — yes, it was Pip the boy with the tambourine the castoff of all whaling expeditions Pippin the forgotten.

The sea horses the mermaids the rays the porpoises the hammerheaded fishes and their appetites their schools kissed his forehead now counted him among them as he drifted out toward the edge of the flat earth just above the waterfall that poured into the celestial emptiness where hunters and prey alike met their deaths he would never see the sun again or know the singing on the green, never know the melancholy in his mother's eyes nor drowse in her arms he was tired he couldn't flap this way a minute longer this chicken-flapping would not save him the flapping of cowardly buoyancy the fishes nibbled the feet from him he could reach down and run his fingers along the shimmering bones and *laugh* swimming in the sky at the end of the oceans swimming in the sky with the sullen purposeful fishes and netted by the white men who would dine on Pip tonight have him in chowder thick and rich in milky broth *don't jump again* these white men in their little ships these men with their night fevers that curdled their brains the way the ocean itself devoured them the ocean itself poured into their eyes — their inhuman jellies — until they too were empty and drowning in the night sky so he called to them *Don't come for me you ship of fools don't come for me any longer because I will ride the sea horses back into the thicket of original names back before you men came to the white hot center of this monarchy don't come here! Desist! Desist!*

Two or three hours had passed. The dark shadow of the long-boat crested another swell. The boat no more than a shadow among shadows in this valley where he'd been paddling. In lazy circles paddling. Only two hundred miles or more to the coast of the Indies. He must have covered *several thousand feet already.* By the time they came for him, then — with the car-cass, too, and the ship in the distance — by that time, the boy in Pip had vanished. When they came for him Pip was no longer just a cabin boy in the annals of this journey, no longer

a mere name in the captain's log. He had expanded across the
flux of the heavenly demiurge. Pip's eyes lifeless, unimpressed,
were like the eyes of the whale itself. *Ho there you little shit —*
effrontery calling across the gloomy ocean night — *ho there you
little black fool we have come for you in our own good time as you can
see and be thankful ungrateful fuck you'll get your share of this cargo
in Nantucket your hundredth part be glad of that* — his hundredth
part of their control of the high seas, his hundredth part of
their great trade, his hundredth part of the meal in which they
served his flesh, served a chowder made of Pip himself, blink-
ing as their great spoons descended upon him.

The harpoonist it was dragged his tiny, waterlogged frame
from the water. The boy's lips chapped and blistered, his naked
body, his shriveled penis, his dead eyes, his senseless jabbering.
They pulled him into the craft feet first. *Didn't want to come,* in
point of fact, so beleaguered, so ghostly. They had to haul him
in by his feet. They might as well have left him too for all the
good he was after that. It would have been more Christian.
They threw a canvas over him where he wept deliriously. He'd
slipped the treadle on his loom, see. That's what it was like.
He'd seen some other ocean, some ocean of fevers where they
spun the tiniest drops of water, where snowflakes got their six
corners and where the bodies of saints were all crucified upside
down. When they got his clothes on him and the ship under
way, the crew didn't talk anymore about it. It was a shame —
how he was after that. Later somebody threw his tambourine
overboard. He couldn't keep a steady rhythm and moreover he
couldn't keep his hands off of it. And here's the end of the
story. After all that, after all Pip's stupid wasting of our time
jumping over the side again and costing us a whale nearly,

after all that, *believe this,* the captain takes the little boy for his *lover. Well, that's what they say.*

when I got back betook myself straight to his cabin the captain's private rooms dressed in the raiment of the ocean deep in the manner of nature's first flowering and offered myself unto Ahab asking no price take my naked shell so that I may know that my sickness is not mine alone not my sickness alone

A
GOOD STORY

1) *The protagonist introduced herewith presentable and competent,*
which is to say youthful, early thirties, attractive, dark hair —
longish but not too long, clothes stylish but not too stylish,
clothes catalogue-ordered to avoid premeditating in matters of
fashion, *viz.* denim trousers that have been creased just so; care-
less enough about grooming to seem impulsive, calculating
enough to let his beard grow weekends; a buyer of compact
discs already well reviewed; a viewer of films with lines around
the block; competent at work, having advanced to junior partner at the firm, anonymous and hardworking; anonymous even
in spite of the unfortunate calamities of the past — for example, an auto accident at seventeen near the country club in
which the girlfriend in the passenger seat suffered spinal
injury — and *reversals,* such as the shoplifting conviction and
the exam-cheating scandal at the Ivy League university his dad
also attended — he learned from the last of these experiences,
worked twice as hard after his brief suspension; *in short, presentable and competent* with numerous women friends each of them
marriageable and most of them willing, a repeater of jokes

from the trading desks of brokerage firms, a decent enough golfer, a lover of dogs, a winter camper, a fine young American, *name of Steve.*

2)   *Landscape as follows:* Having driven from the city, a particular city, a city large enough to have traffic snarls, *viz.* New York City, having driven therefrom, through irritating traffic configurations, to the country, that is to say, beyond the last stop on the commuter rail lines and thus to towns of rural proportions, towns where it actually snows and there is agriculture and historical architecture, having driven in fact to a particular country house, his father's house, a house with paternal authority seated upon a hill in upstate New York, a hill overlooking a pasture, a pasture containing a barn, a barn giving onto a paddock, a paddock giving onto a ring, a ring abutting a meadow, in which three horses idle, two grazing, one standing as if asleep, chestnut mare, palomino, and gelding, respectively, he pulls onto the dirt road having driven three hours in his imported automobile, his car the color of a zinfandel, the horses — according to a telephone call from his father — are where they are supposed to be, *the landscape is peaceful,* stirring occasionally with sparrows, jays, cardinals, crows, and hawks, small game, country mice, the occasional deer, that afternoon peaceful and meditative, that afternoon in late autumn.

3)   A *cast of subsidiary characters including* a) his father, retired, with gout and arthritis, older than he was once, thinning white hair, a vigorous walker in warmer months — gout permitting — an Episcopalian and a conservative, even allowing for the black period in which he and Steve's mother separated and he grew his hair out and dated a woman twenty years his junior

114

(she left him to marry someone her own age) *or perhaps conserva-*
tive because of this period; b) his mother, who owns and maintains
the horses, who loves animals above all, above people —
including neighbors and children — and worldly things, his
mother tall and slightly stooped, a cautious and deliberate con-
versationalist, withholding at the last instant of some warmth,
and yet thoughtful, a rememberer of birthdays; c) the guy with
the backhoe to whom Steve placed the call early that morning,
the guy with the John Deere cap who, for a fee, would drive his
backhoe up from the gravel pit and dig a hole in the back of
the meadow, the disappointed guy with the disabled son, the
son who has cerebral palsy; d) the large-animal veterinarian
from town who has a gold bicuspid and is full of information
(*if the leaves of living maples are blowing upside down in a stiff wind,*
a heavy rain will follow), the veterinarian who will arrive with
an arm in a sling, with a broken collarbone where he'd been
knocked across a stable by a horse not ten days before; and
e) *the horses themselves,* blessed and ignorant, and the patterns of
these horses grazing (seen from a window in the house on the
hill, recollected by Steve), brown, blond, blond; or blond,
brown, blond; or blond, blond, brown, a right triangle, an
isosceles triangle, the horses as they are fed with the carrots
hidden behind the back, sneaking up to the chestnut mare,
Blossom, the grandest and unruliest, and then her chasing
him, Steve, twenty yards across the meadow at a gallop for the
last carrot, trying to drive him away from Millicent, the middle one, the quietest, or trying to drive him away from Sandman, the lord of the manor, king of beasts, Sandman fat unlike
any horse he's ever seen, Sandman's enormous belly hanging
down beneath his head and his haunches like an inadvisable
plumbing configuration, Sandman, and this recollection: Steve

riding him, riding the gelding bareback at dusk through a copse of trees drinking a beer and calling out to a girlfriend sitting on the fence, calling to her, *Yvonne climb on here with me.*

4)   *And a conflict, of course, involving the mortal illness of one of the horses, specifically Sandman,* some equine cancer spreading through his sinewy flesh, his winter coat hasn't even come in, so sick, and the continuous lancing and draining and cauterizing and surgical removal of tumors particularly on the spot where he was initially gelded, his perfectly obsolete phallus, the vet had doped him for surgery a half-dozen times before, his eyes lifeless, his snout dangling just above the dusty earth in the paddock as they used the very tool, a pair of pliers the size of a man's leg, the very tool that gelded him, to cut from him those malignant fruits and then the cycle of antibiotics until he wasn't eating from the drugs and the tumors were growing back and he would lie himself down in the pasture and rub desperately along the wildgrass, leaving a trail of dried blood where he'd been, until Steve's mother asked her husband to make the decision, *You will have to do it because I can't do it,* inconsolable, absent, back in the city, at a museum perhaps, and her husband had in turn called their son, called Steve, *Listen I need you to come on down here and help me with this because I don't know as I can get around well enough to make sure that this is done properly,* and Steve agreed, never imagining that he would be competent enough to undertake such a chore, thus coming to the unavoidable definition of adulthood: *that time of life in which you take care of things because no one else can.*

5)   *From the conflict to the main action,* which begins at the moment when the competent and presentable Steve Abernathy

zips up his brown bomber jacket and climbs out of the Japanese car by the dirt road (two tracks separated by a strip of fine moss) that leads to the barn, Ed Wilson already parked there, standing by nonchalantly, toothpick in one corner of his toothless mouth, Ed watching the horses, who are certainly skittish at the sight of the backhoe; the horses have moved off, as far off in the ring as they can get, some hundred yards off; then *the vet arrives* and the men stand around the back of his jeep as this trained professional prepares the syringe with the tranquilizer, preparing it with much difficulty because of the arm in the sling, and they are all talking about the way in which the action will proceed and then Steve volunteers to go round up the gelding secretly hoping that some impediment will appear, that some contingency will make itself felt, that somehow he won't *be required to perform this duty,* as he puts one leg over the fence, and Sandman bolts, begins to gallop along the perimeter of that fence head down with an urgency surprising in a horse thirty-four years old sick with cancer, for godsakes, the horse circling with effortless grace, and Steve doesn't even have the lead yet, walks over to the stable and gets the halter and the lead and some carrots, crosses the paddock and out into the ring, all three of them, blond, blond, brown, in full gallop — *they know no way to express themselves but velocity* — and he goes after them in his galumphing human step and they are having none of it. Steve asks to be forgiven for administering mercy with a damned carrot; thus they slow down, the horses, at last, because they simply become accustomed to the anxiety, or because he is a somewhat recognizable figure, or because Sandman's curiosity leads him in close enough, because appetite gets the best of this horse and it's a shame, and Steve slips the halter over his ears and leads him to the fence where the vet has the syringe ready, where the vet with his good arm jabs Sandman in the neck, intramuscularly and the old horse rears for a second, and Steve just lets him go, because what the fuck difference does it make, let him run for godsakes, one turn around the back of the ring and he'll be exhausted; Steve says to Ed Wilson, *Well, you might as well go dig a hole.*

6) *A lapse of good story structure involving a digression on holes* because Ed Wilson's moonlighting gig this afternoon amounts to the overturning of earth in the backyard behind the barn, and while this is going on Steve sits on the fence and watches Sandman lollygagging in the field, and in this interval many holes are called forth in Steve's recollection though they are not entertained for long, since the completion of this particular familial obligation can't coexist with a nostalgia for the feck-lessness of boyhood, with a nostalgia for *holes at the beach* deep enough to break ankles of those who don't look where they're going, and *holes in his nylon jacket* in high school on ski trips where they used to flick matches at each other smoking pot in the ski lifts, *holes in the roof* that he used to go up and patch with his dad, *holes in stories* he told in his teens and early twenties until he learned to *straighten up and fly right, holes* in long-range financial planning, *holes in the backyard* from muskrats or were they woodchucks and soaking those motherfuckers out with some pressurized hose borrowed from the volunteer fire department, *holes until Ed finishes the hole,* you know, fifteen across and five feet deep, it is a job of significant dimensions, the mound on the far side of it, bigger than Steve would have guessed, and they're just going to have to fill it in after, with the backhoe at first and then with shovels.

* * *

7)   *Bring the horse here, you narrator,* that horse doped and docile a green foam at the corners of his mouth, that horse vital
and grand, reduced to this, led here by *the one-armed vet,* then
handed over to Steve, who leads him from the ring to the paddock and from the paddock out into the meadow, the sun beginning to dip, the trees empty but for crows gathered silently
there — the other two horses trailing at a discreet distance, Ed
Wilson bringing the goddamned shovels from the goddamned
rack in the back of the goddamned barn and Steve leading the
horse who must surely spook now from a reservoir of distantly
comprehensible signals in him, *stored for this one moment of recognition,* isn't there one signal in him that will direct him away
from this moment? but too tired sagging as he is led along one
hoof following the others in the gait taught him in the year of
Steve's own birth or thereabouts led over this lip of earth, clods
of grass and roots and earth, over the lip and down into the
hole, the other two horses trailing, the vet with another syringe
into the crater where the gelding will now perish, standing
there tranquilized, docile, *standing in his grave,* and the para-
graph now in which I write of the passing of a horse beloved of
my family in this way, the vet trails the other men and the
horse is docile and calm and a car passes out on the road and is
indistinguishable from the breeze and this fellow Steve, so presentable and competent, does what I myself could not do —
and for this I hold myself in contempt — he stays the horse
while the injection is administered the injection at which the
horse winces again but not for long: first one leg goes limp,
front left, trembles and goes limp and then sequentially the
other three and the vet warns Steve, *Watch it, better watch out!*
and Sandman topples over and the three men stand there
watching his breathing go shallow, their eyes don't meet in the

midst of this respite, and then the vet goes down into the grave with a stethoscope, and the other horses close in now, their snouts and the humid air of their respiration right at Steve's back, and the vet pronounces his pronouncements and Ed Wilson climbs back into the backhoe — idling all this time — and begins to push the dirt back over Sandman and dusk falls and then they take up their shovels and pat it down, pat down the mound, it doesn't take long, and Blossom tarries there circling anxious until led into the paddock, *and then nightfall.*

8)   *In the conclusion it appears that* killing things is the job of men, killing things our first talent as adults; we watch death happen, and then we go on to the last vocation, that transmission of the ache of these encounters, the ache, *viz.* the construction of good stories.

THE
APOCALYPSE
COMMENTARY OF
BOB PAISNER

INTRODUCTION: *John, Composing on Patmos*

I use the K.J., or Authorized Version, where the *thees* are *thees* and the *thous* are *thous*. Ever since I was a kid I used it, ever since the sixties, ever since St. Luke's Parish in Manchester, N.H. You don't get the same kind of line in the Revised Standard Version. You don't find "I am Alpha and Omega, the beginning and the ending, saith the Lord, which is, and which was, and which is to come, the Almighty" (1:8), with its Elizabethan implications of damnation and immortality. Which is pretty much how Revelation begins.

Okay, so it was the first century after Christ's martyrdom at Calvary. His followers were suffering. They were spurned, they were flogged, they were flayed, crucified upside down, torn apart by horses, left out to be fed upon by vultures. You name it. Every conceivable torture was visited upon them. Meanwhile, in the

121

midst of this persecution, St. John the Divine goes off to Patmos,[1] an island off the coast of Greece, and begins — in this intense rage — to write a screed on which his reputation rests among fundamentalists. It's about the future of the church, about the coming house-cleaning among the *chosen*. This is the screed called Revelation. It's his prophecy. A prophecy that contains things "which must shortly come to pass" (1:1). "He which testifieth these things saith, Surely I come quickly" (22:20).

Here's what I imagine: John living a life of complete poverty, confined to a monastic cell with only charcoal and parchment to divert him, unfed, unattended, in a building as scorched as the sands of the Middle East. Or maybe he was even one of those cave-dwelling monks. Unwashed, solitary, in retirement from light. In constant fear of the authorities. Panicked at the thought of his own martyrdom. In cycles, John wept, shouted oaths, prayed joyously. He had visions. Because of migraines. I'd say John had a migrainous personality. That's my guess. Anyhow, in the midst of John's rage, in the midst of his abandonment, an angel came to him and said to take up his pen.

MYSELF, *Bob Paisner, in Chapin House*

John saw a future marked by persecutors, false gods, Antichrists, Gog and Magog, plagues, floods, earthquakes. He saw it this way because this was how he felt about the

---

[1]For this stuff about John on Patmos and other information on the book of Revelation and all its commentators, I'm really indebted to David Burr, *Olivi's Peaceable Kingdom: A Reading of the Apocalypse Commentary* (Philadelphia: Univ. of Pennsylvania Press, 1974).

church in the first century. Saw it this way because this was the *moral environment* in which he lived. And of course he's not the only guy that ever had these feelings. Jerome probably felt this way in the wilderness. Nostradamus probably felt this way when he was predicting John F. Kennedy's assassination, the rise of Idi Amin, Ayatollah Khomeini, the invasion of Afghanistan, and the Third World War. Barry Goldwater may also have felt the bruising solitude of moral superiority and maybe he still does. Or take the case of James Earl Carter. And I feel that way too. I feel it now, here in Chapin House at Temple University, Phila., P.A. I suffer with rectitude. I have tunnel vision sometimes. I get these compulsions to drop everything and run, to go in search of a girl with whom I worked bagging groceries in Nashua, N.H. Her hair fell in amber ringlets. She took me into her confidence.

Therefore and thus, I am up at 3:00 A.M. on the night before this religious studies term paper is due. I have taken two Vivarin caffeine tablets. I'm seated inside a large spherical chair — early seventies–type design — packed with cushions, which I, along with Anthony Edward Nicholas (hereafter, Tony) stole from the Graduate Housing Lounge. We had to roll it down College Street. There's no other furniture in my dorm room, now, except for a mattress and a portable cassette player. I'm wearing only worn boxer shorts. I have stockpiled Quaaludes and generic beer.

I'll just briefly expatiate on how I ended up living alone. The room is a double. Tony moved in. It was a week after school began (Sept. 1980). His shit was everywhere. He had a plug-in pink flamingo. He had congas. Bowling shoes. Hawaiian shirts. He left his records on the floor, out of their sleeves.

He didn't bathe. And then, just as suddenly as he moved in, he moved out. Maybe a month later.

I *thought* we got along pretty well. He agreed to dine with me in the refectory each night. We chain-smoked. True: I gave him a number of polite but direct suggestions about that lingering hacking cough of his and about his frequent nosebleeds; I offered to separate the whites from the colored items that lay strewn all over our little room. Maybe I wasn't too politic sometimes — one time when he came back from a frat party with some floozy I barricaded the door. I couldn't stand to *overhear that groping.* One night — it's true — I even threw some of his shit out the window at him when I saw him passing below. These things come over you sometimes. I offered apologies. After Tony left, the housing office moved in a rugby player *actually named Scooter.* He didn't last long either.

So here I am.

This solitude I've described counts among the similarities between myself and St. John the Divine. There are additional concordances[2] between my life and the prophecy written down in the book of Revelation, to which I would now like to draw your attention. My comments on them will form the major work of this paper. Blessed is he that readeth.

---

[2] Joachim of Fiore in his *Expositio in apocalypsim* (manuscript in the Vatican someplace) believed that there was an exact concordance between the events of the O.T. and the N.T. To him I owe this concordance idea. And I'm aware, if my life is mapped onto Revelation, that there must also be a concordance between my life and the O.T., and between your life and mine, and between the Bible and the Koran, etc.

The Angel Appears to John

"What thou seest, write in a book, and send it unto the seven churches," the angel commands John in the first chapter of the final book of the Bible (1:11), and later, "Write the things which thou hast seen, and the things which are, and the things which shall be hereafter" (1:19). The appearance of the angel bearing the word of Christ is intended to foster in John the act of writing scripture.[3] But the way I see it, the testamentary approach, this emphasis on *writing things down,* is important not only to Revelation but to the Bible as a whole. The Bible is about writing, about persuasion and the dissemination of belief and practice, and its subject is *praise,* pure and simple, praise for God's stuff. The stuff he made.

Moreover, the Holy Bible, of course, was the first book ever printed with a printing press — the Gutenberg Bible. The revolution of dissemination brought about by the printing press came first to sacred ground, get it? and that's not just coincidence. All books, as a result, refer back to the Bible and to the truth contained in it, just as all writing refers back to divine creation, and, by extension, all critical papers ought to be contained in this concordance too. Between all covers, joined by all bindings, sewn, glued, or Velo-bound, is the word of God, like the movement of radiation out from Ground Zero.

---

[3]Likewise, Jacques Derrida, when writing of Jean Genet's method of composition, found traces of the Apocalypse: "Why not search there for the remains of John (Jean)? The Gospel and the Apocalypse, violently selected, fragmented, redistributed, with blanks, shifts of accent, lines skipped or moved out of place." *Glas.* Paris: Editions Galilée, 1974. Trans. by Robert P. Paisner.

And that, you see, is what John's *writing* is about in the Apocalypse. Christ is the "Alpha and Omega, the beginning and the ending" of all alphabets (and all words) and all books and all society and all of society's works.[4]

Now, let's examine me for a minute. Ever since I was a little boy, I have felt the significance of the printed word. I read *a lot* of science fiction. But as for writing, I avoided this shit like the plague. From the age of twelve, when I went away to boarding school, I was exposed to classes in rhetoric and composition. I didn't enjoy these classes. I think I might have a learning disability. Really. When I have to write something, I get really bored. I never wrote my parents or my uncle, and they never wrote me. (My father[5] lived in a tent — heated, with electricity, outhouse in back — at the furthermost corner of our property. Early mornings he would stride across fallow acreage with a shotgun and his dog, Claw. As the sun teased through the remote woods of New Hampshire, my father would fire off round after round at the crows on his property. He took shots he could never make. This was his kind of dissemination. The dissemination of buckshot. His oaths of rage crackled across the White Mountains.)

---

[4]Note also that there are *books within the book* called Revelation. There's the book with the seven seals "next to the one who sits on the throne" (5:6), and there's the book "which is open in the hand of the angel which standeth upon the sea and upon the earth" (10:8).

[5]Some more information on my dad appears in my Deviant Personality final, December 6, 1980. I received a C-minus — partly because I had stayed up till 4:00 A.M. buying drinks for Annie Parsons. Later she used her hand on me, in the hall of her dorm, as revelers stumbled by. The exam was a few hours after that.

In the weeks leading to the deadline for my religious studies term paper, I know I am compelled to write in order to proceed to my junior year or at least in order to pass this class, and yet I can't do it. I want to write, but I can't. I'll do anything to avoid it. I'm wandering around dangerous parts of South Philly in a torn overcoat throwing rocks at stray dogs. I'm sleeping in public places. And then — all at once — a paper on Revelation comes to me, *all at once,* in a convulsion of inspiration, *in a revelation you might say,* just as the angel comes to John. It's not that I set out to write down the story of my life this semester, I'm just trying to think up a good paper topic, like, say, *Christ as literary character in the three Synoptic Gospels.* But instead the words just tumble out, as if it's a fit or a seizure. As though I'm taking dictation. My dorm room is a grotto and I totter around in it like an autistic until that moment when suddenly I can't stop myself from writing.

Without too much of a stretch, therefore, we can see that the angel's injunction to compose (in 1:1) can actually refer *to this very religious studies paper,* and to problems in its composition and in my life generally.

The Letters to the Seven Churches

The seven churches to which John is enjoined to write by the angel are in Asia.[6] Here are their names: Ephesus, Smyrna, Pergamos, Thyatira, Sardis, Laodicea, and *Philadelphia.* The

---

[6] My close friend Shusaku C. Sunami (who is Asian) dropped out of school just about the time this story takes place, just before exams last fall. After a long, expensive cocaine binge, he skipped his exams and took the first train home to NYC.

point here is pretty obvious, right? John's letters to these churches are intended to reward and punish the various successes and failures of these institutions. The language of each letter is dictated by the angel of 1:1.

My paper — this very paper — is being written in *the city of Philadelphia, Pa.* Here's an excerpt from John's letter to the church of this very name (3:12): "Him that overcometh will I make a pillar in the temple of my God, and he shall go no more out: and I will write upon him the name of my God, and the name of the city of my God, *which is* new Jerusalem" (italics in original). Therefore, all that I'm telling you is true, *it fulfills prophecy,* and plus, it all happened in the one-time capital of the United States of America.

I came to Temple in the fall of 1979 after being rejected at Brown, Yale, Hampshire, Haverford, Union, and U.N.H. My first year was uneventful, although I did meet a guy, Malcolm, who eventually became my pharmacist. In the spring of that year, I began the frequent use of Quaaludes. My first bona fide blackout — loss of memory from the combination of drugs and alcohol — followed not long after. I was getting ready to go to a bar at the Tyler School of Art (it's all the way across town). Then, however, a gap in the narrative of these events ensues until the moment when I found myself suddenly, inexplicably, in a men's lavatory wearing a gray suitcoat with both sleeves torn off. I was shirtless underneath this garment, and I was also — I noticed in the smudgy mirror before me — wearing lipstick and eyeliner. I reviewed the facts. I had been drinking on top of downs, I guessed, and was luckily at the very bar to which I had set out. To a guy urinating in the stall behind me I gleefully shouted the following:

— I don't want to seem like I'm giving you a pop quiz or

anything, friend, but do you happen to know anything about what time it is or what day it is or what presidential administration is currently tangling things up or whether there's selective service registration yet? Is there anything you might know about these things?

I cackled good-naturedly, but my new acquaintance left me (in haste) to my confusion. I decided, because of my condition, to make my way back to my dorm, a journey of forty-five minutes, where, along with Shusaku Sunami (see note 6), I got into the systematic destruction of my college-issue furniture. The desk and desk chair, the chest of drawers, etc.[7]

The Throne of God in Heaven

What can I tell you about the Tap Room, as Tyler's bar was called? When I was there, when I was immersed in its liquid dankness, its crimson lighting, its unlistenable music, I felt like I was *breathing properly,* I felt that people weren't whispering invidiously about my wardrobe and comportment. I loved and revered bars in freshman year and I still do. I seemed, in spite of my faith in the community and fellowship of Christ, in spite of my belief in an eternal life as promised by him, to need to degrade myself with drink (and compulsive masturbation). Again and again I found myself scamming, pretending to be a Tyler student in order to find a way into the Tap Room. It was a tiny, rundown space, with no more than six or seven booths,

---

[7]I've considered the possibility that John suffered with some kind of alcoholic or drug-inspired vision, maybe toxic withdrawal. This would account for the "four beasts full of eyes before and behind" (4:6) and like imagery.

maybe twenty-four seats in all. (And twenty-four, just by co-incidence, is my very age as I write this paper — because I took two years off bagging groceries and receiving psycho-therapy.) An enfeebled citronella candle dwindled on each ta-ble; a mild adhesive varnished all surfaces. You had to yell into the ear of the person next to you. The men sometimes wore skirts; everyone wore black.

I fell on my knees in places like that. I succumbed to a joy in my heart. I heard God whisper the good news. Even if they could tell there that I was a liberal arts guy. We were inter-lopers, those of us from Temple and Penn, in tweed suits from the fifties and skinny ties and peg-legged pants. They could tell us apart.

Compare this bar and its charms with the fourth chapter of the Apocalypse: "Round about the throne *were* four and twenty seats: and upon the seats I saw four and twenty elders sitting, clothed in white raiment" (4:4), and, later, *"There were* seven lamps burning before the throne, which are the Seven Spirits of God" (4:5).

The Seven Ages of Church History

Seven lamps, the seven letters to the seven churches, the seven seals of the Great Book — there are even seven visions in the book of Revelation as a whole. With these sevens in mind, I will now briefly discuss the work of Petrus Olivi, the Francis-can biblical commentator.

Olivi, before being condemned posthumously in the early fourteenth century, was notable for insisting on a seven-fold division in church history to accord with the system of sevens in Revelation. He also insisted on a threefold division — borrowed from a Franciscan predecessor — to go with the Holy Trinity. The three ages went roughly like this: God the father went with the age of the Old Testament, Christ went with the age of the New Testament up to about 1300 A.D. (the time at which Olivi composed his *Lectura Supra Apocalypsim*), and the age of the Holy Ghost was, according to Olivi, to last from the time of his composition (1300) for about 666 years — the number of the beast — until circa 1966 A.D. *Or roughly ten years after my own difficult childbirth at Mass General in 1956.* This third period would accord more or less with the sixth age of church history, in which, according to Olivi, we would find the war between the Holy Ghost and Antichrist.

If we consider that Olivi's first defense of his views before the Franciscans occurred in about 1292, not 1300, we can see that the Apocalypse and with it the end of the reign of Antichrist may well occur on or close to the year of my own birth. All baby boomers, therefore, the countless offspring of the late sixth age — of that great period of darkness, the fifties — will be around to see the Apocalypse. In recognizing this concordance, I'm also alluding to another trinitarian construct — the three writers and prophets: St. John the Divine, Petrus Olivi, and Bob Paisner.

And here's one last interesting equation! The first Olivians, the followers who made pilgrimages to his grave, were burned at the stake for heresy somewhere between 1314 and 1318. If we take these dates (instead of 1300) as indicative of the onset of *the sixth age* (the beginning of the reign of Antichrist before final Judgment), and add to them the 666 years signifying the beast, then we can see, of course, that the Apocalypse arrives between 1980 and 1984.[8]

The Book, Its Seven Seals, and an Angel

What happens next in Revelation is that John, in the throne room of heaven, is given a chance to view the great book of prophecy spread wide on an ample table there. "No man in heaven, nor in earth, neither under the earth, was able to open the book, neither to look thereon" (5:3).

I've told you about my own reading habits — mostly s.f. and light psychology books, although I am also a big fan of the writings of Ayn Rand. And there is this little "book" I'm writing here, this book of my own life, which I hope will top out around the required twenty-five pages and be done about three hours from now. But none of these books seems to resonate with the book described above in Revelation.

In fact, I would submit to you that a real book is not intended here. Sometimes you have to admit that Revelation has both a literal and symbolic level. The truth of Revelation floats between the two registers like a mostly submerged iceberg. In the case of the book referred to here, I think we can confidently speak of the symbolic. The book John intends to anoint as the highest book of prophecy and the book of Judgment is not a regular *book,* a product of the printing press. It's the ancient and all-powerful book of the affections. The book of life, as described in 20:12, is *the book of love.*

---

[8]On the other hand, Olivi's posthumous condemnation by the Pope wasn't completed until 1328, which would slide the whole thing back to the early 1990s.

I know a little bit about it, about love. For example, my roommate Tony Nicholas and I had had a few drinks one night. At the Tap Room. End of fall semester 1980. After Tony had moved out. And we had smoked some pot, which was always bad for me, since in its clutches I imagined not only that people but tables and chairs, all the objects in the cosmos, were secretly passing messages about my mood and complexion, my family, or my sickly childhood. That night I had smoked this marijuana and was suffering with the predictable *referential mania*. A malefic world spun out around me. I was powerless over it. I drank to cut the edge of this bad noise. Tony was telling me in some litanical and repetitive way about a stylish mystery film he wanted to direct. The eternal globe-trotting semiotics of mystery. The hermeneutics of murder and power pop. It all sounded the same. I was drinking faster. I had aphasia. I was nuts.

The music in the bar, some fusion of punk and funk that was going around then, obliterated all the ambient noise. I couldn't hear anything. I couldn't see anything. But I could tell, suddenly, that Tony wasn't talking to me anymore. It dawned on me. Through some sixth-sense heartache. He *hated* me. He was five or ten minutes into a conversation with a woman in the next booth. Five or ten minutes? Or longer? He had actually slid into the next booth and was chatting her up and I hadn't even noticed.

That was Judith. That was the first time I laid eyes on Judith. What did she look like? In the dark? Greater forces than my brute desire directed me at the moment, so her beauty wasn't uppermost in my mind. I can't tell you what she looked like, therefore, and her face was mostly turned away. She was chatting amiably with my former roommate. Still, I knew her immediately for who she was.

She was the angel of the seventh seal. She was Mary and Mary Magdalene, she was my mom before my mom got sick, but that's not all, she was like Christ, she was Francis or Gandhi or Thomas Merton, she was the grinch after his heart got bigger, she was Patti Smith after the broken neck, she was the transcendental signified, she was the thing that rid me of Tony Nicholas, she was the thing that was going to thaw my ache, and I *knew*. I'm aware that it sounds pretty sudden. But consider the evidence: "And there appeared a great wonder in heaven; a woman clothed with the sun, and the moon upon her feet, and upon her head a crown of twelve stars" (12:1). Judith's address at the time was 1212 Rodman St., Philadelphia.

My head cleared when she turned — from where Tony was yelling something in her ear. They were in the next booth. Backs to me. And she turned. As if according to some higher purpose. She turned and looked at me. My head cleared. Something tricky was going on in my life. There was contempt in the air, Tony's contempt, but contempt couldn't last in that furnace. I felt the absolute and irrefutable faith in an instantaneous bond. Love at first sight. My feelings would be boundless and exact and I would grow fat and bald cherishing memories of Judith. I would comfort her even when she was really wrinkled. I knew all of this by the time she was leaning over the booth:

— Hey . . . Hey, what's your name? You're a friend of Tony's, right?

She screwed up her face. Her smile was dimpled, uneven, overpowering. She evidently thought she was really having some fun. I nodded.

— Tony here says you were raised by wild animals.

She started to laugh. Couldn't stop laughing. And I could see Tony looking away, too, shaking from the effort to control himself.

Look, I know when I am the object of fun. Often I can laugh right along. But the little romantic skirmishes of the past, the meager recon missions of my heart in which I risked nothing and lost less, they didn't prepare me for this. This was a comment like a blow dart. I had to respond. I got right up in her face, leaned toward her and took hold of her bangled wrists. Tightly.

— Listen, you don't go in for this bait-the-misfit stuff, do you? Because you don't look like the kind of person that would, right?

Then I bowed my head in a prayerful way. I was wobbling and bowing.

— I dare you to treat me like a human being, I said. That's my dare for you and Tony . . . I dare you. And I'm sorry you're both so hard up for fun. I'm sorry about your *empty lives,* okay?

I knew how it would turn out, you know. I knew she would overcome my barb. She thought she didn't care about me, but when she turned nervously back to her conversation with Tony there was no conversation. Tony and she sat there, backs to me, like they'd never met at all. The space between them had widened. My chatter, meanwhile, was with the stars.

Believe it or not, this is how the book of the affections gets opened. It's right there in the Bible. Deep calls unto deep, across expanses of loss. In the course of my stupid life, I've tried to crack the seals of this great book, the way a kid might, six times I have, with six girls I guess you'd say, each with her different lances and charms and sadnesses, a woman with balances, a woman with hell behind, a woman who carried the souls of the dead with her, and a woman who felt earthquakes when we made love.[9] The seventh was Judith.

Now I'll tell you the number of those lost to heartbreak in all of history because this number is worth remembering: *a hundred and forty-four thousand of all the tribes of the children of Israel.*

The Half-Hour of Silence

On the way back home from the Tap Room I had another blackout. Or this is my guess. They were getting worse. I was slipping into bad situations the way others in my family had. The next morning, I showed up for Semiotics Twelve coming in and out of consciousness. I was still tanked. I napped facedown on my desk. Migrainous auras, flares, and lights burst from the margins of the passage we were reading (in Saussure). And the worst thing was that I regretted what I'd said to Judith. Not only that, I knew I was going to be troubling her again in the future.

St. John: "And when he had opened the seventh seal [of the book of love] there was a silence in heaven about the space of half an hour."

The Seven Trumpets

We're down to only a couple of hours remaining, so I'm going to have to summarize the five months that followed. In December 1980, in a sudden display of collegiality and mirth, Chapin

---

[9]Their names were as follows: Susan Ward (in fourth grade); Lisa Burns; Debby Madden (in eighth grade), who replied to my request to go steady, "Lisa Burns says you are a fag and I agree"; Liz Overton; Laura Drummond; Liza Benedict, whose dad caught us trying to do *it* (my first time) in the basement.

House, where I live, anointed me dorm president. I was elected by acclamation. Unopposed. In my new post, I would be making a number of important decisions, such as what parties we would be giving, how to deal with communal problems like loud stereos, whether to have special study hours, and so forth. I called meetings on these subjects, which we held in our ample, unfurnished common room, but I could never get a complete set of officers to show up. No one would come to the dorm meetings either. In the absence of consensus, therefore, I went ahead to make a few decisions myself.

My first act was to propose a house party entitled Inquisition Night. It was to take place in January, after Xmas break.[10] The party would feature period costume. We could burn effigies on the lawn in front of the dorm. Crucifixes everywhere. Drinks dyed red to simulate the running blood of heretics. We'd haul up people on false charges.

Not surprisingly, the other dorm officers wouldn't agree to the party, especially when it became clear I was serious. They would, they said, have to *run it by the deans, health services, security.* And then they told me that my election had been a big joke in the first place; they told me that I had misunderstood a simple prank. My powers as president were thereby completely revoked. But I simply proceeded without my housemates. I printed up fliers. The design, if I do say so myself, was lovely,

---

[10]My mother, who has been pretty sick for a long time, was, over the holidays, readmitted to a private psychiatric hospital in Concord. We spent Xmas morning with her in the visiting room. She was disoriented. I brought her gourmet cheeses. I held her in my arms while she slept.

featuring a photocopied woodcut (from an art history text) of Francis bleeding from his stigmata. I stapled these fliers to locations far and wide, including 1212 Rodman Street, which I had learned was Judith's address — from Tony Nicholas, in one of our last conversations. I plastered her street with handbills. Inquisition night! Rodman Street, a barren lane of overturned grocery carts, blind cats, and leafless trees, provided ample surfaces for my literature.

And though I had been forbidden to hold the party, the night on which it was scheduled to take place eventually arrived. I purchased, for the occasion, some luminous food colorings and in my empty dorm room I mixed up a shaker full of red vodka and tonic and crushed valium. While no one joined me for my advertised party, I managed to have a good time —

That is, until I found myself, in a bathrobe dyed black and worn backwards — apparently to simulate priestly garments — at a party miles from my dorm at which a venerated local band, The Egyptians, was playing. (They turned out these angular dance tunes, really loud — one of which, "Ancient Times," can still move me powerfully: "Oh, I wanna get a boat and go to ancient times; / Go any farther gonna lose my miiiiiinnnnnd."[11]) Luckily, however, Judith was at the party. Wearing black paint-stained jeans and a white thrift-store dress shirt. She also had on a white leather jacket. Her hair was a long hennaed tangle, madwoman-in-the-attic style. She looked like a go-go girl ten years into a devastating nervous

---

[11]Another song I liked by The Egyptians was based on a painting by Hieronymus Bosch: *Cure of Folly*.

illness. I reminded her that Tony had introduced us a month or so earlier and she was obviously happy to see me again. I gallantly volunteered to walk her home (though, in my bathrobe, I was a little underdressed), but she said she wasn't going home. She was catching a train that night to Trenton or Pittsburgh or something.

— What's with the bathrobe? she asked.

— I'll take you to the station.

— I'm taking a cab.

— I'll join you.

She smiled.

— Look, I slurred. I'm not going to hold you down behind a bush and assault you or anything. I just want to have a conversation.

There must have been some credible or deeply heartfelt catch in my voice, because she suddenly changed her mind and admitted she *was* going home. I won't try to excuse my behavior. I remember, unfortunately, every garbled sentence of this encounter. I know, for example, that at one point I quoted Revelation to Judith: "And I will give power unto my two witnesses, and they shall prophesy a thousand two hundred and threescore days, clothes in sackcloth" (11:3). I told her that our association, therefore, was circumscribed by Scripture. This line was supposed to be romantic.

She said:

— Even if you weren't completely nuts I would still say you are expecting too much, you know? I've talked to you, what, two times?

Okay, this was probably true. But I must not have cared then, because soon we were in the laundry room of the apartment house on Rodman that Judith shared with three other

Tyler students. We were sitting on the cement floor — it was really cold — and I was trying to persuade her, in a language that was awkward and desperate, that she shouldn't go upstairs to her apartment. In fact, I told her she couldn't leave until she agreed to let me hug her. I asked for this hug many times. Seven times.

— Forget it, Judith said. Look, I don't want to be rude or anything, but if you think this is the way to get through to me, if you think this'll win me over . . . you're completely wrong, okay? Do I have to be clearer?

— Just a hug, I said. A hug, not anything . . . more than that. Just a hug.

— Come on, she said. This is embarrassing. It's stupid.

Mine was a sad story, but it didn't move her. I remember when she moved up onto the coin-operated dryer — still warm from a recent load — she fell into banging the backs of her heels against the front-loading door.

— It's cold, she said. How long do we have to sit down here?

And then she said the worst possible thing, a sentence of death and confusion. These dismal, lacerating words banged around in that reverberant space:

— And anyway, you know, I'm seeing someone else.

I brushed it off at first.

— One hug? I mumbled. One little hug . . .

You want to know why it was so important, that hug? May I answer a question with another? Why does the wilted house plant need its weekly flooding with the Philadelphia Phillies plastic pitcher? Why did St. John look for the resurrection to come? Why was Judith still in the basement with me? She had her reasons. I had mine.

She slid off the dryer and the tail of her untucked shirt fluttered behind her.

— What the fuck.

See how easily the weather changes? She had to reach up a little bit. I was that much taller. My constitution improved immediately. I saw the generations of causation, from the great first cause, lined up behind me. On the other hand, maybe I was just a lonely guy. I wish I had been more awake for it, my cheek flush against hers, her hands around my waist, a strange supernatural pounding inside the ineffectual radiator on the wall. Footsteps in one of the apartments above.

I said:

— Lemme come upstairs with you.

— Forget it.

— Then promise me you'll . . .

— Forget it. Out. Now. Out. *Go.*

— Then let me come see you at your . . . at your studio . . . tomorrow . . .

— Not until you promise to leave. And even then I'm not promising anything.

I hung my head. And in that lapse of vigilance she skittered upstairs. In the moment of my shame. I idled in the basement. Then, in my priestly robes, I weaved up and down deserted streets blessing the night and the inhabitants of night.

The Number of the Beast

According to most scholarship, it's *not a number at all,* but a sequence of letters. It's likely, therefore, that 666 probably represented initials of some kind.[12] A lowercase beta, e.g., from the Greek alphabet. In English we would use the letter *b*. So for my name, Robert (or Bob, if you prefer) Benson Paisner, you have two *b*'s and a *p*, which is really an upside-down and backwards *b*. I'm leaving the conclusion here to the reader. I didn't feel too happy with myself the morning after the laundry incident.

The Seven Plagues

At 12:3 in the Apocalypse a giant red dragon appears with seven heads and ten horns, to threaten the chosen, "That old serpent called the Devil, and Satan, which deceiveth the whole world" (12:9). The nature of his leadership is discussed by John in the next chapter, "He that leadeth into captivity shall go into captivity: he that killeth with the sword must be killed with the sword" (13:10).

You get a pretty good idea about sin, about life in the sixth age, from this description. Sin is like a vigorous movement away from the freedom of everlasting life (as described, e.g., in the Synoptic Gospels). In contrast to *affection*, especially as it has played itself out in my life, sin (and its agents, Satan and Antichrist) represents a contrary movement toward . . . well, toward separation, apartness. In the place where Satan's followers dwell, the smoke of those in torment "ascendeth [from Hell] for ever and ever: and they have no rest day nor night,

---

[12]Some of my thinking about the number of the beast derives from a fine Gregory Peck vehicle entitled *The Omen*.

who worship the beast and his image, and whosoever receiveth the mark of his name."

Sounds like a college environment, right? And which of us students is numbered with Satan's legions? I'll give you one example. Steve Dodgson, the bisexual sculptor/performance terrorist from Tyler School of Art.

Judith's boyfriend.

First, his gums were really bad. (I can find a couple of oblique references to bad skin or gums in Revelation, of which the best is 16:2, which speaks of the first plague of final judgment as consisting of a "grievous sore upon the men.") Dodgson always buttoned his shirts all the way up to the neck and greased his hair in the rockabilly style. His face was round and cherubic but also with a deeply angry cast. It was the face of a murderous shoe salesman. He had, as far as I could tell, no human compassion of any kind. In his effort to assure himself that he was not really attracted to men, Dodgson exercised a vigorous control over Judith. In his presence, she was to wear her hair tightly bound into a bun. She was not to wear slacks of any kind. He abhorred, at the same time, any situation in which he had to watch her eat. (I learned all this later.) When she was at his house, she ate in a room off the kitchen, at least until he realized that he hated *hearing* her eat. He asked that she *suck* her potato chips. Similarly, he asked that she avoid him during the worst part of her menstrual period. She was to keep any razor that she used to shave her body hidden from him at all times. She was not permitted to wear any shade of violet or purple, because, he told her, it was the color of the anus. And, above all, she was not to speak to other men, whether attractive or threatening, whether gay or straight, whether jock or artiste or academic, whether tall, short, fat, lean, desperate, androgynous, or anything else.

No men. Judith hovered in the periphery of his vision at all times and her brilliant smile became infrequent under his control. Dodgson said once, in public, at a party, *See this girl here? See my girl? The mother of all abominations!*

The Lamb

The hug in the basement (in the deep of night, in the trance of love) wasn't the only thing that stuck with me in this academic year, but it was right up there. As demonstrated above (mspp. 15–16), my experiences with women weren't all that broad. And though I knew about Dodgson, though I knew he was calling Judith and seeing her and dropping by Store 24, where she worked as a cashier, I tried to pretend it wasn't happening. I too began to stake my claim upon her attentions, standing in the back of the all-night convenience store, with the guys thumbing copies of *Motor Trend* and *Juggs*. I found a way to visit her each day.

She was seeing Dodgson, theoretically, but he was frequently distracted, it seemed, or out of town, or simply breaking into houses on the Main Line or shooting speed or whatever it was he did. And Judith and I were having some laughs. She tolerated my visits to her on the job and to her studio and my telephone calls all hours of the day and night. I was twenty-four years old and I didn't see how I was going to get along with people — it was a skill I didn't have; I had imagined that, after capitulating to the decline of my family, I would be hospitalized or would move into the deep woods, into a shotgun shack with no electricity or running water; but here I was *exploring intimacy* with one person, with Judith, and I didn't care if she was a little preoccupied, or peculiar looking, or anything else, because she had forgiven me for that hug.

But when I got back from spring break I called and she broke me the bad news. She'd told Dodgson about me. He had returned from his breaking-and-entering spree, and she'd told him. She'd told him *she was friends with this guy.* She'd confessed a fealty, a devotion. I didn't know whether to take or lose heart. Dodgson made it clear immediately that she was never to see me again. She was to expunge our conversations from the record of her life. She was to deny me.

— No no no, I mumbled into the phone. No. Let me see you just one more time. *Just one more time.*

— Can't, she said, can't do it.

But two weeks later, after a lengthy negotiation with her criminal boyfriend, she agreed to meet me in a public place, Airport Lounge at Temple University, for exactly fifteen minutes. She had arranged with Dodgson that she would call him at the beginning and the end of this conversation, she would *bookend* it, in order to demonstrate its precise duration. They had covered, Judith and Dodgson, every aspect of this event. They had thought it out. Our meeting was to be bounded by the ordinary, by Temple students dragging their knapsacks and buying packs of Marlboros, by kids sprawled on modular sofas, by security guys and snack bar employees (work-study slaves) coming on and off break. I arrived twenty minutes early. A trebly radio at the snack bar played the college station. The carpets were trampled down. Paths of grime led to and from that lounge of dreams.

The Fall of Babylon

"Therefore shall her plagues come in one day, death and mourning, and famine; and she shall be utterly burned with fire" (18:8).

So much of our lives take place in the *spiritus mundi,* in the ether of the numinous, under the pressures of Antichrist and his servants, with the music of Heaven drifting toward us distantly as if overheard in an agreeable daydream. We're little puppets playing out the drama of the sublime. It's no wonder therefore that my conversation with Judith was difficult. The entire spiritual chemistry of the age hung in the balance. We were whispering. Judith looked all wrong. Her hair was pulled back tightly; she was wearing some cheap polka-dotted dress she'd bought at a thrift shop. Our meeting was all full of false starts. What's going on at school? How is your painting? What did you do over spring break? What music are you listening to? Then it got into harder stuff. I took her hands. I grabbed at them greedily and held them in my lap. *Why wasn't I good enough?* I asked. Why couldn't I be closer to her than I was? What was I doing wrong? Why was I so bad at human commerce when it was the thing I wanted more than anything?

Then I asked:

— Why do you let him do this to you? I wouldn't do this to you. I wouldn't treat you like this, pen you in.

Her expression didn't change.

— Because I'm in love with him, she said. I'm in love with him and I'm *not* in love with you. Simple as that. You're always making things bigger than they are, or harder than they have to be, so you don't even know what I'm talking about. Besides how could you know what's going on with me? You couldn't. You have no idea —

Of course, this is just how college kids talk. Their language is crude and simple, like the language of ancient practitioners of physick, medieval guys, when considered by the scientists at

Lawrence Livermore Laboratory. College students can't talk about their own feelings. They blunder around or cut themselves off. I bet they don't know anything for a good ten years after those *best years of their lives.* I don't hold it against them. Their feelings might as well be in Aramaic. But I can tell you what college students *mean;* they mean that grief follows grief like the tides running in and out; they mean that feelings are just a code for the intentions of God; they mean that numbers or letters or decimals can be attributed to feelings; they mean that the words of love and loss are just labials, dentals, or gutturals;[13] they mean that these words are pronounced with the hard palate or aspirated and that the revelations fashioned from them will outlive this sitcom of today. That's what I have to say about feelings.

CONCLUSION: *The New Jerusalem*

Then Judith and I backpedaled, talking about movies, about painters, about the Egyptians. In the middle of this, the fifteen minutes was suddenly past, though we'd said nothing, really. Our meeting was over. Abruptly, Judith took her hands from mine and moved off to cloister herself in the phone booth outside the lounge. I could see her shoulders and the back of her hair.

That was eleven days ago.

---

[13]See, e.g., Ferdinand de Saussure's *Course in General Linguistics.* In his later years, Saussure became obsessed with anagrams, word games, with systems, with codes, with the worlds that he felt were hidden behind our words, with all the life that was beyond his reach.

After that, after I skirted around the phone booth where she was huddled — protesting and denying to Dodgson — I was on my way back to the dorm when a sudden rain, a freak sunstorm, fell glistening on my face and hands. The cursed pansies pushed up their perditious heads all along the margins of my path. I said, *Alleluia!* I said, *All salvation and glory and honor and power unto the Lord our God!* Well, at any rate, I *thought* this stuff. The completeness of my solitude prevented me, that afternoon, from making a scene.

So: youth is apocalypse.

When the great whore, Babylon, is finally fallen, St. John the Divine enters into the New Jerusalem, into the seventh age, where God and Christ will reign eternal over the faithful. Heaven and earth pass away. God wipes away the tears from the eyes of his flock, announcing that there will be no more death and no more term papers. The foundations of the new city are garnished with gems and the nations that are saved walk in the light of the Lamb. A pure river of water of life, clear as crystal, proceeds out of the throne of God and of the Lamb. There are no more curses and no more night. We're all innocents. Then the Lord says to John, "Blessed is he that keepeth the sayings of the prophecy of this book. If any man shall take away from the words of this prophecy, God shall take away his part out of the book of life, and out of the holy city, and from the things which are written in this book. Surely I come quickly."

This is how the Bible ends. This is its terminus. It's a big ending, a crowd scene. John knows this too. He knows there is a powerful prophetic dimension to endings. And I know that I have come to the end of my education. And to the end of childish longing. This draft will have to do the trick, because the sun has risen over the burned-out frats on the quadrangle, Professor Soren, and I have to get this over to you, to the department office, in less than an hour. Sorry there's no bibliography. That's the least of my concerns. In this afterlife.

TWISTER

A long gap in the conversation followed and then he told his father about the tornado at school that day. They were out on the patio in back, facing the street. The father smoothed a long strand of hair over the barren part of his head and returned to the plate of macaroni and cheese in his lap.

One of those Garden State twisters, his father said, mouth full.

He nodded.

A car passed on the street kicking up fallen leaves in its treads, and he told his father how they were all sitting out behind the observatory, as they did on those irresistible days, discussing the will of man and the will of nature which was the subject of the course, when the gravel in the parking lot, and with it, stray newspaper and Styrofoam cups swept upwards in a stiff opaque gust.

Nodding, his father loaded another forkful.

The gravel and dust rose up in front of the class. There were the hedges off to one side, running alongside the recital hall, and on the other side the observatory, and in the middle of these the unpaved parking lot, and amid it, amid the cars, the cloud borne upwards turning and turning back onto itself, a barber pole swirling upwards.

It roared in their ears, a calamity from another time, like glacial movement or tidal waves, and their casual interest, as though the twister were simply an audiovisual aid, turned to alarm. The instructor fell silent. The funnel swept across the street toward the athletic fields. Good thing no one was practicing yet.

His father lurched too late to catch the elbow noodle slipping from the plate and soon it was lodged between his thigh and the metal folding chair. He stood. He craned to see where the macaroni had gummed up his flannel trousers. Go on, he said.

Now the twister had made its way to the bleachers at the border of the gridiron, and effortlessly it upended the kelly green woodwork there. Into the air the stands wobbled and swam, and flopped to the ground after, like a marionette unstrung, and then it doglegged to the right to pick up another set of bleachers, this one lifted higher than the first, a full ten feet or so, to be wrecked as forcefully as a sea vessel flung against a rocky coast. A single beam lingered in the air for an impossible time, straight up thirty feet in the blue it dared gravity, stuck for a moment before tumbling like waterfowl shot from the sky.

He stopped there. He fingered the hole in the knee of his worn denim pants. Ran his fingers along paint stains there.

The father set his plate down on the flagstone. A breeze stirred the backyard. Activity besieged each of three birdfeeders. The father tasted his drink and set it between his legs.

Then what? he said to his son.

That was it. He told his father that was all. An empty calm. The class awaited the next signs of destruction, trees snapping, roofs flying off like the tops of jack-in-the-boxes, but nothing happened. The twister ran out of steam. Vanished.

The son smiled with accomplishment.

The father drank.

There was another silence.

The first lie that troubled him, the first lie about the twister, was the one about its having happened that day, when the actual date was maybe two or three weeks before. He had a dog-eared copy of the school paper to prove it. Photos of the kindling, and the fellow on the dozer waving his hardhat as he prepared to nudge the splintered grandstands over beside the observatory, where they had sat since.

The second lie was that he was there. He hadn't been there, although he was very close with a bunch of kids who were, well, not exactly close but he had almost taken the course. He had interviewed two of the kids who *had* taken it and who *had* seen the twister, before the editor of the school paper ran his own account, along with the photo of the dozer. Well, he didn't interview them really. He didn't feel comfortable asking, he never did. Although he overheard one guy and this guy said he had felt closer to the others for a couple of days, like they were a real tight group, but now when he sat next to them in class it was just like sitting next to anyone at all.

Do you want anything? the father said and without waiting he overturned the last amber inch in his glass, spilling it out onto the edge of the lawn, and headed back to the house. A pair of yellow jackets circled around the plate he left behind.

The son didn't say anything. Started to and then stopped.

And there were other lies too, these were not the first, some

153

of them too minor to mention but some not, some that dogged him, like how he had told his father he could swim when he had almost drowned during a swimming test once; how he had claimed to have lost his virginity to the daughter of a certain woman his father had dated, when this daughter wouldn't even speak to him; how he pretended to remember the faces of people in their family long ago lost; how he pretended to misunderstand a poem in a book he had, so that his father would sit with him and offer an explanation when the poem was as clear as change jangling.

A squirrel dove from a branch to the gutter pipe. Birds roosted on telephone lines. A car passed on the street and the rustle of leaves beneath it rose and fell like surf.

He wondered if he told these lies about the twister, the very existence of which was in doubt because of his record where lying was concerned, simply out of fear. He thought it was that but also more.

The porch door screeched. Why don't you come inside? the father said. It'll get chilly soon anyway.

The father stood where he was, holding the door open. The sun dipped in the direction of all great tornadoes, where towns had been splayed and scarred by the truth of tornadoes, and in the opposing skies, the moon, from where it was stuck on the end of a maple branch, rose.

And the next day the father would pass the twister off on a buddy at lunch. And years later the son would unearth it for a woman he trusted.

THE RING OF
BRIGHTEST ANGELS
AROUND HEAVEN

I.

The Ruin — where my friend Jorge Ruiz spent some of his nights — was decorated in twisted car parts and fruitless conversation and postindustrial clutter, in the collision of strangers and in the flicker of lost opportunities. Some of it was decoration; some of it was left over from whatever manufacturing operation had occupied the space in the early decades of the century. There were, on the walls of the Ruin, the melted shapes of obsolete computers, suspended from the wall from old meat hooks. Those early desktop Macintoshes — Typing Tutors or Flight Simulators or unfinished novels still flashing anemically, in green, on their screens; motherboards splayed on counters and at tables with microchips scattered around them like a new currency. Gutted stuffed animals stapled up on the walls and mangled dolls. Floors covered in straw and fiberglass and asbestos and metal shavings and bent nails and tattooing needles and syringes. There were the rusted steel shovels of ancient backhoes: gladiatorial burial vessels. Volkswagen Beetles attached by chains to the ceiling: splendid and degraded chandeliers. The design vocabulary of the meatpacking district — the meatpacking district of New York City — made the Ruin what it was. It seemed hard back then to imagine clubs, these kinds of clubs, without the meatpackers. The meatpackers, the ranchers, the butchers. The broad clean wound that the butcher, ankle-deep in blood, opened in the animal's arteries, the head toppling from the calf — in Texas, in upstate New York, or wherever this butchering was taking place — the neck stump quivering before him.

The butcher and his victim weren't all that far from the guy at the Ruin who left at home a disconnect notice or an unemployment voucher or an unhappy marriage or even a double-booked dinner at the Four Seasons or Café des Artistes so that he could open his mouth and quench his thirst on another man's waste.

The action was in the stalls. Were these *actual* stalls, Jorge wanted to know, at first, like stalls from your public school, transported into the Ruin after they had outlived their usefulness over at P.S. 103? Or were they carefully decorated stall facsimiles, with artificial yet highly suggestive stall graffiti? The designers, as clever as they were angry and remorseful, would never tell. People had come this far and they were paying a lot of money for nonalcoholic drinks and they sure as hell wanted everything, even the graffiti, to be contributing to the pungent and bracing sleaze of that club, the weird sadness that lay in the air like religious incense, like smells and bells. So if they weren't real stalls, Jorge thought, they were at least designed by people who had spent their time in public schools and who knew the code of sadism that lay at the heart of public school corridors, who knew the erotic power of hand tools and dental drills and heavier machinery.

The logistics of *home,* the logistics that oppressed the regulars at the Ruin, could only be solved in this theater of detritus, of glory holes, of discipline and submission, of piss and shit; so they wanted home near and far, oppressive and yet declawed. They wanted stalls, they wanted industrial spaces, they wanted uniforms, and (in part) the threat of deadly diseases, but the sight of a balance sheet, the sound of a cash register, or the ebb and flow of ordinary conversation, these were the things that really ruined these patrons, that caused them mortal discomfort.

The guy on the table being fisted by two men at once, two men wearing black leather face masks with zippers across the mouths; the woman with the penciled-on sideburns, with the dildo that glowed violet, glowed with a strontium 90 kind of light; the woman who lightly, desultorily whipped herself, while mumbling an alphabetical list of sexual insults; the guy suspended in the cage with the daggers sheathed in his pectorals, *in his pectorals* — the possibilities seemed endless at first, but they weren't at all. The possibilities were marked by the faint, beveled edges of modern imagination, by the devouring ennui of the straight culture that the Ruin honored by opposing all the time, in every way. I mean, after a while, Jorge knew that the guy getting fisted was named Malcolm and that he was an assistant stage manager of off-off-Broadway shows and that he had a brother with cerebral palsy, just as Jorge knew that the woman with the dildo — who said her name was *Huck* — was from San Antonio. Actual name: Doreen. When she was a kid, Jorge had learned, she had been a Deadhead and an environmentalist, an artist of batik and macramé.

Every day the Ruin stayed open was a miracle of invention; every day it threatened to get old, to run its course, to file for bankruptcy, to liquidate its assets, and still the regulars came. They waited for nightfall, for the early part of the evening to pass, when the breeders had all gone home to their genetic responsibilities. They waited eagerly, but without a choice. The Ruin was like the psychiatric hospital where some of them had done time. It was a last-chance joint with directions to the next last-chance joint; it was rock bottom with a trap door in it — Jorge told me so — and, after all, he knew about eschatology. He detoxed himself in the psych ward and came out again to tell of it. He got a prescription for that crystal, lithium. He had come to the end and found there were innumerable other ends in the cauldron of his city.

When Jorge Ruiz wasn't visiting sex clubs — and it was the question you always wanted to ask about the people you met there — he lived on Times Square. Middle thirties, medium height, perilously thin, hair in tiny steel coils, a large burgundy splotch on the left side of his face, a birthmark, a speaker of Spanish and English and Spanglish. He had left his mom, who lived alone in Union City, to come to Manhattan. That is, he had left behind the outlying dilapidation for Manhattan. And Times Square was where he ended up, where it was cheap enough, where there was a high turnover of real estate because of death, terror, illness, and the sex industry. *You know the throw weight of chance in these decisions, the decisions about where to live,* Jorge told me, the kilotonnage of chance — you come one day looking for an apartment, two other guys are looking at the *Voice* the same minute you are. There are thousands of people looking at the *Voice,* really, but these two guys, these other guys, in particular: one guy ends up living in Harlem, one guy ends up living in Chelsea — and this second guy dies young — one guy ends up in Times Square. You all look at the same apartment one day, though you never really meet. Next day, you step on the same gray, stringy piece of Trident gum on Seventh Avenue and Fifty-third Street; the same desperate panhandler, in the upper forties, asks all three of you for change (he's a guy I knew in college, who is now schizophrenic); you fire the same real estate agent. But you never meet.

And in this way you figure out after a while how the people around you, in New York City, are like so much *dark matter*. You don't know who they are, you never meet them, but they shadow you. Your movements implicate one another; your good stretches and disconsolate moments are one and the same.

Other New Yorkers, they are exactly like your friends, *your* New Yorkers, except for one small detail — Jorge explained — they were born in the D.R., not Puerto Rico, maybe, or their hair is a lighter brown, or they really prefer tea to coffee, or prefer boys to girls or girls to boys, or they prefer Techno to House or House to Techno, or they live in clubs like Lebanon, where people get stabbed, clubs that only last a year or two and then are gone. These New Yorkers have three brothers instead of two. Or they never did drink or never did start smoking that shit or they never did finish school. Or they went to graduate school and now can participate in grand discussions about the city's duty to house the homeless or about the dialectic of literary-something-or-other that has, at one end, formalism, and, at the other, *hermeneutics*.

These people look exactly like other people you know. That guy passing on Forty-sixth Street looks exactly like that guy you met on line at the Ziegfeld. That guy looks like someone from your gym. He's even carrying a gym bag. And in fact the two of them, those two guys you just saw, those guys who look like other people you know, they also look like one another.

In this city of the Ruin, *an entire manufacturing run of human beings was completed,* Jorge said, *and then the molds were all used two, three, maybe four times, to save money on newer molds, and if you are lucky you never meet your own double. If you're lucky.*

Which is not to say that we don't grow into the particulars of our environment. Twins grow apart; identicals grow apart. Ultimately we and our doubles are seized by vain, idiosyncratic quirks. Landscape works on people the way diet does, or the way local television broadcasting does. People grow apart. Like it says in the Gospels: *Fortunate is the lion that the human will eat, so that the lion becomes human.*

So Jorge Ruiz, who lived in a neighborhood with a thousand kinds of nakedness, came to see nakedness as his vocabulary. With it, he tried to explain things, his merciless depression, for example. Jorge lived over a store that sold knives, just around the corner from a pickup spot called Sally's. The new Sally's, that is. (The name was lettered in the window on Forty-third in browned, unsticky masking tape.) Sally's was as venerable in the world of transsexual hustlers as, say, the Algonquin — only a few blocks away — was venerable to the charlatan writers of the sixties and seventies. The old address, the old Sally's, had burned somehow. Before Jorge got there. Suspicious activity. An unhappy or confused trick. A shortfall in protection money.

Around the corner from Sally's was the Peep World, a midtown sex establishment of enduring popularity. It too had burned once; it too struggled back from this calamity. *Peep World! Hot! European! Gay! Kinky! Bizarre! Rubber Goods!*

Marital Aids! It was all mirrors and antiseptic spray. It was all lockers inside, like some demented public high school, like P.S. 103. There was a guy whose job it was simply to hose down the video booths afterwards, but sometimes he was backed up or on break and you slid, or your sneakers squeaked, in fresh extract. Jorge had been inside, of course, had sampled video booths both straight and gay, had even made the acquaintance of this bored young man with the cleaning agents. His name was Ray and he stood off to one side like any other minimum-wage laborer — checking and rechecking a plastic, five-dollar watch.

And across the street was the Priapus, an all-male erotic film center. *Army Brats. Trucker Studs. Trap Door Treats. Locker Love. Prison Guys. Hard as Stone.*

At first, Jorge liked to watch the kinds of artificial expressions that played across the faces of the men, and even the women, who ventured past the neon entrances into these local enterprises. He was eating a Sabrett's hotdog, say, and leaning against a destroyed parking meter, watching. There was a certain way consumers of the erotic pretended that they were fortuitously drawn there, a certain low gear in which they traveled, a certain look they had that said — Jorge told me — *The office where I am dropping off this important document seems to be right by this suggestive nude poster.* Or, *There happens to be someone I recognize inside, glancing at that rack of . . . videotapes!* At first, these superficial acts of dignity pleased him. Or at least his apprehension of them, of their hypocrisy, pleased him.

Until he was going in there himself.

Because after a couple of months in Times Square, he was going in, too.

Like this: In front of the Peep World, the sky was the blue

of colorized films. The traffic moved like it had never moved before. Somewhere the mayor of New York City was dreaming of pitching Manhattan to the Democratic National Committee or to the Grammys. His pulse raced in this dream. The mayor napped and dreamed of public check-signings and flawless photo opportunities and a Manhattan that operated like a Japanese factory, and just for one afternoon his dream had come true. It was a miracle. The cars were racing past the Port Authority Bus Terminal as if there were a civil defense emergency uptown; the homeless, including that guy I knew in college, had stirred themselves from their vents and grates because it was so beautiful. And that afternoon Jorge had followed up on a half-dozen leads for jobs, including a promising opportunity teaching English as a second language. True, he had a friend with that horrible kind of pneumonia; and his mother was old now, and wouldn't live long, especially not alone in New Jersey, but the breeze in the air nourished him today, he was like some purely aerobic organism, and that evening's full moon would hang above Times Square like the most fabulous neon. That day, no decision seemed wrong. The operations of chance were like a fine harvest.

There was a girl in some salacious poses on the billboard out front. She was the girl with the hundred aliases — Trixi, Candi, Belle, Wanda, Ginnie Mae — and her retouched curves adorned the doorways of every pornographic outlet on Eighth Avenue. Jorge saw a couple of guys in UPS uniforms check both ways and roll into Peep World, and in spite of the good luck he expected that afternoon — he was even imagining tomorrow's *Post* with nothing but good news in it — in spite of everything, he was following them. His hand was on the slippery stainless steel door handle — you had to open that door, you had to manifest your intention to enter —as he strode across the threshold. *How do they decorate a place like this? I was always curious.*

Inside the Peep World or the Show Center or the Nude Revue or the Triple XXX Lounge, Jorge learned, the girls were like the rest of the citizenry of New York, all exhausted, over-worked, frightened of the future, cynical, bitter, looking to cop. He talked to them, sometimes, the ones in the double-occupancy booths, or the ones who writhed on felt-covered tables, though he wasn't terribly attracted to them, though he had some deficit in sexual desire now, and this in no way endeared him to women who were working. He had little money to tuck under the elastic of their G-strings. And anyway, in conversation, Jorge was worse than awkward. He was an educated guy who looked a little weird, a little pasty, kind of ill, but also gentle and knowing and forgiving. Jorge told me himself that he talked the way a confidence man talks, trying to catch you in some well-traveled fallacy, or like a religious zealot, unyielding and lost at the same time.

— I guess this is supposed to be when I take my pants down, he said to the girl in the double-occupancy booth, that confessional. She was tricked up like a dominatrix. She frowned.

— You can do whatever you want, she said.

Sound of her voice muffled by plastic.

— Is there some . . . is there a kind of routine you do if I don't know what to ask you to do?

— Uh, sure, I guess . . .

— Touch, uh, touch yourself and . . . No, wait. Wait. Just wait a second, okay.

He sighed deeply.

— You don't have to do that, he said. You don't have to . . .

— Look, she said, if you're not going to . . . If you don't wanna . . . If you're not here to *get off,* why bother?

— My money, Jorge said. My money.

A silence, as though they were closing in on something. Then at the same moment the invisible factories of chance manifested themselves. Like a lethal blade, the window guard slid down between them. Rustling on the other side of that impenetrable wall. Time for more tokens.

It was later, or it was another day. He didn't talk to the girls, the lap dancers, or whatever they were that year, he looked at the ones in the booths. Or he didn't even look in the booths, he looked at the video screens with their innumerable parameters of chase and entrapment. A hand grasping. A cock, as large and brutal as some amputation stump. He simply wanted to see what was on every channel. It no longer had to do with wanting to see a woman *dowsing* with some bruised-looking phallus, or with some guy sitting on some other guy, taking the thing into him. Or a young girl moaning breathlessly. It was all just *want and flesh,* bodies melding in some cold fusion, bodies without borders, bodies eager for the subterranean passage that led beneath and beyond New York City.

Jorge hustled from the video rack to the booths to the rubber goods, those handsome Caucasian- and African-simulated penises, strap-on harnesses, those ticklers and pincers and rings and clamps and devices of the rougher trades. Inflatable women, the sort without politics, pillowed, vinyl facsimiles of kindness. He hovered everywhere like a yellow jacket in autumn trying to get the sense of Peep World, he wanted to know, wanted to know. He was shivering with excitement, and somehow the shivering seemed to have its own separate strategy. Or, as Jorge said later, *The thrill of pornography, well, it was around a long time before pornography ever was.*

Then he was back in the booths: Ray, the purveyor of antiseptic reprimanded Jorge for accidentally pressing a button unlocking his booth too soon. Toothlessly, Ray mumbled, his lips folded back in disappointment and contempt to reveal the black rinds of his gums: *Don't open the fucking door till you're done.* Jorge settled himself again into the video booth, and he was finally able to stroke himself to the point of points, to the *summa,* and he was grateful.

He was grateful that the atomization of city life could be dealt with simply on this cash basis; that the cobwebs that had decorated his oldest fantasies, the stuff he thought was his burden alone, could be cleared away just by turning some dials and spitting into your palm; he was grateful that the workers in the sex industry had, he was sure, kind bones. What more compassionate people were there? Who was more accepting of the desperate and lonely? As a profession of kindness sex work was easily more inclusive than either social work or nursing. He was suffused with a feeling of gratitude that was all out of scale with the brusque, impersonal machinery of Peep World.

And the feeling didn't last very long. It didn't even endure beyond the premises of the establishment, in fact. The expanding streets of Times Square — bubbling up and cracking, engulfing and digesting — had not evaporated while he was inside. That brief afternoon interval of municipal fellowship and teamwork had vanished. It had just been coincidence. Jorge was back in the old New York, the quarreling New York. What he wanted, what he desired, the city was taking these slowly from him.

He killed time, like other users of pornography, between the glittering entrances to Times Square. There were gyro restaurants — *Gyros! Pitzas!* — and passport photo shops and the video game parlors and back-dated magazine shops, the Best Western for foreign teenagers, cheap bars for the theater district, and stores with sold Broadway memorabilia and knives, and cheaper bars for the hard-luck binge drinkers. Lingerie stores for transvestites. Liquor stores with bulletproof glass and little slide-thru slots for pint bottles.

And here was what he felt when he came out of Peep World (a couple of drops of seminal fluid riveting his shorts uncomfortably to his thigh): he could feel the charcoal and polonium falling from the sky, he could feel urgency in every conversation, he could see that men walking the streets were fitting brass knuckles on over their arthritic joints. He knew why people went into Peep World. Because they were feeling really good; because they were feeling really bad; because they had had trouble at work; because they were having trouble with their girlfriend; because they had no girlfriend; because they had two girlfriends, or two boyfriends, or a girlfriend and a boyfriend and they didn't know how to choose between them; because they were lonely; because they never got any time alone; because the world was full of hypocrisy; because it was not; because they weren't caring for the people they loved; because they were tired of caring for others; because the skies were blue, or their car had a dent, or their cat was sick, or they'd had an argument on the subway, or they wanted to live in the country and own a trailer, or they hated tuna, or they loved rock and roll; or because they had no money; because they had too much; because they were honest with themselves; or because of chance — Jorge said — *because of chance.*

The neon of the gyro place, the neon of the shoe repair store, they were all the neon of Peep World. Jorge confused the thresholds of these businesses. They were identical. Just like, after a time, strangers and the people he knew were one and the same. The neon that called to him in Times Square was all one sign. It said: follow your itch, hasten your descent. Go ahead, dive.

His mother helped him out some. With money, I mean. She had some social security and some money given her by Jorge's dad, an Eastern European man from Edison who had abandoned them when Jorge was just a baby. Occasionally Jorge put in a little time here or there — in a travel book publisher once, temping, doing some clerical work at a clinic in Times Square. These jobs did not last because Jorge had trouble getting out of bed sometimes. It was Epstein-Barr virus or pernicious anemia or maybe just an attack of nerves. His mother had cures involving various spices. Bills and equations were tightening around him like the leather restraining straps you might see in the Ruin, or maybe they had always been there, he told me, tightening around him, a part of his life, bills, and math and algebra and all that stuff he couldn't really learn in his public school, the school with the sadistic stalls. He saw the forms of these equations on his walls, he had actually selected a wallpaper with 1040-EZ forms on it — he had good taste in decorating; he was a tasteful guy, when he had the energy — and sometimes when he was particularly upset, he tried to fill in these forms. Or so he told me. He used red laundry marker, the pen of choice for suicide notes. He never could get these columns of numbers to add up the same way twice, as he was

often late with the rent and often finding bills that were black
bordered and threatening. *He couldn't work, he couldn't work.
Work exhausted him.* Then he'd go to the Triple XXX Lounge.

Somewhere in the midst of these months tumbling inertly into
much longer stretches, he picked up the other most economi-
cally important commodity of his neighborhood, the name of
which is such bad luck that it's scary to pronounce it here. I
like its name, though, its first and last names — so many hard
c's. A name that was made to sound good in English. In the
romance languages, it would sound ugly and hard. But here in
the New World in the languages of native Americans, the An-
asazi, say, it would perhaps be the lovely name of an estuary or
a long, rolling meadow. It was made for this continent. It was
made for this place. Despite bad luck, then, I will write its
name down: *crack cocaine.*

The street hustlers — the prostitutes — and the dealers in
Times Square were all attached by coincidence, chance, and
circumstance. They were all acquainted, as in any other New
York City business, and it made convenience shopping for vice
that much more pleasant. Jorge had hustlers sleeping in the
doorway of his apartment building, girls and boys, teenagers
who wore the same clothes day after day, who had lice and
open sores, who were hives of HIV. These kids were hustlers
only in the most limited definition of the term. They would do
whatever you wanted for a price, *they said,* but they wouldn't
do it, really; they would get scared in the end and say that you
couldn't fuck them in the ass — yo, it's *dangerous* — or could
they just jerk you off, or they wouldn't say anything at all, they
would assume a stony and resentful posture until you just gave
them the money anyway.

They were just junkies, in Jorge's view, crackheads, garbage heads, cross-addicts, call them whatever you want, they were ghosts, they were the afterimages of people once photographed or yearbooked or fingerprinted or otherwise entrapped in a devouring system of images. Ghosts, children already dead to their parents, dead to their principals, ministers, social workers, friends, fuck buddies, running partners, dead even to their dealers, ghosts who would for drugs assume corporeal form, as if crack cocaine was some conjuring stone. They were ghosts like he was a ghost, like Jorge was a ghost, and later an addict, too, living far from his own neighborhood, far from his mother, sleeping all day, drawing the blinds, and then going to the Priapus to watch a double feature in which a dozen robotic actors with large mustaches pretended to be camp counselors or infantrymen and then unsheathed themselves.

So this shit these hustlers were smoking, it was available right in the doorway of Jorge's building, because the dealers and the hustlers were all mutually implicated somehow. They appeared at the same time each morning. They hung around in the same way. And that shit they smoked was cheap the first time around. So Jorge, after some months of refusing, gave it a try. It was cheap when you first learned about the way its network stretched out around you, about its system of distribution and shipping and sales and marketing, and about the way it traveled in your neural pathways, Jorge told me, *which was an exact replica of the chart of its distribution* — it was all bait and switch, divide and conquer, symbolic and imaginary, you were talking, you were talking, and the sentences were getting longer and longer and you were saying stuff to this dealer, who was also smoking this shit, in impossibly long sentences, sentences that mixed something that masqueraded as euphoria with the most venal cruelties — Jorge was laughing as the guy called his girls *crackhead bitches* that first time, Jorge was saying that Dominicans was the crassest motherfuckers in the city — and the shit was dancing in your bloodstream like rogue cells metastasizing, and you were thinking, hey, this is pretty good, and then you were going to the A.T.M. on Ninth Avenue and Forty-second for the fourth time that night, *that night,* uh huh, because it was almost sunrise and you hadn't slept yet and your money was going to this guy who wasn't getting much of it because he was a low-level employee *nothing more* and his profit was going to this guy back in Jackson Heights and his money was going to the guy who was *flying this shit in* and his money was going to some other guy who lived in the jungle who was using some of it to pay off the military government of his country, which was trying to pay off loans that your bank — the one where your A.T.M. is — made to this rain-forested country, and you, meanwhile, had one of those crackhead bitches in your bed, *gimme one of those crackhead bitches,* or one of those crackhead boys, sucking on your *dick,* didn't matter which, boy or girl all the same, the mouth around you right then was just a mouth — *suck my dick, you crackhead bitch* — and your *dick* had no *self-respect* left in it anyway, there was nothing left in you in fact you are impotent and it is morning and you haven't slept and the blinds are still drawn and you loathe yourself more than you can say, fucking right you do, only that's too simple, self-loathing because your revulsion for yourself is bottomless, could power a hydroelectric generator, and it sounds this morning like someone is trying to open your bolted windows with a rusty tire iron, *someone is coming in,* and the screech of city buses braking sounds like your name, *Jorge,* on the wind. New York City is a slow corruption. It is time to find some work. To find some money to buy some more of *that shit* from that guy who lives on his feet at the bottom of your stairs. Jorge told me.

After that, after that first time, Jorge would have liked to have said that he stayed clear of the drug. He would have liked to have visited his mother in Jersey. He would have liked not to have his blinds drawn again and his cat tipping over cartons of half-eaten Chinese takeout, his cat chasing the cockroaches. He would have liked to say that he had bathed or that he had read the paper or even circled some Help Wanted ads or cleaned the tub or done a dish or taken the filter out of the coffee thing or that he at least had one of those compulsive cleaning sessions that visited him when he had a hangover, when he went looking for every trace of the night before in his apartment, a night he only remembered in part anyway, shining his apartment, buffing it, polishing it, on his knees, short of breath.

But after a while he didn't even want to straighten out so much, Jorge told me. Getting clean required an effort he no longer possessed. This *aperçu* was the kind of thing people might whisper in the sex clubs. Someone sits down next to you and says, *My life is really coming to an end, if you want to know the truth. Don't say anything. Don't patronize me. Don't try to convince me otherwise.* Stage-whispered over the music. After a while, Jorge's resolve had gone the way of other New York resolutions. It became the style of some other Jorge, some other New Yorker, some guy who looked like him but didn't have his bad luck. The Jorge who had health insurance.

So he was at Sally's II one day when he had come up for air, and he was talking to a very nice girl named Crystal with whom he shared this penchant for grand dramatic statements. Crystal said, having just met him, *My life is fucked up when I am not high. I am simply at my best when I'm high. Being a man was just a way of slowly dying for me, I may as well just tell you. I am a girl like other girls. I would just like to have a husband and live a life in the Catholic church.*

Crystal's complexities, her physical inconsistencies, didn't bother Jorge. And he knew that Crystal would come with him on the promise of crack cocaine. And they walked up Forty-third Street, the way of champagne dreams, the way to all Las Vegas weddings, and they walked right up to the little guy sitting on the hood of a car in front of a place where they sold fake identification cards, and this guy said to Jorge, because Jorge was now a regular customer:

— What the fuck you come up to me like this, what the *fuck?* You crazy? What the fuck? This my *business.* You're an asshole, man. What the *fuck.* What the fuck you doing?

He was gesturing ominously, violently at Jorge, who couldn't figure how he had done anything out of the ordinary. The dealer led them around the corner onto Forty-third Street, heading toward Ninth, making a number of lascivious comments about Crystal, about the size of her breasts, and, because he sensed it was a big night for Jorge, he quoted a price higher than usual. For the *crack cocaine.* So Jorge refused.

At this moment his luck turned almost uniformly bad.

Now Jorge and Crystal were standing there with commuters swarming around them — toward the bus terminal — and she was yelling at him, What is the matter with you? She yelled anxiously as if what troubled her were not the crack cocaine, as if there were something much deeper, some life-threatening thing for which this moment was merely emblematic. Her voice plunged down into a lower register. She had a robust voice, a singer's voice. *Boys with breasts,* Jorge told me wearily, *they are angels and when they break your heart they take you closer to God.*

It started raining. It was raining and they were standing there, and then she was swishing off in her high heels and Jorge was limping after, No wait, *Honey, no, wait,* thinking she looked an awful lot like someone he had known when he was young. In spite of all her operations and medical procedures, she looked like a girl he had known from Newark, the first girl he had loved, Kristina, who had eyes like colored beads. Crystal. Kristina. Which was which?

So he jogged back and gave his last few dollars to the hyena in front of the ID parlor. Paid the price. It was that kind of a night. The dealer was laughing at him now; he was pronouncing grim prophecies in a dead tongue, as Jorge disappeared up the block. And then Jorge and Crystal were back at his place and they were griefstricken, yes, it actually came over them like a contagion and they were crying and somehow they had gotten the rock and they were smoking it and they were making these rash promises like *their marriage would be a grand affair, with a reception that would go on for days,* and it wouldn't matter that Crystal couldn't afford the kind of gown that would have best suited her, and then she started to go down on Jorge and it was an act of mercy, really, not much else, and he put his hand down between her legs, because in spite of everything else, in spite of the fact that he was sweating profusely and grinding his teeth, he felt this was somehow a real chance to exercise those atrophied muscles of compassion, it was the last night he ever felt love, maybe, and he actually said this really stupid thing to her, he actually said these words, words with their own intentions and syntax, *This is the last night I'm ever going to feel love,* he told me, he told her, and he reached down there to the little chrysalis-shaped stub that had once been Crystal's penis before all the hormones and stuff — it was roseate and shriveled and it didn't exactly snap to attention — and he tried to coax something from it, some shiver of recognition about the structure and implication of contact, about sex and its relation to human kindness. Because at least he wanted to give something to someone else. Because if he had become impervious to his own feelings, he at least felt like he could give something to someone else. Crystal moaned as though she might come, but he knew that nothing of the sort applied. They were right near Broadway after all, and he was sleeping with a *guy who was more or less acting the part of a woman,* a top-flight performance, a Broadway performance, and the moan was to attest to the success of Jorge's own erotic masquerade and how it made Crystal feel, ostensibly, well, kinda sexy.

And still he came. Depressed when the moment arrived, with none of that *cocaine self* after orgasm, none of that grandiosity. Cocaine had emptied him. There was simply less of him than there had been in the early part of the day. No tranquilizer was going to restore that deficit. He was grazing bottom. His testes emptied their freight. He reached his arms around her. They held one another. Yes, and then they gave up consciousness.

In the morning, Crystal was gone. She had stolen the last few valuable things in his apartment: some silverware his mother had given him and an antique vase his father had sent him once.

I don't need to tell you of the grim movement of the next month or so, the way the utilities were getting shut off, the

income tax people bringing up stuff from years ago, the land-
lady threatening. These particulars are not unusual and so I
abbreviate them. Jorge said that he *preferred to read by candlelight,* as solitary readers had done for centuries, and he had no
need for a phone. He called his mother from the street.

He began shooting heroin as a matter of course. It was the
equal and opposite reaction to what I have been describing. It
was just another thing to do, heroin or speedballs, and it
actually served to broaden him in a way: it got him out of the
house. It got him into Harlem, where one of those guys he never
met, the guy who looked at his apartment right before he took
it, was also shooting dope. It got him into the East Village,
where there were a number of other people he would never meet
but who were quite close to him — a friend of mine, in fact,
Dave, with whom I went to college, and a girl Dave almost went
on a blind date with once, and a painter from the gallery Dave's
never-to-have-been blind date once worked at. All these people
were in Harlem or on the Lower East Side, putting money in a
pail that a guy was whisking into a rundown tenement building. Heroin got Jorge into the East Village, from which it took
him a really long time to get home when he was high. And it
got him, in the end, into the Ruin. His habit wasn't gigantic,
but he was starting to take risks with it. His arms were pocked
here and there. The Ruin followed directly from that. It was no
longer a matter of any bio-electrical orgasmic *spike.* Orgasm was
out of the question. The Ruin was the place where Jorge felt
relaxed, to the degree that relaxation was an idea he still understood. Listen, he said to me, *Times Square is a place you live because
it's the only place left where you feel like you are comfortable. And this
is true of this club, too, and maybe even true of all of Nueva York.*
He could have lived in San Juan, say, or in Bridgeport, or

Toronto, but the ebb and flow of macroeconomics had brought him here and he had relaxed into chance the way one grows attached to a shirt that is a size too big.

Maybe he heard about the Ruin from some of the women at Peep World or Sally's (where he went to look for Crystal, to beat her senseless, though he never did find her), or maybe he was just drawn there by walking aimlessly along the desolate streets beside the West Side Highway. He was wearing khaki pants and a Hawaiian print shirt and a belted leather jacket and a gold necklace. He had a beard now and his eyes had that disembodied, unsouled look of junkies, and he recognized no ordinary human boundary in conversation. *I've been looking at you all night,* he said to me. And then he told me what I have told you. There was no emotion in him, he was as gray as a blank screen, but at the same time there were in him all the regrets of this city. The story of his decline and fall was marked by repetition and coincidence. The same opinions again and again, in further states of decay, the same complaints about the city, about how the museums were fascist and all the good clubs were closed, and how the best neighborhoods were off-limits for a person of his origins.

What happened to him after that night I met him at the Ruin I am able to tell you. What happened to him after he started shooting dope and before he detoxed himself, Jorge's story, or the part of it that I know, ends this way: we talked above the din of industrial racket. There were dancers in studded leather underwear. A night in June. Jorge disappeared into one of the stalls. When he came out again he was jaundiced. I was thinking about going to an after-hours bar. Jorge said he was going home, but instead he went down to the East Village, to a *cop shop* he had heard about. This I learned later. It was a bakery on Eighth Street and Avenue D that was a front for a heroin operation. Jorge didn't really know the East Village all that well, though, and so when he got off the subway at Astor Place, he wandered block after block into the rubble of that neighborhood trying to find that bakery. It was deep in the night now and he was trying to find it, the silhouettes of these abandoned blocks were ominous, and he was feeling sick and shaking, and he didn't think he was ever going to sleep again, going up and down Eighth Street, thinking about how he was going to get out of this neighborhood and back into Times Square without being bashed or robbed or murdered or anything else, and also not thinking about it, but thinking — with the one last flickering neurotransmitter given over to ordinary human curiosity — *how was the place, the bakery, going to be decorated?*

Starless sky. The only pedestrian traffic was working the same line of business in which Jorge was engaged. When he finally found the bakery, by chance, oblivious to a sudden confluence of meteors above the city, he was as lost as he would ever get in his short life. He was sick, he told me. *I was sick.*

II.

Look, not everyone in New York City goes to sex clubs. Above Fifty-seventh Street on the East Side they march to and from hired cars as if the subway and its contents were television fictions. There is the guy with the private life up here, with the call girl problem or the fucking-boys-in-a-motel-in-the-Bronx problem, and there is the ragged teenager whose ambition is to throw off his or her Upper East Side address, the kid who takes the limo to the shooting gallery on Lexington and 125th, but truly this Upper East Side is a separate city, where only the occasional skirmish with the New York of this story takes place. The Upper East Side has its loneliness, it has its isolation, it has its lost opportunities, its disintegrating families, it has its murder and its addiction and its adultery and homosexuality, sure, but all this is *cushioned*. Disconsolation drifts out of the Upper East Side, in some river of chance, drifts neglected like discarded packaging, until it lands somewhere else.

So another friend I knew from that time, Toni Gardner, went to a club called Wendy's. Saturday nights in the meatpacking district. In the same space as the Ruin. A club for women. *Private sex parties.* They had auctions. You could *auction yourself.* There was a line of those willing to be auctioned. It snaked back to the black plywood bar. A lot of people wanted to participate. If you were willing to wait for a while, you could know your value.

The auctioneer, a woman in her forties, specialized in a certain stage patter that was ironically imitative of the classic auction-house style. The Christie's and Sotheby's style. She was well-dressed and knowledgeable and articulate about the artifacts at hand. Her argot was full of hyperbolic folderol, jokes and salacious commentary, and it was delivered at a nearly unintelligible pace. She enabled, through the blur of her rhetoric, a host of ritual couplings all based upon principles of chance and economics. On the other hand, maybe she was like the country auctioneer sending off the calf to be made veal: *Woman of the age of twenty-five, hair the color of cinnamon, eyes an arctic blue, height and weight, well, she's of a certain size — she's in tip-top physical condition — note the breasts, the fountains of maternity, which I can only describe to you by falling into the use of those old metaphors — perfect fruits — and an ass to die for, yeah to die for — yes this dyke can sing, I can promise you that — in these black jeans, well she will do whatever transports you, this young dyke of twenty-five — I can promise you, and let's start with an opening bid of a hundred and fifty dollars for the evening; do I hear a hundred and fifty, yeah, one-seventy-five, who will pay one-seventy-five for this auburn beauty from the country, from the . . . from the state of Maine, that's right — never visited these precincts before and ready to be broken on the rack of your choice, fresh from the unforgiving and dramatic coasts of Maine — unwise in the ways of Manhattan — do I hear one-seventy-five, one-ninety, do I have one-ninety, two hundred dollars — she assures me she can take a dildo all the way to its rubberized base, two-twenty-five, do I hear, two-thirty — a bottom, yeah, she's a bottom of compliance such as you have never experienced, SOLD! YES! SOLD!* And so on until the obscure and almost unlit room rocked with the dynamics of ownership. Her voice now a whisper in the microphone, devoid of affect, the words delivered without feeling at all, just the words, a perfect simulacrum of auction slang and then you were owned. You were owned.

Toni was from the Upper East Side by way of the suburbs — she had never been to Maine at all — and she got out of that New York neighborhood as soon as she could. Took the bus down Fifth Avenue and only went back for holidays. I met her at Rutgers. When she auctioned herself after a few drinks, I was with her. She'd had a hard time persuading them to let me in. They quizzed you out front if you were a guy. If there was a moment's hesitation in your responses you were gone. *Are you a fag?* If you even quarreled with the usage, you were alone walking past empty warehouses. Way, way West. No cabs. No buses. No subways.

Back then, Wendy's was just coming into prominence as an event. It was making a transition from a prior location, and the fliers were getting more and more aggressive: *Wendy's, the dungeon of destiny for discerning dykes.* Or: *Wendy's, Cruising, Dancing, Humiliation.* Toni had recently stumbled into the new room in the back, the one with the vinyl bed in it, and she often found bodies writhing there, including, once, the body of a composition professor we'd had at Rutgers. *She gave the stupidest assignments.* Wendy's sprouted these new rooms, like a starfish regrowing itself. Private rooms down this long, gas-lit corridor. Like the steam tunnels under the Rutgers campus. Tunnels like architectural diagrams for the uterine and fallopian insides of the customers. Wendy's was a mystery. You could never tell if the pool table would be there, if the cages would be there, if the bartender who was alluring last week still had her shift. The specifics came and went. Including the pertinent information. Wendy's only operated on Saturday nights, as it had once operated only on Thursdays; it changed locations. It had a phone. It didn't. It had live music. It didn't. Sometimes it was in the meatpacking district and sometimes it was gone altogether.

Likewise being auctioned that night were the services of a first-rate dominatrix, who would demonstrate her gifts on the premises, later in the evening. A tattooist and scarification expert auctioned some work. One of the bartenders auctioned herself. They were supposed to use *play money,* simulated legal tender bills that had been printed for the occasion, but the artificial bills diluted the effect of the transaction. Therefore, a subterranean market existed featuring real cash. Toni got into this long unruly line — she was soon to be the cinnamon-haired beauty from Maine — after we had sat there a while, excitably. And it wasn't so strange that she did it, really. The auction wasn't that far, say, from a *coming-out party* back in Montclair, where Toni had lived as a kid.

Things weren't going well for her professionally. She didn't really know what she wanted to do; she had spent a couple of years now talking in therapy about *Vocational Choice Anxiety*. And she had flipped a car in Long Island visiting her parents' summer house. She owed them a lot of money for it. She'd moved out of the Upper East Side after being engaged to a nice boy with a legal practice. Toni auctioned herself to slip these binds. She did it for fun, an amnesiac fun.

She danced in a go-go cage, beside the auctioneer, dressed in black jeans and a tank top, she made sure to sport her tattoos, and she affected an insouciant look, as if daring a bidder. This was *the* look among the lots at Wendy's auction — a look that mixed subject and object, *sub* and *dom* — and therefore not terribly novel. Toni didn't garner the highest price. That went to a woman in a sort of librarian costume who seemed to weep nervously as a pair of anxious bidders competed aggressively for her. She brought a thousand dollars for the night.

The music was speed metal. Speed metal with girl singers. Toni danced. At last, the bidding was completed. Two hundred and fifty dollars. A scattered and diffident applause. The crowd parted a little bit, and in a sort of movie slow-motion the employees of Wendy's waved Toni over, waved her over to the edge of the stage, waving like construction flagmen, where *two women were waiting for her.* Two women had bid together for her. A consortium. They were fucking cheap, was Toni's first feeling, she explained it to me later. *They were fucking cheap, they couldn't even afford to buy their own slave for the evening — they had to go in on one.* No way was she going with them. No way. They were cheap.

But then Toni began to warm to the idea a little. She was charmed, it turned out, by their garishness. By the ugly complexities they presented. She hated them at first and then in her disdain she started to like them. At the bar. As she stepped from the stage, Toni took one hand from each of them — from Doris and Marlene — and they repaired to the bar. One of her owners was a good lesbian and one was a bad lesbian. The good lesbian was Doris, and she came from Bernardsville, New Jersey, but she didn't go to Rutgers like Toni Gardner did. *She went to Princeton.* Doris's parents were disappointed when she made clear her object choice to them, Toni learned later, when Doris told her parents that *she was in love with a woman.* But they were supportive (her mom was especially supportive now, because she was in therapy, with Dr. Bernice Neptcong, who had an office right in Princeton), and they supported her efforts to find a loving, caring relationship.

Unfortunately, Toni told me, Doris didn't want a loving, caring relationship exactly, or perhaps these terms were simply more elastic to her than might be supposed by Bernice Neptcong. To Doris loving and caring always seemed to have a certain amount of trouble attached to them. So Doris formed an attachment with Marlene, the bad lesbian. Marlene was a tall, exotic sex worker — Marlene was not her real name — who had platinum blond hair and coffee-colored skin, who slept with men at a reasonably successful escort agency and who came home aggrieved by her profession. She drank a lot and dabbled with harder drugs.

Marlene's cheekbones were like the sharp side of an all-purpose stainless steel survival jackknife, and her eyes narrowed to reflect disappointment and loss, which, when combined with her biceps, her violent and toned physique, made for a compelling female beauty. Doris, meanwhile, looked like an Ivy League intellectual. She had thick black glasses and she shaved the back of her head. She wore maroon velveteen bell bottoms and had a navel ring. She was a little older than her clothes suggested.

Marlene and Doris, Toni realized, didn't have much to say to each other. Toni didn't know, yet, that Marlene had just come back from a hard day at an escort agency where she had to fuck a whole bunch of strangers, guys for whom deceit was a simple fact of their day, who wove deceit and its responsibilities into their schedule like it was just another calendar appointment. And she didn't know that Doris hated her job at the women's magazine where she worked on the copy desk — she aspired to write articles for *Camera Obscura*. Toni thought Marlene was the harder of the two. Marlene was like a tea kettle almost boiled off. Anything could upset her, it seemed, any little stray remark. But in truth Doris was harder. Doris was detached and skeptical and full of calcified antipathies.

Their apartment was in the Clinton section of Manhattan, also called Hell's Kitchen, where Jorge Ruiz lived. On the night that Toni was auctioned off to Marlene and Doris, Jorge, as I have said, was arguing with a pre-op transsexual, Crystal, about whether to buy crack cocaine from a guy on Forty-third Street who was out to chisel them. At that very moment, while Jorge was just lifting the hem of Crystal's cheap synthetic miniskirt and pulling delicately on the mesh of her white fishnet stockings, Doris, Marlene, and Toni were throwing lightswitches a couple of blocks away.

It was a small one-bedroom and it was draped in leather

items, in stuff from the Pink Pussycat or the Pleasure Chest. There was restraining gear, and they even had a gynecologist's exam table with house plants on it. The table had stirrups and everything. There was another decorating strain, too: Bernardsville chic. It was a kind of homely, countervailing sensibility. Doris hadn't been able to shake it yet, though she was in her thirties. She had a few museum posters, Monet's years at Giverny or the Treasures of Egypt, and some handsome black Ikea furniture, and a lovely imitation Persian area rug made in Belgium. Her parents helped her to buy these. Doris and Marlene also had one of those little yapping city dogs, a corgi or something, named Bernice Neptcong, M.D. Doris would say, *Get out of the way, Bernice Neptcong.* The dog was vicious. It was an attack rat.

Marlene had clamps, Toni told me. She liked to have you apply the clamps to her nipples and then, also, to her labia, though the best part, Marlene said, and Toni repeated to me, *I'm telling you — the best part is when they come off.* She also used clothespins, because you could take a little of the spring out of them, bend them back and forth a few times, and they didn't hurt quite as much. The three of them had already had enough drinks to loosen up — it was maybe three in the morning — so their clothes were off in a hurry. They'd barely turned the dead bolts. Except that Marlene had this idea about donning other clothes. Once she had her clothes off, she was striding, like some carnivorous game animal, across the room toward the closet. She had a closet full of the garments of the diligent bondage fantast. So they took off their clothes and they put on these leather chaps in which their asses were exposed. Shredded T-shirts through which the edges of leather brassieres or the slope of a breast were evident. On Toni, the costume was kind of large. She was normally in the petite range. Doris seemed to make her own selections wearily, as though this part of love-making were as new as selecting a temperature for a load of laundry.

Marlene had Doris and Toni attach the clamps to her body. She whispered brusquely. They observed a clinical, professional silence as they did it — because the procedure involved pain and had the sobriety of pain. Toni performed her role intently as though the process were curative or therapeutic and because she didn't know Doris and Marlene well enough to chatter anyway. Toni hadn't told them anything — they knew noth-ing about her except her nakedness, the shape of her tattoos: the Ghost Rider skull on her shoulder blade, the Minnie Mouse on her ass.

Though now they knew she liked novelty. Toni went down on Marlene. It was pretty hard to avoid the clothespins in that posture, but brushing against them turned out to be part of the point. Marlene let the breath of God pass from her lips. She seemed a little dizzy, and the region that was clamped became enlarged. It must have hurt like shit, Toni told me, *because those things were on there pretty well and she was grinding up against me and they were getting caught in my hair or I was pushing them aside and she was just moaning in that way people do, moaning like this was the straight, vanilla thing.* This went on for a while and finished with Marlene producing a formidable strap-on dildo from a Doc Martens shoebox under the bed. Marlene reached and shoved the box back under the bed. A ripple of pain seemed to overtake her as she did so, and she huffed once with it, as though this were a brisk sort of exercise.

Marlene arranged the dildo harness *over* the clamps, organiz-ing these hazards disinterestedly. They might as well have been curlers. She stood. She stepped out of the leather chaps and into the black Lycra garment with a real weariness. A couple of clothespins sprung loose and she let them go. Then she guided the dildo through the hole in the harness. Its pinkish, Caucasian color was ridiculous. She had a large bottle of Astroglide already waiting on the floor beside the bed, and she told Doris to lean over and grab it, and then, while Toni was doing busy work on her breasts, fingerpainting them, she lubricated her lover's ass and vagina both, as though she were baby-oiling an infant — with just this detachment — and bid Doris kneel at the edge of the bed. Marlene, standing, fucked Doris in the ass, while Toni got around front and fondled Doris's clitoris. Toni was doing the same to herself. *It was like jazz-dancing,* Toni told me, *it was all these moves and steps all figured out like that bitch in Montclair, Mrs. Beatty, tried to ram into my head when I was in Jazzercise on Mondays and Wednesdays when Mom was doing the day-care center thing.* But the fact was: Toni liked it. It was thrilling the way the last reel of a film is thrilling. You just want to see it all played out.

Doris, on the other hand, seemed to be walking through it a little bit. *Penetration, you know, isn't always the coolest thing among women,* Toni said. Doris held clumps of Toni's cinnamon hair in her hands as she, Doris, was being fucked by Marlene. She gently tousled Toni's hair, mumbling slightly, with a kind of sexual agitation that had a little sadness in it too. The amazing thing, though, was that Marlene was getting the whole thing up into Doris, *grinding up into her with those fucking clamps and clothespins all over her!* Finally, though, Doris seemed to have enough of it, and she pulled the thing out of her ass with a sigh, reaching behind her, looking behind her in this vulnerable way and then, pulling the thing out of her, she stood and pushed Marlene down on the bed, masturbating the rubber dick attached to Marlene, as though it could feel, pulling the condom off it, yes condom, and jerking it off, grinding against her lover's hips until Marlene seemed to be in some thrall of shuddering and pain, kissing Doris on the mouth, reaching up to gently kiss her goodnight. *Oh, God,* Marlene said, as Doris removed the clamps one by one, first the nipple clamps, and the skin underneath was bruised with red rings around it. Even on Marlene's dark skin you could see the welts rising. And then the clothespins from her labia. Marlene fingered the damage in an inebriate swoon. *Oh, God.* Toni and Doris stood around her, around the foot of the bed. Marlene probed with her long dark stalks for the evidence of the clothespins. Then she lay back on the bed. Doris wiped her hands on the comforter at the foot of the bed, almost as if that simulated thing, the simulated dick, had ejaculated onto her, as if she'd had Marlene's very semen upon her.

And then she turned her attentions to Toni. She said something that Toni didn't hear, because the two of them were angling around one another like wrestlers now, angling as if to grasp one another, and then the words became clear, their quaintness, Doris wanted to be held, *really,* Toni told me, *believe it or not, she just wanted to be held,* so the two of them were hugging, and Toni really felt like she was Doris's dad or something, holding her, and then this paternal kindness or whatever it was gave way to another set of roles, another set of styles. They were lying on the bed next to Marlene, who was in some narcotic semi-consciousness, and they were facing one another, head to foot, going down on each other, because the just holding each other part was okay, but it led elsewhere right then. They were unclothed now, the pile of fantasy gear sitting atop their street clothes like an upper layer of sediment. Doris tasted musty to Toni, as though forgotten in all the rush to arrange things, and Toni felt badly for her. So pity became a component in this secondary tangle of erotics. Pity in there too, like yet another partner, an unwanted partner. Toni's first and only instance of transportation of the evening was a little ripple, really, and she made more noise with it than it required. She faked it. *By then, there really wasn't anything going on that was doing it for me, so I faked it,* she told me. Doris in the meantime was having the revelation of the shy. All the contentment in the world seemed to come out of some locked basement and crowd around her. There was sentiment everywhere; the world was her damp handkerchief, her multivolume diary. It was the kind of orgasm, to Toni, that was promised by the good-natured phonies who wrote sex manuals. *Loving as Lesbians (By and For and How To).* Or: *The Gay Woman: A Manual for Lovers and Friends.* Come out of your cellar cabinets of shame, *womyn,* and *celebrate!* Know the community of love!

— Wow, Doris said. God. Wow.

— Mm, Toni said.

Now they lay beside one another in the light of a single bedside lamp.

— Don't worry about her, Doris said. Out cold. Once she's out you could jump on the mattress and she wouldn't notice.

— This is a —

— You want to spend the night?

— Can we all fit on here?

They could, sure, even though Toni wasn't totally convinced she wanted to spend the night. She was kind of hoping they couldn't all fit. She kind of wanted to go back to her own bed and sort through the fleeting recollections of the evening: dancing in the cage, putting on the bondage gear, fitting a clamp onto another woman's nipple, the exponential complications of a threesome. She felt overtaxed, like she'd sat through a double feature in the front row. She was cranky, short-tempered. It didn't make any difference. Toni was worried about hurting Doris's feelings for some reason, for some stupid girl reason. So she stayed. Soon all three women were arranged in the enormous bed. Marlene's lungs wheezed like an old bellows. Doris, on the other hand, was a light sleeper. Toni was between them and she couldn't get comfortable all night — the gravitational yank of those bodies was too much for her. And Doris kept throwing a leg over her, pinning her, as though Toni were there for good.

A diner on Ninth Avenue. After a silent and hungover breakfast, the three of them made another date for the Thursday following. *Would you want to come visit us again?* Marlene said. And Marlene did indeed seem to want to try it again. But there was another part of her — Toni told me over the weekend, when she and I went to a bar on First Avenue and St. Mark's called simply *Bar* — there was another part of Marlene that was suspicious somehow, evidently suspicious, that the two of them, Toni and Doris, had been *fucking around without her.* Taking advantage of her intermittent consciousness. She must have had some infrared surveillance device, Toni thought, watching out for her interests. Or else she was just keenly attuned to the inevitability of heartache. *Rejection sensitivity.* So what if Doris and Toni *were* doing it? It was part of the problem of three people. *You really gotta trust each other,* Toni told me. *Cause there's always two on and one off.* But Marlene couldn't withstand the implications, and as the thought took root, it sent forth these poisonous boughs.

That was no surprise. The picture of Marlene got worse as Toni learned about it. Marlene flew into a rage if the place, if the apartment in Clinton, was not swept clean; if the dog, Bernice Neptcong (a male) had not been walked; if the pictures were crooked, if Doris happened to show any interest, conversational or anything else, in any male who didn't wear dresses and have breasts; if, even for a moment, Marlene had the sensation that Doris was preoccupied with another woman. Or sometimes Marlene flew into a rage just out of confusion, just out of daily confusion. And when Marlene flew into a rage, *she sometimes beat Doris.* This is what Toni found out before the second date ever took place, when she met Doris for a drink, because Doris called her at work and said, *I have to talk to you. Let's meet at this bar on St. Mark's. It's important.* Her voice was hushed as if even the security on her work phone had somehow been breached.

This fact of battery seemed to slip almost casually from Doris and Marlene to Toni and Doris and then to Toni and me, the enormity of it almost routine or incidental at first, as if it were not about people at all, as if there were not bruises on Doris's china features, as if it were about a way that people lived in New York City, an awful way that people lived, where women beat their children in public, and men beat one another on the subways. Toni told me and I said nothing, because this beating was a vacuum, a lifelessness that I couldn't really adjust to at first, and then I passed it on, passed on that silence to someone else, who in turn passed it on, the idea that good people, principled women, occasionally beat one another out of confusion and sadness and loss and thereby put the purple, the hematoma, in the flag that hung over city hall.

Bruises had appeared all over Doris. She frequently wore sunglasses. She spoke of falling down stairs and walking into doors. It was getting difficult at the office, as it had been difficult at offices in the past. *I've been fired from jobs before,* Doris said, her hands trembling as she lit a cigarette. Her voice was dull and methodical; she smelled clean, obsessively clean, to Toni; her skin was the palest white, the color of gallery walls.

— I can't lose another job because of her. I'm not functioning as it is. You know? It's getting a little embarrassing. I'm tired of going through it. . . . It's humiliating and it's really tiring too. I'm tired of living like this. There's this dull way things go around and around again and I'm almost thirty-two years old and I don't want to live like this anymore.

Doris would veer off in another direction, onto another subject, and then come back to it. And then another refrain emerged. *She asked Toni if she knew anywhere they could cop some cocaine.* They were drinking and having a conversation that veered from the tragic to the mundane, from battery to discussions of rock and roll bands, and then suddenly Doris was trying to procure. No delicate way to announce it, like there was no delicate way to say that you have been beaten by your lover and that you haven't exactly done anything about it yet. Doris said, *Do you know where we could pick up?* And since Toni lived in the East Village she did know where to buy drugs, though she was no regular customer, she knew where, because you passed it every day. Wasn't terribly complicated. So they walked down Twelfth Street and copped some rock from the first cluster of dangerous-looking boys they saw. That simple.

The boys took their twenty dollars and came back a little later with the vials, the vials with their little red plastic caps. Doris and Toni smoked it together in a basement stairwell.

Then the complaints were spilling out of Doris's mouth in long, artificial strings. How had she assumed this role, this victim role? What kind of mystery was there in her *family of origin?* Where could blame be apportioned so that her burden would be lighter? She was victimized by Marlene. Marlene pulled all the strings. She was thinking back to her parents' *concept of child-rearing and its hidden language of coercion.* Doris was powerless. She needed to *share her truth.* To set *boundaries.* The passions of battery were stirred way down in the unconscious, in the history of the species, not up where Doris or anyone could control them. She didn't know if she could shake it. She wanted to leave but she didn't know if she could. There was something operatic about Doris not walking the dog and getting hit. There were all kinds of hatred between Doris and Marlene. Marlene was systematically trying to *murder* Doris. Doris had actually woken to find Marlene holding a pillow over her head as she slept, she had found Marlene tampering with jars of prescription medication that she had in her cabinet — *I have these attacks of nerves,* Doris said. And Marlene couldn't handle in the end, that Doris's family had money and that hers did not; the differences between the classes was too much for her, though Doris herself felt she understood the misery that Marlene had come from. She could see how her life had been devoid of any model for affection. *But she didn't have to murder her for it.* She didn't have to buy a gun, which was what Marlene was talking about doing, to defend them from the fucking creeps in Hell's Kitchen, *fucking creeps.* And then just as suddenly, Doris was in love again. She had not exhausted all of her affection for Marlene. Marlene was radiant when she was happy, she had a smile that would stop at nothing. When she was happy, her face seemed to open and to reply in the affirmative to everything, to the abandoned buildings, to the crack dealers, to the repulsive men who paid her. Her face said *yes* and it was clear how revolutionary and dangerous was the *yes* of a woman who was *grabbing the world by its dick and yanking*. Marlene happy, Doris said, was as dangerous as a souped-up automatic weapon. But then on the other hand she was dangerous when she wasn't happy and that was where all the trouble started. Marlene was dangerous. She was just thinking out loud. Marlene was dangerous. (Toni was telling me in the bar.) And that was when Doris began to think about what she might do about the problem. Maybe there just wasn't any way around it.

They went to Wendy's together, the next Saturday. All three of them. For a minute, everything seemed to be going all right. There was a new room where a woman in thigh-high boots and black leather gloves was throwing darts. There was another auction and the three of them discussed buying a fourth woman. They were particularly fond of a little girl in a white party dress who shivered and grimaced like a child abandoned in a department store. This little girl would have waited days among the men's shirts for the mother who would never return.

But they didn't have enough cash between them to really pay for the girl, who was a hot item. Top dollar for this girl. They were back at the Clinton apartment; it was only 12:30. The dog was walked, the apartment was clean. The three of them were there in the apartment, and already the process of unclothing themselves seemed ritualized. Something had gone out of it. Toni knew she was just chasing kicks and it didn't make her feel that good. Marlene seemed intent on being the passive recipient of whatever fucking was going to take place that night. She had a tableau in mind; it was theatrical. She was actively arranging for her passivity. Through some superhuman effort, Doris managed to keep the whole thing together for a time. She put on the pink dildo and fucked Marlene in the missionary position, but both of them seemed sad and distant, and Toni lay around drinking beer and lending a hand now and then. The air was hot and still. The heat was a malevolent force in the apartment. By the time they climbed under a lone sheet, the three of them were covered in the sweat of exertion, the sweat of connections not entirely made. They were each a little drunk.

When Toni awoke, the sun was muffled in humidity. They had coffee and she wondered if Doris was imagining the whole thing. New York City was quiet, it was Sunday morning, people were absorbed with that newspaper and no ill feeling would spill onto the streets of the city until noon. Vice was canceled for a time out of respect for a few regular churchgoers. When Toni went home, when she called me later to go for a drink, she had a feeling this auction vogue had run its course now. She could go on to other things. *Sex just isn't that important,* she said. *You can get into it for a while and then you can get into something else.* She was thinking about going back out to Long Island for the summer.

But that night Doris called again. She had to see Toni right then. Right away. She was a mess. *I've broken my wrist,* she said. *My wrist is in a sling.* Doris couldn't go to work the next day, looking like one of those women who, in dark sunglasses, stands by her man, who limps slightly and walks very slowly.

Her wrist in a sling. Something about the night before. Marlene had just flipped out. She was coming at Doris with a lamp, one of those halogen lamps. She was going to break a fucking halogen lamp over Doris's head. They had been kissing while she slept, Marlene cried, Doris and Toni had been fucking without her. *And we hadn't!* Doris said, as if Toni needed to be conscripted into her version of the story somehow. *And I told her that!* And Marlene started bringing up crazy stuff. Stuff that happened months ago. Why was Doris leaving early for the office on a Tuesday in March? If she actually went to the gynecologist in April did she have any proof? Marlene was bringing up things that never happened, totally imagining things. So Doris did what she had never done before. *She took a swing at Marlene.* Hit her in the arm and broke her own wrist. Just like that. Broke it like it was the tiny limb on a sapling. Marlene didn't have anything more than a bruise, but Doris's arm was broken and Marlene wasn't talking to her anymore. Marlene was shattering furniture in the apartment. Marlene was silent and implacable and breaking things. Oh, it was horrible, it was horrible, New York was horrible, and life was horrible, full of compromises — she was crying now — and other people controlled you, people you would never know, never even know their middle names or what their vices were, the stuff they never told you, the real pornography of sensitivity, the pornography of love and affection, the pornography of plain old bliss. . . . You never knew anything and you passed into old age knowing nothing except the color of some *fucking bathtub toy from your childhood. Let's go get high,* Doris said. *I want to get high. I just want to get high.*

Doris made this plan. She told Toni. Their anniversary was coming up. She and Marlene had been together two years. She would make a plan to set things right with Marlene. It involved taking Marlene to see a play. The theater. *Shakespeare in the Park.* Yep. In New York you could work your way past the homeless people in midtown and the homeless guys sleeping in the park and the guys who were auctioning off their tragedies, their TB, their KS, their HIV, their veteran status for alms, and you could go see these plays in the park. *Shakespeare in the Park.* Anyone could go. And though Marlene had not had much formal education, Shakespeare moved her — all those old tragedies with their sins of pride and their purgations. She especially liked strong women characters. Lady Macbeth and Cleopatra. So they were seeing *Lear* and Doris knew she was a Regan or Goneril; sharper than serpent's teeth, Toni told me, because at that very moment the other part of the plan was taking effect. Because Doris was leaving. Doris was leaving. Doris was springing it on Marlene. And Toni was agreeing to help. Out of pity.

So Toni and a team of illegal aliens were breaking into Doris's and Marlene's apartment, and were feeding the dog, Bernice Neptcong, with fresh steak, actually feeding the dog steak like in some PG-13 heist movie, because the dog, raised by Marlene, would fasten its jaws onto any intruder, and they didn't want to have to kill it, and while the dog was eating the steak, a fine cut, I would imagine, lean, lean, lean, Toni was directing this team of illegal aliens who had no real interest in the haste or deceit involved in their work because they just needed the work; Toni was directing them to what she believed were Doris's furniture and CD's and books and sexually explicit videos and pictures of Monet's years at Giverny, and was putting them into an unmarked, rented van that was double-parked in front of the Korean deli below. It was too bad that it had to be on their anniversary, Toni told me, but Doris couldn't think of another way to shake her, another day, another perfect time and place. Or maybe the cruelty that was involved in this plan was very much on Doris's mind, for the two years of cruelty she had received, and this was the best way to work it out, the most perfect way to make her point, a point thematically coherent and consistent, like a play itself, a point featuring the coincidences and destinies of a play.

I guess I have to admit here, too, that as a friend of Toni's I served as an accomplice to this crime. I served as a lookout, just in case Marlene or one of her friends (though she didn't have that many friends actually) might have some synergistic understanding of what was going on, some sudden impulsive need to go see if Bernice Neptcong, M.D., had enough water in all this heat. Shamefully, I stood on the street as the Hispanic guys, their faces twisted into the solemn, sensitive gazes of funeral parlor employees, carried the furniture out of the apartment at a trot.

Finally, there was an intermission at *Lear,* between the third and fourth acts, and Doris told Marlene, giving her an affectionate little peck on the cheek, that she had to go to the bathroom. Doris's lips were not thin lips, as I might have imagined the lips of preppy women from Bernardsville to be. No, through some strange genetic twist, she had been given the broad, full lips of a lover, and even at the beginning Marlene had adored these lips, Toni believed, had adored kissing Doris. So Doris's lips were now descending on Marlene's razor cheeks, and Marlene, as a matter of course, was pretending not to care entirely, though inside perhaps, where things were all tangled up, there was some interior paroxysm of joy or gladness at the bounty of love, though this paroxysm was smothered by the cool of New York. Then Doris gave her a little hug. She was wearing a black tank top and black jeans, and Marlene was, too. Marlene was wearing almost the same thing, and Doris gave her a little squeeze, and said she had to go to the *comfort station*. She laughed and said it, *comfort station*.

And then she took off. She was sobbing like a baby, sobbing like that girl left in the department store, sobbing in a way that can't be ameliorated by the stuff in this world, no matter how much good happens. But by the time she met another friend, Debby, over by Tavern on the Green, by the time she met Debby she had settled down a little bit. Debby had borrowed a car, a black Toyota Celica with plastic wrap in the rear windows from where they had been shattered, and they were driving straight to Newark airport, where Doris was catching a flight to New Orleans to stay with some cousins for a couple of weeks.

Elsewhere, with crack timing, the illegal aliens and Toni were driving Doris's stuff to mini-storage over in the west teens, just above the meatpacking district.

Marlene in the meantime was sitting on the blanket under the trees. Just a regular old blanket from the apartment, nothing special. And she was eating a cheap piece of cheddar cheese on a Triscuit and watching the edges of the audience fray as people came and went, and thinking what a great breeze, what a killer breeze, and then wondering, when the play had begun again, where Doris was, but just wondering briefly, not giving it that much thought, and then watching some of the play and getting concerned, packing things up as if she was going to leave, wondering if leaving was the right thing to do, if staying put was maybe better, because if Doris was lost — as she was often lost, a little absent-minded — it would be better if one of them weren't moving and then getting pissed off, really pissed off, *fuck,* and getting up and blocking somebody's fucking view of *RAIN RAIN RAIN,* or some such passage in *Lear,* and sitting back down, and then getting worried because the rage that Marlene felt was in part worry, rage blanketing worry based on experience, some experience of loss, and so she was getting up and walking fast, now, purposefully, in a way you might have found scary if you were watching her, walking fast toward the PortoSans, or whatever brand they had installed over on the other side of the field where everyone was sitting, and looking at the line of people there, unable to ask any of the women there, the overdressed women, the society chicks who had read *Shakespeare in college* if they had seen a woman in black jeans, suddenly unable to do it somehow, unable to do it, shy or something, and then wandering around the PortoSans, in the woods, out of the woods of Central goddamn Park, wandering, past Tavern on the Green, and back to the play, hearing applause, not paying any attention to it, seeing a dozen women who looked like Doris, looked exactly like her until you got up close, until you could see up close that they had one birthmark that Doris didn't have, or they held one opinion that was not Doris's, or that they were fucking boys instead of girls, although otherwise they *were* Doris, seeing them and working upstream to the spot where she and Doris had sat and not finding her, in the dark now, getting dark, worried, concerned, enraged, yeah, murderously enraged, worried, Doris's headless, raped body in the Ramble, raped by some fucking pervert, worried, and then walking out of the park, empty now, followed by cops on horses, not cops that you would ask to help you, though, they were no help, cops, gangsters attached at the waist to horses, so worried, walking back toward the apartment down Eighth Avenue, down through the sleaze, down Eighth Avenue, walking automatically, not thinking at all, not feeling, just thinking the worst, but in a disembodied way, permitting the worst just to swim in her wherever it would — Doris's headless body. Doris's headless body, her jeans and her breasts and then no head, just bones and tubing and pink gelatinous stuff, and then turning up the street and fitting the key in the lock that was broken anyway, and checking the mail just because *Doris liked to get mail,* checking the mail just for Doris, and climbing up the poorly lit and warped steps to the third floor, and fitting the key in the door, not knowing right then how time was stretching out in this moment, not knowing how long it was taking to turn that key because she was imagining the worst but in a detached way, in a way while she was planning to go to Wendy's that night, or in a way while she was thinking about her job and almost crying with how much she hated it and how the guys thought they could just do anything . . . and regretting all the trouble with Doris, regretting it and not being able to explain it, not even being able to admit it exactly, imagining trouble but not seeing the real trouble that lay right in front of her. And then turning the handle and seeing the blankness, the emptiness in that space.

The apartment was just about cleaned out.

Doris on her way to New Orleans: she was having a drink on the plane. And then she was in the Big Easy. The second day there she went to Mobile. To the Gulf Coast. The sun was high and it was humid and the water was a fabulous blue. It was nothing like New York City. When you were in Mobile, New York City just didn't exist at all. It was somebody's fever dream. And then she called Toni that night, because she hadn't left Toni the number, knowing that Marlene would be calling

Toni wanting to know if she was a part of it, the conspiracy, if she was responsible for it, and sure enough Toni said she had called weeping, hysterical, *How could you do this to me how could you do this to me how could you do this to me how could any human being do this to another human being?* but Toni had the machine on and had gone to stay with Debby, who also had her machine screening. Marlene's hoarse, throaty screams. Beyond the frequency that telecommunications can handle. Marlene's shrill recognitions drifting out over New York.

Actually, by the time Doris was in Mobile, Marlene was already dead. Doris was on the plane when it happened. The exact moment was lost on her; she felt no shiver of symbiosis. She felt no paranormal sadness. She was over Tuscaloosa. Or she was at the baggage check when Marlene hanged herself. All of this is *true,* I can tell you that. Marlene hanged herself. This is what Doris did — she abandoned her girlfriend at a performance of Shakespeare in the Park and then flew to New Orleans — and this is what Marlene did afterwards. She hanged herself with rope she got at a hardware store right next to the Best Western on Eighth Avenue. She left a crumpled twenty on the counter. The guy in the store didn't even notice when she overlooked her change. When Marlene did it she was alone, and she wasn't discussing it with anyone. She had to make sure the bar in the closet was sturdy enough. She would have to really make her mind up once and for all, because it was pretty low, that bar, and hanging yourself in there would take a lot of work. She left no note, as Doris had left no note explaining her own disappearance. She used the handcuffs in their apartment, which once had bound her and Doris together while they made love, to cuff herself behind the back, and another set on her ankles. She put the ankle cuffs on first, then the handcuffs, and then she put her head through a slipknot. A regular old slipknot. And then she threw herself off balance and gasped as she fell over, stumbling to her side, kicking around the boots on the floor of the half-empty closet, kicking over boots and bondage gear and the other stuff Doris had left her, wanting to get up but all tangled and having trouble getting up, desperate to get up now, weeping, but not getting up. The energy to do so dissipated. Shocked in the last second, terrified, and then resigned, powerless. Her last breath spread in an even film in the still air of the apartment. She too settled down to room temperature.

The closet door was open. The dog paid no attention. He had been fondled and loved that afternoon by Toni and the guys from Ecuador. He'd eaten steak. But then, when she was dead, Bernice Neptcong, the dog, became somehow uncomfortable. He went and sniffed at the long dark legs half-folded awkwardly under Marlene. And then he curled up by one ankle for the long wait. When they found her days later, when the neighbors complained, Bernice was shivering and hungry, but he struck out blindly nonetheless at the super, the police — the interlopers in this drama of neglect — baring his teeth, and protecting the lost lives that had prized him. This was his kingdom now.

Three weeks later Doris was walking down Eighth Street late at night. The streets were empty. She was on her way to Avenue D. Ten days back in the city. She had tried to get in touch with Toni, but it wasn't turning out exactly as she hoped. She hoped that Toni would be around when she got back. In New Orleans the unspeakable drama of her predicament created a space between her and her cousins. She found this space again in Princeton. She was more alone than ever before, though she had fled Marlene to escape loneliness, though she had opposed loneliness with what strength she had. Death mocked all this stuff. These weeks made clear the over-pressure of her situation. She'd taken too much time off from her job. She didn't really have anywhere to stay. She certainly wasn't going back to the apartment. And Toni wouldn't see her. So she had come to this address in the East Village. She had come by herself, feeling nauseated and lost, for the dull thrill of carelessness.

In the bakery on Eighth and D Doris waited in line like everyone else. The woman in front of her actually bought some bread to go with her heroin — it was a demonstration loaf of stale Italian — but Doris wasn't here for bread. She was here for a dime bag. In front of her in line was Jorge Ruiz. His clothes were shabby. Throughout the transaction, he never once raised his eyes. Neither did Doris. She wouldn't have recognized him anyway; she wouldn't have seen anything, lost in the flow of her own disgrace.

III.

Randy Evans didn't know that that girl on Ninth Street had been directing a film for two years. That girl, Yvonne. He thought she just sold hash. She was small and pale. She had sloppily dyed platinum blond hair. Roots showing. She was spending money on what? On leather miniskirts and stuff and on hash when she was supposed to be selling the hash instead of smoking it, selling it in order to finance a film she was making. He found this out later. Yvonne was going to be his wife, although he wasn't quite sure when or how yet. She didn't know anything about it. And he didn't know it either, on Ninth Street, when they met. In front of a store that sold

Populuxe lamps and plastic handbags and photos of Marilyn and Elvis. He didn't know it until he ran into her a few times at clubs in the neighborhood, most of them gone now. At 8BC or Pyramid. He didn't know until a sort of pattern was established. A pattern of meetings.

He clubbed and so did she. Although he liked *nice* clubs — Interferon or Area — where the cash dwelt, cash and speedballs and stuff like that, he also slouched around in twilit venues like the Crypt and the Manhole and the Ruin. He was flashy, he liked to throw a little money around, but late at night he found himself watching guys getting flogged at the Ruin. He was making some good money working up in the garment district, had his own showroom for a while, in fact. The Evans Line. Borrowed some money from some garment industry backers and started this showroom, which was a little cut-rate, priced to move pretty well, and he was hoping to get some of it into department stores. At first he was. He was getting it into some places. Alexander's and Gimbel's.

Then at night he bought cocaine and he went to Area. And some time later in the evening when he was teetering between drunkenness and mania he went to the Ruin. There he watched the sleepwalkers in the oblivion of the masochist's craft, with their dicks in their hands, circulating around the room, or around the stage where a guy with a ponytail was getting whipped on the ass by a dominatrix. This guy must have hung up there for half an hour. When he was released from his torture, he was covered with welts. Black and blue all over his ass. And the guy just smiled. Randy liked it. He liked to watch the sleepwalkers as they inclined, lips pursed, toward the toes of women lounging at the bar. They'd wander around sleepily jerking off and then they'd ask a woman if they could suck her

toes. He laughed at all this stuff. He'd stay at the Ruin sometimes until dawn.

Anyway, he met Yvonne at 8BC. He didn't tell her about
his late-night exploits. She didn't tell him about her film. In
fact, Randy's interest in B&D was something that he dis-
avowed generally. It occupied a corner of his life that he did
not dwell upon. He was sometimes afraid of who he might
meet at the Ruin. His nightlife was only partly under his control. But that night he was at 8BC. There was this band playing. They had no name. The only way you knew if they were
playing was if one of the clubs left a conspicuous absence on
their calendar. Or there would be a listing, *Closed for Private
Party*. That was how people referred to them sometimes. They
said, Oh, I'm going to see *Closed for Private Party*. Randy was at
8BC with his friend Noel. Noel from England. They went to
Pyramid. Or was it somewhere else? Who could remember?
And then they came back, and when they walked into 8BC it
was like something had changed in Randy's life. There had
been some subtle movement of chance and suddenly the whole
topography of his life was different. Or that's how it felt. *Holy
shit,* he said to Noel. *Holy shit, who is that woman across the room
and how could I have missed her the first time?* She was standing
under this neon fixture, and it turned out he had met her once
before. Yvonne. In torn black leggings and blond hair and a
black crucifix and a black brassiere with a black sweater unbut-
toned over it.

To Noel he said: *Think I will have to use that line about how I
have met her somewhere before. It only works if you really have.*

Because he had met her on the street that time. And he
invited her to do a line with him and she agreed, even though

she hated Eurotrash and would-be Eurotrash guys. American guys who thought that everything was okay if they just flashed a little green. American guys with platinum cards. American guys too stupid to know that Europe had nothing to offer now but Swiss watches and deconstruction. American guys who actually invited in these colonialists with their dead cultures. *She must have wanted the drugs,* Randy told Noel later. *I don't care how the job gets done as long as it's done.* But the truth was Yvonne was just collecting material for her film. Everything was material, the dullest moments, the most ornate fancies. After Yvonne and Randy did the lines in the men's room, they left behind Yvonne's friends Debby and Noel.

In the neon shadows in the back of the club Yvonne cheerfully admitted to Randy that she dealt hash. Which he knew already by hearsay. She produced a pipe. They smoked some of her product. It was old-fashioned and quaint. The conversation was lurching along; there was neither agreement nor discord. And then they slipped out the back door into an alley. Somewhere along the line the hash hit, they were laughing, giggling, totally stoned. Laughing about something — he couldn't even remember. Wait: laughing about Eurotrash and Ecstasy and House and Japanese people invading the East Village and buying all the real estate out from under the slumlords and about the tanks in Tompkins Square Park. Just laughing. He hadn't had such a good time in a while. So they ditched Noel and Debby altogether, at 8BC or Pyramid or wherever it was, and went to her apartment, right near his on Ninth Street. It was all coming back to him now. He had met her a couple of times before. It was the greatest thing. She was the most beautiful woman he had ever met in his entire life. She was going to be his wife. He would have a wife *and* a secret life. Yvonne was hard to talk to — she missed all the ease in a conversation — but she was beautiful. They stayed up and did some more cocaine and watched the sunrise on the roof and he didn't lay a glove on her and they went to a coffee shop on First Avenue. He poured black coffee over the ground stubs that had been his teeth the night before. They smarted. He was tired as shit. He was giddy.

Later that week, he was back at the Ruin, watching an old fat guy lean into the bullwhip as this woman named *Huck* really let him have it. The fat guy had a lifeless, undersea expression on his face, and no kind of erection that Randy could see. It was hard to tell whether pleasure was involved for this guy or not. And then he got the itch to see Yvonne again. There were a few other women on the roster, but he moved them around a little bit. He didn't know why they were suddenly of less interest, these other women, but he wasn't worrying about it. He was just improvising. His mind was on the Evans clothing line and on hitting the clubs. He didn't think too much about other stuff. He called Yvonne's number at the Ninth Street place. She was probably working some gallery job during the day or for some nonprofit theater company. She probably had jeans with paint stains on them. He realized *he didn't even know what she did during the day.* He wondered if dealing hash was her principal line of business. How did she organize her clients? Did she keep a file on computer? What kind of overhead was there in an enterprise like that?

Then she got pregnant. There's a gap in the story here that doesn't concern me, a gap with its conventional romantic navigations of approach and retreat. The fact is that a month or two later Yvonne found she was pregnant. This was about as stupid as anything Randy had ever done. They had slept together, of course; they had been sleeping together off and on for two or three months. They had fucked without a diaphragm or a rubber or anything, and they had done it a number of times, on a number of occasions, maybe even too many times to remember. And they hadn't thought about it too much because they had just come from some bar or club. She said, *I will not take the fucking pill,* and who could blame her? She smoked several packs of cigarettes a day. She had one of those lavender packets of birth-control pills on her bedside table but it was neglected. They had used condoms, but he didn't like them — *worse than a wet suit* — and then she had become pregnant.

She didn't seem concerned with her pregnancy either. She had been selling hash in order to make a movie about the East Village, about the people in the East Village and the coincidences that overtook you in a place like the East Village. You could miss someone by seconds, you could turn a corner and this incredibly pertinent information would be lost because the person you were about to pass, whom you did not see (because in Manhattan you always looked at your feet), was now lost to you. In this film, Yvonne liked to say, *you could see how much larger the pool of potential facts is than the pool of facts that actually turn out to be true.* You could, in this film, turn a corner on St. Mark's Place and First Avenue, say, and just miss your ex-boyfriend's ex-girlfriend who was actually related to you in some way, who could tell you something about your ex-boyfriend that you never knew, who was going up First Avenue toward Fourteenth Street. You could just miss her. In this way there was much that you failed to know. You failed to know, for example, that a man who had once been important to you was now ill with that horrible kind of pneumonia. But you wouldn't know this, because you were walking the wrong direction. Or you wouldn't know because you had been ducking, for a week, the barely functioning answering machine in your barely furnished apartment.

The film, however, contained all these possible outcomes; the film that Randy still didn't know much about was being filmed on a *shoestring budget,* in various bars, with the cooperation of various bartenders. Yvonne would venture into these locations with a loaner camera — she was always charging it on the AC adapter back at her apartment — and shoot interviews, just little snippets, or false pieces of narrative material, late into the night, after closing, after everyone slunk off to the after-hours joints. She had no idea how any of this material was going together. She had a naive optimism that she would figure it out eventually, and that it didn't matter that the neighborhood was changing around her and that her film now represented an East Village that was no longer located in this spot. And all the money from the hash and the waitressing was supposed to pay for this film that was subordinate to everything else in her life, for processing time on the Steenbeck, for the transfer from video back to film, for the sound edit, but she was smoking the hash and borrowing money to pay back the guy who sold the drugs to her in the first place.

And now she was pregnant. She told Randy over the phone, and they had their first big fight. He was from a good family from Atlanta, this decorous family with whom he was not really in touch anymore, and he thought having a decorous family of his own wasn't such a bad idea. He could see that there was a convenient aspect to this calamity. Now he had an argument for marriage and family. They could just fall into it. So he went over to her place to break this news to her. To break the news that he was ready, at twenty-four, for domesticity.

They slept together first. They slept together before talking, and it was really, really sexy, the way he saw it. It was like the first time. He took off her skirt slowly. He liked to see how slowly it was possible to make love. He kissed her so slowly you didn't even know his lips were moving. How slowly? His movements were in increments smaller than millimeters. *The band with no name* was playing on the old, beat-up tape player, and the video camera was standing on a tripod, pointing out the window, and he was proceeding across her lips as slowly as possible. It could take hours before he would creep down along her neck, after pausing to dig an incisor into her earlobe, after pausing to suck on her tongue. Hours before he was aimlessly encircling her breasts with his fingertips. And then further down. He liked every second of it. He even liked unlacing her Doc Martens. Nakedness was never so naked. And then he touched her stomach. Women had gotten pregnant because of his irresponsibility before, once in boarding school, once after a weekend by the shore in Mobile, but he had been young then. This was his first time as an adult. The fact of it, the fact of fertility, was enormous and perfect like the shape of a particularly dangerous storm.

Her belly was small and trim. She didn't eat too well. *Just eat to avoid fainting,* she said. *Nothing more.* He traced his finger across her stomach as if he were painting cave paintings there, as if trying to render the moment of conception in some pictorial writing. As if trying to capture all the lives bound together in this notion of conception. What was so sexy about all this? What was hot about coming to the end of the profligate and wandering part of your life? What was sexy about suddenly wanting to accept responsibility? Maybe in part what was sexy was all the bad news, all the risk, all the difficulties. Maybe he wasn't thinking clearly about it at all. But maybe he was. Love was something that had the threat of bad news with it. Love was risk and obligation and caffeine addiction. Love was like watching the Tompkins Square riots on television. It was like hearing a guitar amp explode. It was like shooting coke for the first time. It was like watching the demolition of a tenement building and it was like remembering these pleasures years after they are gone.

And that was when she introduced the device.

— Hey, look, I have this thing I have to show you . . .

She reached over beside the bed where an ominous looking electrical kit was waiting.

— What the fuck is that?

The shame of being found out, of being located and then conscripted into the league of kinks, of being a guy who liked devices *and* wanted a family, this shame overcame him first. His resistance was first. He knew, in some atavistic part of his unconscious reserved for the pursuit of bodily woes disguised as pleasures, he knew what it was. He didn't know how it was going to work, but he recognized the control knobs on the box. They resembled the knobs that had driven the electric trains of neighbors in his boyhood. One of the dials was marked "course" and the other "adjustment."

— This is an electrical stimulation box, she said. It's for the film. See? I'm getting interested in this idea that I can have like some sex club stuff in it. I could have, you know, couples using these marital aids. Like this one or Electra or something.

From Orgone Romance Systems of Las Vegas. These ones here are the *instant kill switches* and those are the *indicator lamps* to monitor the control of the voltage.

— That's —

— Uh huh, she said. It's for fucking.

And from a small cardboard box lying on its side on the faded and dirty Indian rug *she produced the combination vaginal plug and cock ring attachment.* The attachment was made of a sturdy and durable transparent plastic, and, like the finest Steuben sculptures with their hints of silver and gold sunken in the glass renderings, the wires in the attachment, those glorious conductors, were glimmering in the plug and the ring. Yvonne had batteries in the device — it was running on battery power —and she juiced it up with the knobs and held the probe by the end.

— How are you going to use this for the movie? he said. You're going to get friends to use this and —

— Just touch your finger to it quickly. It's on the lowest setting.

— What the *fuck? Where did you get this?*

— I borrowed it. I'm thinking we should —

— Oh no, Randy said. If you think I'm gonna let you electrocute me with that thing, so that you can . . .

She touched it herself. Touched an index finger to it. There was a velocity to the way she was avoiding *the question in the air.* He had come over to talk about her pregnancy, to talk about the future, to raise practical questions, but instead they were here with the electro-stimulator. There was a velocity, a speed and a direction, to her avoidance. She was using the device — that facsimile of the most potent Latin American political torture machines — to stray from *the implications of things.* And she wasn't foolish: she knew what she was doing. She touched the plug and he could hear its faint buzz, its melancholy hum. She held her finger there.

He took the thing from her and set it aside.

— Hey, Yvonne, Randy said. I got a more important question. That's why I came over here. I came over here to ask you something.

The plug snapped and fizzled on the edge of Yvonne's comforter.

— I came over here to ask you to marry me. That's what I came to do, Yvonne. We could get around this *problem* in a way you're probably not thinking of. The baby, I mean. We could just get married.

And he had the engagement ring, in his pocket, an antique silver band that had been in the family for a while. Impulsively, though, before taking the ring out of the tangle of khaki trousers on the floor, he took the cock ring from the electro-stimulator and *set it on her ring finger.*

She laughed. A nervous, high, piccolo laughter. He reached for the "course" knob.

— No way, she said. I'm too young to get married. I'm not carrying your fucking little *junior* around for nine months and fucking up my body and my hormones so that you'll have a peg to hang your hat on or someone to take care of you when you get senile. I don't want to spend my life with anybody, I can't even think of what my life will be like next week. I can't even imagine that I'll *have* a life next week. *Forget it.* Honey. Forget it.

Randy got really angry. He turned the stimulator all the way up. She laughed again. He brushed the device off the bed. They started to shout. They actually threw some stuff, some books and lamps, what kind of relationship was this, and what was she going to do, let this bad luck drive the last bit of fun out of their relationship when it could make them closer, and didn't she want to share anything with him, didn't she want to know that even on the lowest day she wasn't alone, didn't she want to wrinkle with someone around who loved her, didn't she want to file a joint tax return? But she wouldn't do it, wouldn't do it, wouldn't do it, and he couldn't believe that he had been so stupid that he thought this woman who sold hash and claimed she was some kind of filmmaker, that this woman was going to do this marriage-and-family thing with him, how could he be so stupid, and then they were fucking again and in the middle of these attentions some key of persuasion was turned in the lock and she was able to convince Randy that the electric stimulation device was an adventure, a gamble, a temporary shelter. In the penumbra of rejection he agreed to it. That was the decision that came first. In that penumbra, in the penumbra of late night, she had the tape player on and she had the *fine adjustment* on the stimulator control panel turned down as low as it would go and she had the video camera turned on, she had swiveled it on the tripod to take a closeup on Randy's face, and she put the cock ring around him now, though his cock was only halfway hard, and then she turned the knob up slowly. It was just like being drilled by the dentist at first, it was that sensation of wrong, of inappropriateness, and then there was a white alarm in his head as she turned it up and the sound of the capacitor inside dampening it and then the device scorched him like there were electro-magnetic teeth ripping into his dick and he tore the thing off with the urgency that one shoos away an ornery wasp that has already deposited its venom and he collapsed on her bed for a second to catch his breath, to let the shock disperse itself throughout him. It was as though he were joining his friends the sleepwalkers as they too were bent upon the rack, *the rack of reactivity,* desperate simply for sensation in a monochromatic and decontextualized city. Yeah, it was right that he be here in this way, with the Ruin only a couple of nights behind him, with his fascination for the sleepwalkers and the transvestites and the perfect toes of the women at the bars. And he waited for the voltage to fade in him, until its absence was a sort of pleasure a sort of relief, and then he noticed her arm around him over his back and her voice in his ear saying *okay, okay,* that's right it seemed she was agreeing suddenly, she was changing her mind, *okay, okay,* yes she really was, *okay,* and so marriage was an interim government between them, and you could say all this lifelong and ever after stuff, but if it didn't work they could throw in the towel. She loved him in this vulnerable tableau with the electro-stimulation box beside him. She loved him. They would work it out. The kid would work it out. They would have the kid and the kid would understand that she had other ambitions. The kid would figure it out. Kids were like Super-balls or something, like high-concentration rubber objects. Kids could learn to adjust. *Okay.* She lit the pipe. She toked on it. She passed it to him. Now it was her turn. She handed him the vaginal plug and lay back against the pillows.

Their marriage consisted of a civil ceremony on Staten Island, where the line at the courthouse was shorter. A friend of Yvonne's, Mike, filmed it, though none of the footage worked, really. It was nothing she could use, except for a brief shot of the justice of the peace straightening his tie.

Randy didn't tell his family. They would just have come up from the South. They would have hung around. Yvonne didn't tell her family, in Syracuse. She *forgot*. The two of them didn't really tell anyone, except Noel and Debby, who came to be witnesses. And Mike. There were all these coincidences on the way to the ceremony, people they met, people on the streets, people on the Staten Island ferry. New York seemed that day to be nothing but a system of low-probability coincidences. But then she had agreed to have the baby, too. Or at least she had agreed temporarily. Yvonne agreed to have the baby because she was tired and depressed, and she didn't want to think about it. Most days, she tried to renege on the decision. Some days she wanted to have it and then, after feeling sick, she vowed to abort. She should have gone for the abortion in the first month, when she was feeling especially bad, but somehow she didn't get around to it. This lack of decisiveness seemed to Randy to mask an excitement about the baby. Still, they were arguing so much about whether or not to go through with it. She hung on, looking for some kind of perfect advice from her friends or from her own mom — who thought she was out of her mind — or for some sign in the grid of order and disorder that was Manhattan. Walking the streets, turning the corners: *What should I do?* By then the baby was *close to quickening* as they said in British law. Somehow she didn't see how she could snuff it in the second trimester.

At the same time, though, she started getting a little further into particular kinds of East Village life, into the substance abuse parts of East Village life, started getting into them because she was nervous and scared and sad about how she had slid into all this, slid into some middle-class thing that she wasn't prepared for. It was all about this stupid film that was sitting in a metal box in her secondhand desk. There was the metal box and a bunch of old videocassettes. She *used to think* that it was all about the film. They were married. This had happened, although Yvonne couldn't figure out how it had happened. They lived pretty much the way they had lived before, except that they shared an apartment. Now he was always on top of her with his insecurities, with his practicalities, and Yvonne was really upset that she had never made the movie she had wanted to make, and she never had any time to herself, and she never *was* herself, and soon, on top of everything else, she was going to have a baby. She wasn't supposed to smoke or drink, but she sort of *was* smoking and drinking, anyway. And that wasn't all. Just a little bit really, just the occasional lapse in the area of harder drugs, for the really special occasions.

And instead of making more of the movie, instead of just going out and buying the film, which Randy might have contributed to, instead of finding someone to do the sound for her, she felt like she had to perfect the fifteen minutes of it she had. The continuity was all fucked up because it had been shot over the course of years, and some of the sound wasn't synchronized. Over and over she would do this opening, borrowing time from friends who were still editing or P.A.-ing instead of going to law school like you were supposed to do in your late twenties. It was really kind of good this first five minutes, if you were into a sort of totally random New York chaos. Full of jump cuts and repetition and shots of the microphone boom and a sequence with a dog hair on the lens. It doubled back on itself, this five minutes, this documentary, or whatever it was, though it was never going to be much of anything really. Two lives in it might mean different things at different times. They might be the same life, they might be twins. Toni, this woman, seemed to be straight in one scene and gay in another. People looked like one another, or like other people, and the structure of the film was going to be like the structure of Manhattan. Laid out in a grid, except for the parts that weren't laid out in a grid, totally repetitious, except for the explosions of violence.

Then she became obsessed about the sound track. She decided she had to secure the finest sound track composers possible for this film that was never going to be finished. It had to be *the band with no name.* She went to a party at the house of this music columnist for the *East Village Eye* — some neighborhood periodical — Jeanine Love. So they were at the party, which was on Avenue D, in a cramped apartment that had a porch with a great view of the Con Edison power plant on the East River. Yvonne, who had let Randy go out to some club, Pyramid or 8BC, to re-create the wild days of his bachelorhood, went up to this guy from *the band with no name.* He was from Massapequa, Long Island, and rock and roll had transformed him from a guy from Massapequa into a person with charm. Standing there in these rags and looking like his guitar had scorched him and he had been thereafter embalmed. He seemed not to have any emotions that she could discern. She told him, *I really like what you guys do and I think it's got a really experimental kind of thing . . . kind of feeling to it, and I think it would really be good for like a sound track or something, um, playing the guitar upside down and everything and well I'm making this movie about the East Village it's like an archeology of life in the East Village and I was wondering, I mean I was thinking maybe you would . . .*

The guy just grunted. He knew, as anyone looking at Yvonne would have suspected, that nothing was ever going to happen with this film. At the same time, she was preoccupied with the fact that his skin was an incredible blue color. He didn't say anything, made no commitment of any kind. But Yvonne understood that she was to follow him into the next room where the drummer from the band was tying off his arm with a handsome Velcro tourniquet so that he could pop a little bit of that grade-A Lower East Side dope underneath his baggy skin.

Jeanine Love, the hostess, was peripherally involved in the sex industry, in addition to being a music critic. She gave performances at the Ruin on occasion, and she wrote a little *sexually explicit material,* except that she didn't like writing it, so she hired ghost writers to write it for her. Because of her affiliation, however, on the floor and on the bed in the bedroom (where the guys from *the band with no name* were shooting heroin) there were cut-rate, rough-trade skin magazines piled everywhere. *Juggs* and *Cheeks* and titles of this sort. And while Yvonne was trying, politely, to discuss music with the guys in this band, they were flipping through the magazines and chuckling ominously. Then the guy from Massapequa, who had no expression whatever, who looked a lot like the boys that Randy was right then watching amble around the Ruin, was motioning to her. He was going to take care of her. She didn't know if she should do it. He would do it for her if she couldn't do it. In fact, there was no decision involved. Or it was a decision not to make a decision. It was a relaxing, an acceptance. It was caving in. Letting go.

— Really, I'm mostly into . . .

Then she let him do it.

And the light over the power plant on Avenue D was like fucking celestial lights, like the angels on the head of a needle and Randy was where? Who knew? She was puking in Jeanine Love's bathroom, and Jeanine was saying, *Come on, you guys, come on, I'm really tired, I just don't want to stay up anymore. I don't want to* . . . And one of the guys from *the band with no name* was still there and he was going to leave Yvonne there because he was a little guy anyway and he wasn't going to carry her anywhere and he had to be up the next day for a Saturday shift at the copy shop where he worked. But then for some reason he was overcome by charity and soon he helped Randy's pregnant wife to a cab where he repeated the address she whispered to him to the cab driver. Kissing her on the lips and putting his finger to her lips — *don't tell* — and then repeating her address to the cabbie.

Then she miscarried.

The period of the marriage and pregnancy in which she was killing herself with dope would have been tougher if Randy hadn't been killing himself too. The movie was nowhere to be found now, it was in some dead-letter office somewhere, some imaginary film library of imaginary projects. What movie? There never was a movie. There was Randy and Yvonne going out to clubs, her in some kind of fashionable black maternity dress even though she wasn't really showing yet, but just because she liked the maternity look, some maternity dress that he'd gotten from a friend at another company. And there were no plates or sharps left in the house, because their arguments were too wild. And he was as strung out as she was sometimes. And he was pretty sure the books at his business were cooked, but he wasn't concentrating on it, exactly, he was going out with Yvonne and leaving her at home sometimes so that he could head out to the Crypt or the Ruin and watch the silent participants in the games there. He ground his teeth into a paste. And he was really into the electro-stimulator, though she had become bored with it. When Randy did come home to their meager kitchen, he would find her already high, with that empty look in her eyes, eating a single carrot. Blasting some noise on the old, beat-up tape player. He had a bad feeling about it all.

— Don't you think you could lay off just until after the baby is born? Wouldn't that be a little safer?

— Huh?

— Wouldn't that be the polite thing to do? For the kid?

— I don't know what you're talking about, Yvonne said.

This period ended with her hysterical call. At work. On a Wednesday.

He told her to call 911 and he would meet her at the hospital but she was really scared. She was really really scared, he could hear how scared and so she asked him to come pick her up instead. *Please. It's a mess.* He made the emergency call himself and met her at the apartment before the ambulance arrived. Her skin the color of slate. There were trails, archipelagoes of blood in the bathroom, the mildewed bathroom, on the dirty towels. She was crying. Her hands were bloody, and he couldn't tell how much was from the miscarriage and how much was from needles. Abscesses. He knew. Right away he knew how bad it was. How lost the kid was. How lost she was. How bad.

— I was never supposed to have it anyway, she mumbled. Tracks of tears. I was never supposed to have it.

— Oh, shut up, he said. He hugged her and they waited. What was already obvious was then officially pronounced by the medical authorities.

The argument then spilled over into the deep part of several nights. It wasn't an argument about anything special now. It was an argument with *things in general*. Her breathing was so shallow he couldn't believe that oxygen ever grazed her bronchia. But her cells didn't need anything now but what dope could give them. All the same, he couldn't believe that lying came so easily to her. On the other hand, maybe she could lie without even noticing her lies. Maybe the possibility of truth was dormant within her now. And this is how she was after pregnancy, managing an ever increasing stream of lies. The current between the two of them dwindled under the burden of these lies.

— I'm not high, Yvonne said. I'm being really careful now, honey. I want to have a baby. *I want to make another baby.* Really, I'm telling you the truth.

He watched her sleep sometimes and he watched her puke in the morning and it was impossible to say whether it was from this miscarriage or from the drug. Or both. He cleaned up a little bit of her puke before going out to the office. He took a damp paper towel across the surface of the toilet seat.

And maybe she could have ridden the wave of her addiction through another childbirth. She didn't seem especially to care about pain anymore anyway. Her body was an obligation insofar as it played host to the brain and the brain's store of flattened affections and blunted nerves. Otherwise who cared? She was a brain in a vat. She was working on throwing off her body somehow; she was putting it in cold storage; she was decommissioning it.

He came home from work and played spouse with her, hoping that she was going to bounce back, that the old fun was going to bounce back. His business went under not long after, and that made it even easier. He had a huge bank loan hanging over his head. He would have to get another job eventually, a job working for someone else, but not for the moment. For the moment he lay around the house. They had come to the end of club-hopping. They had come to the end of it. Randy suspected that his wife had shot up while carrying the baby. She said she was *only snorting,* as though that excused it. No, really, she was only snorting coke. Not even heroin. No, really, she was clean. Really. And she'd disappear at night and he'd yell at her but sometimes he'd get that yen too, that yen to go out, and he'd do it. He didn't care what time she was coming in. And he would drink and tell someone on the next stool all of this. All of what I've told you. In fact, he told *me.* At the Ruin. They had come to the end of their marriage. It had lasted five months. It was time for him to leave his wife. This was not difficult to accomplish. Because Yvonne wanted to pursue, unencumbered, her own muse, the muse of her inactivity, the muse of her silence.

Later. Third week of June 1987. (Hot and humid, low visibility.) *The amphetamine of loss* with its jacked-up system of attribution and detachment roiled in Randy Evans. He was driving around lower Manhattan in a van he had rented to help move some stuff for the Japanese clothing line he just started working for. He was driving with the radio up loud. WFMU. They were playing something from *the band with no name.* He wondered if the guys in the band were still alive, if these were new songs or if the guys in the band were infighting acrimoniously about an upcoming tour, if they were thinking of tossing one another out of the band. One of them, he had learned once, was the son of a major stockbroker. The son of the head of some brokerage house. The rich dad had bought them all the PA equipment and a studio to record in. And the son, the son of this wealthy broker, was shooting dope and living in some rundown East Village basement apartment with nothing in it but a futon and a CD player. This kind of life gave *the band with no name* a lot of credibility.

And the song didn't sound like their songs had sounded to him two years before when he first heard them. It sounded different, as the whole East Village seemed different. It wasn't galleries and clubs anymore. The East Village was chain stores and crack dealers. People were getting sick, and Randy had taken the test too and had waited the three weeks it took then to get results. He couldn't imagine why he was negative. He and Yvonne had shared needles with a few people, definitely, with Jamie Lefferts and Donna Harvey and Mike and that other guy Mitch who came over with him to the house that time. And they had all gone to a really creepy shooting gallery off Delancey with someone named Juan. Who knew who they were sharing with? Back then you didn't think about it as much. Where the needle had been was somewhere you yourself had been, and the trail of that needle, the trail that led to the shooting gallery, was the history of your footfalls and of the people whose lives were a part of yours. Where you had walked was what you believed in and it marked you and your DNA and it left information for your children, for when they would want to know the truth about you. The past and the future were in Randy's every move, in the imitation Syd Barrett sound of *the band with no name,* in the Veselka, where he had spent, over the years, maybe a thousand dollars on pink borscht, in the fresh-vegetable stand where, ten years from now, he would go with his son, the son he would have, and select the best carrots for a soup. But right now Randy's van was in the stream of the loneliest New Yorkers, those grasping, reaching for anyone in arm's length, hugging them close, pushing them off. Starting over. Falling into the disease, climbing out of it. Starting over. That's what the song by *the band with no name* sounded like. And that night Randy could have driven all night, on and off the FDR watching the lights on the Williamsburg side of the river, he could have driven all night, never gone home to the new girlfriend, the new hostage, where he now lived in Brooklyn, because he had the past on his mind and the way the people from the past were not really past, the way they crowded around him on the streets of Manhattan, the way he was always running into them. And he had a sort of agenda too, because he was driving down Eighth Street, west to east. He got on it at Third Avenue, and then he drove the block past Trash and Vaudeville where he had bought a leather jacket and past St. Mark's Sounds and past the bar called simply *Bar* and then around the park, where a gallery called Gracie Mansion had once been, and into the deepest East Village, where 8BC used to be, and then he was in front of the bakery at the corner of Avenue D.

The projects were on one side of the avenue and on the other side it was all empty lots filled with temporary shelters of cardboard and plywood and decorated with giveaway blankets and plastics. Randy's van was in neutral and idling quietly near the corner and the radio was whispering some chant — some New York prayer, some specifically local ritual for the dead that doubled as a solicitation or an advertisement of some kind. He watched the entrance of the bakery, watched people going in and out.

Jorge was there, of course. Jorge Ruiz, who was going back to live with his mother in another year, after his detox in Hollis, Queens, after barely avoiding being locked up in

Creedmore; and Doris Frantz, of Bernardsville, New Jersey, and Princeton University, who was thinking about picking up some cash on the side doing dominatrix work, just sort of turning the idea over anxiously. These two shadows came along the poorly lit streets, staggered by several minutes, walking slowly so as not to attract attention, so as not to appear to be in a hurry of any kind. Their hearts were in a terrible rush. They entered the bakery — Doris carrying a paper bag as if she intended to buy rolls — to give tens and twenties to people who would before long be arrested for trafficking — this arrest having no effect on neighborhood traffic.

Randy was hoping in a way that Yvonne *wouldn't* turn up. And that was when he saw her small, emaciated figure coming down the block. He didn't believe it at first. He didn't believe it was this easy to track somebody down, that junkies were so predictable, that he himself had been so predictable. He didn't believe that statistics and addiction were so navigable, that the arc of need was as orthodox as the law of falling bodies. No matter: there she was and she was *moving pretty fast.*

He left the van without even locking it, without turning it off. Material things had no place in that moment. The blackness of the sky was perfect and enduring. These shades came from the bakery and darted up the street looking for the first possible spot where they could tie off. And Randy was trotting across the street like he too was desperate in that way, toward Yvonne, and he had his hand out to touch her. He had a windbreaker tied around his waist. And his hair was really short and he didn't look like he had looked the year or so before. When they met.

She didn't either. Yvonne looked like she'd been orphaned by war; she looked like she suffered with unimaginable grief.

When he spoke to her there was a long moment before she seemed to recognize that she was stopped now, that someone was talking to her, holding her up. She grimaced. She didn't seem to recognize him — she knew his face and who he was, but she didn't recognize any freight in the encounter — as if chance had been the only thing between them. She wanted to get into the bakery. He was an impediment. The way she wheezed and coughed proved it. She was nervous. But the weirdest thing was that she was smiling. She was grimacing and smiling.

— Well, Randy said, coming to the end of an awkward politeness. Well, I just wanted to . . . to see you. Listen . . . Jeez, you know, I don't want to say it, but you *just don't look that good.*

Her own words seemed to drift up into her throat as if they had a separate set of controls, as if she were the dummy for some ventriloquist.

— What are you talking about?

— Forget it, Randy said.

— No, she said irritably. What the fuck are you talking about?

— Listen, he said, if you want any help, if you ever want any help or anything . . . just let me know. I don't know . . .

— I don't have time, she said. Anyway, *I don't want your pity.* You're a fucking *junkie,* too.

And then she left him there. She hurried on. She took off.

He was stricken. He was halted. He was going to say something. He was going to defend himself, to defend his self-evident pride. But what could he say? He was standing there like a beseeching panhandler. Hadn't he been one of those club rats for whom all human folly — the suspension and flogging of men several feet above a stage — was the stuff of fun? Then why couldn't he let Yvonne *go on her merry way and finish the job?* Why not let all these people go? Let this stuff, these places recede into whitewashed accounts of youth he would present to friends when provoked momentarily into some foolish grandiosity about having simply *survived.* Why not let it go?

He called after her. Just as Jorge was coming out. Sweating quite a bit. Jorge, sweating like it was deepest July and he had no A.C. Randy was calling after his wife, oblivious. On an empty street. On a moonless night. She never looked back. He was standing there watching. She never looked back.

There was one more time, a few years later, that he saw her again: when she had finally gotten clean, when she needed to discuss completing the divorce. She had Kaposi's sarcoma, and her face, into which a lively human rose color was at last returning, was freckled with lesions.

And there were others caught in the vine of those five minutes of June, in front of the cop shop on Eighth Street, in the moments just before and after: Buck Miller and Susan Ward and a guy whom I used to see at the Marlin Café; and Debby, the girl who drove Doris to the airport, who also knew Yvonne; and Ray, the guy who hosed down the booths in Peep World; and Crystal, the preoperative transsexual who slept with Jorge one night and then stole all his stuff; and the auctioneer at Wendy's; and the woman, Huck, with the dildo that glowed violet neon; and the guy getting fisted by two men at once; and Randy's friend Noel; and the men who had fucked Marlene when she was a hooker, most of whom didn't know she was dead; and two of the guys in *the band with no name* (the third had been shipped off to an expensive rehab). And some people I know whom I have not mentioned yet, like Robert and David and Frank from the Mudd Club and Dan and Crutch and Bob, Julia, Karen, Kenny, and Kate. Lizzie. And there are other names I don't know yet. And myself. Me. I was there. All of us strode up and down Eighth Street like it was an actual artery in some larger life form, in some larger organism. As one of our number slipped into a storefront along Eighth Street, another passed by. None of us seemed to know the nature of the coincidences that bound us together, as I know now, or that junkies and masochists and hookers and those who have squandered everything are the ring of brightest angels around heaven.

And just by chance a bunch of these characters turned up in Yvonne's documentary, which had been transferred to film and then back to videotape and which now languished in a foot locker. Each of them was captured in and around the bars that Yvonne frequented when she was just out of school. I remember what she looked like then. When her face had an openness like good luck, like the big puffy clouds you see over the desert. I remember how bright her eyes were; I remember how excited she got by stuff, how a movie at the Film Forum could change her for weeks, how a certain record with just the right snare drum sound and a little bit of anger could keep her going all night, writing.

And the end of the film, the end of it for now, until somebody completes it for Yvonne, was like this. At a party crowded with the characters in this story, or other characters not unlike these, at a party at the Ruin weeks before its closing, with stalls strung with Christmas lights, surrounded by half-clothed erotic dancers, *the band with no name* struck up some kind of evolved march thing. In the basement of this wretched club. The music was fast. Everyone knew the song.

The room was lit poorly. You could have slept with anyone in the room. You could have thrown your arms around anyone and it would have been okay. It would have been nice. The frame was frozen for a second. Then there was a jump cut and the band was throwing down its instruments and there was some buzz in a Fender Twin reverb amp, a little feedback, but the guys in the band weren't paying any attention to it. And there was a close-up on Randy, laughing. His smile taking up the whole screen. And then it just ends.

I am going now. I am leaving.

PRIMARY
SOURCES [1]

Abbé, William Parker.[2] *A Diary of Sketches.* Concord, N.H.: St. Paul's School, 1976.

---

[1]Born 10.18.61 in NYC. Childhood pretty uneventful. We moved to the suburbs. I always read a lot. I did some kid stuff, but mostly I read. So this sketchy and selective bibliography — this list of some of the books I have around the house now — is really an autobiography.

[2]Art instructor at St. Paul's School when I was there ('75–'79). Abbé was an older, forgetful guy when I met him. He was in his late sixties probably. He lived alone in an apartment above the infirmary at SPS, an apartment that had burned once. The fire took a lot of Abbé's paintings, and I believe this accounted for the halo of sadness around him. He could also be infectiously happy, though. His house was full of jukeboxes, dolls, and electrical toys. Games of every kind.

One time I showed him my *Sgt. Pepper's* picture disc — remember those collector's gimmicks that revolutionized the LP for a few minutes in the seventies? The famous jacket art was printed on the vinyl. Abbé laughed for a good long time over that. He sat

Bangs, Lester. *Psychotic Reactions and Carburetor Dung.*[3] Edited by Greil Marcus. New York: Knopf, 1987.

Barnes, Djuna. *Interviews.* Washington, D.C.: Sun & Moon, 1985.

Barrett, Syd.[4] "Golden Hair." On *The Madcap Laughs.* EMI Cassette C4-46607, 1990 (reissue).

Barthes, Roland. *A Lover's Discourse.*[5] Translated by Richard Howard. New York: Hill & Wang, 1978.

----

in the old armchair in my room, the one with the stuffing coming out of it and laughed. He loved that kind of thing. He had a lot of Elvis on his jukeboxes.

[3]Lester's last published piece, in the *Voice,* appeared in my senior year of college. I moved back to NYC a little later, after six months in California, where it was too relaxed. By the time I got to New York, the East Village galleries were already disappearing. Lester was dead. The Gap had moved in on the N.W. corner of St. Mark's and Second Avenue.

[4]In 1978, back at SPS, I took six hits of "blotter" acid and had a pretty wrenching bad trip. Eternal damnation, shame, humiliation, and endless line of men in clown costumes chanting my name and laughing. That kind of thing. I turned myself in, confessed, to a master I liked, the Rev. Alden B. Flanders. Somewhere in the middle of the five or six hours it took to talk me down, I asked him if he thought I would remember this moment for the rest of my life.

[5]"The necessity for this book is to be found in the following consideration: that the lover's discourse is today *of an extreme solitude. . . .* Once a discourse is thus . . . exiled from all gregarity, it has no recourse but to become the site, however exiguous, of an *affirmation.*"

Bernhard, Thomas. *The Lime Works.* Chicago: Univ. of Chicago Press, 1986 (reprint of New York: Knopf, 1973).

Book of Common Prayer and Administration of the Sacraments and Other Rites and Ceremonies of the Church, According to the Use of the Protestant Episcopal Church[6] in the United States of America, The. New York: Harper & Brothers, 1944.

Borges, Jorge Luis. *Labyrinths.*[7] Edited by Donald A. Yates and James E. Irby. New York: New Directions, 1964.

Breton, André. *Manifestoes of Surrealism.*[8] Ann Arbor, Mich.: Univ. of Michigan Press (Ann Arbor Paperbacks), 1969.

Carroll, Lewis. *The Annotated Alice.* Edited with an introduction and notes[9] by Martin Gardner. New York: Clarkson N. Potter (Bramhall House), 1960.

---

[6] I didn't get baptized until I was fifteen. The minister, who had buried my grandparents and my uncle and performed my mother's remarriage, couldn't remember my name. Right then, the church seemed like the only thing that would get me through adolescence. I was going to get confirmed later, too, but instead I started drinking.

[7] Cf., "Eco, Umberto," and also n. 9, below.

[8] The band I played in in college was called Forty-five Houses. We got our name from the first Surrealist manifesto: "Q. 'What is your name?' A. 'Forty-five houses.' (Ganser syndrome, or beside-the-point replies)." Our drummer, Kristen, preferred women to men, but I sort of fell in love with her anyway. After we graduated she gave me a ride on her motorcycle. It was the first time I ever rode one. I held tight around her waist.

[9] See n. 20, below.

Carter, Angela.[10] *The Bloody Chamber and Other Adult Tales.* New York: Harper & Row, 1979.

Cheever, John. *The Journals of John Cheever.*[11] New York: Knopf, 1991.

——— . *The Wapshot Chronicle.* New York: Harper & Brothers, 1957.

Coover, Robert. *In Bed One Night & Other Brief Encounters.* Providence, R.I.: Burning Deck, 1983.

Daniels, Les. *Marvel: Five Fabulous Decades of the World's Greatest Comics.*[12] With an introduction by Stan Lee. New York: Abrams, 1992.

---

[10]The first day of Angela's workshop in college a guy asked her what her work was like. She said, "My work cuts like a steel blade at the base of a man's penis." Second semester, there was a science fiction writer in our class who sometimes slept through the proceedings — and there were only eight or nine of us there. One day I brought a copy of *Light in August* to Angela's office hours and she said, "I wish I was reading *that* [Faulkner], instead of *this* [pointing to a stack of student work]."

[11]As a gift for graduating boarding school, my dad gave me a short trip to Europe. Two weeks. I was a little bit afraid of travel, though, as I still am, and in London I spent much of the time in Hyde Park, in a chair I rented for 15p a day. The sticker that is my proof of purchase still adorns my copy of *The Stories of John Cheever,* also given to me by my dad. I haven't been back to the U.K. since.

[12]We moved a lot when I was a kid. In eighth grade I had a calendar on which I marked off the days until I'd be leaving Connecticut forever. My attachments weren't too deep. I spent a lot of time with Iron Man, the Incredible Hulk, and the Avengers. I also liked self-help books and Elton John records.

Danto, Arthur C. *Encounters and Reflections: Art in the Historical Present.* New York: FSG, 1990.

"Darmok."[13] *Star Trek: The Next Generation.* Paramount Home Video, 1991, 48 minutes.

Davis, Lydia. *Break It Down.* New York: FSG, 1986.

De Montaigne, Michel. *The Complete Essays of Montaigne.* Translated by Donald M. Frame. Stanford, Calif.: Stanford Univ. Press, 1958.

Derrida, Jacques. *Of Grammatology.*[14] Translated by Gayatri Chakravorty Spivak. Baltimore, Md.: Johns Hopkins, 1976 (originally published as *De la Grammatologie* [Paris: Editions de Minuit, 1967]).

Elkin, Stanley. *The Franchiser.* Boston: Godine (Nonpareil Books), 1980 (reprint of New York: FSG, 1976).

---

[13]Picard and the crew of the *Enterprise* attempt to make contact with a race of aliens, the Children of Tama, who speak entirely in an allegorical language. Picard doesn't figure out the language until the captain of the Tamarians is already dead. A big episode for those who realize how hard communicating really is.

[14]One guy I knew in college actually threw this book out a window. Here are some excerpts from my own marginalia: "Function of art is supplementalism though devalorization of weighted side of oppositions"; "Attendance as performance: more absence creates more real presence." I'm not sure what I meant, but I loved Derrida's overheated analogies: "Writing in the common sense is the dead letter, it is the carrier of death. It exhausts life. On the other hand, on the other face of the same proposition, writing in the metaphoric sense, natural, divine, and living writing, is venerated" (p. 17).

"Erospri." In *The Whole Earth 'Lectronic Link,* [15] modem: (415) 332-6106, Sausolito, Calif., 1986–.

Feelies, The. *The Good Earth.* [16] Coyote TTC 8673, 1986.

Fitzgerald, F. Scott. *The Crack-Up.* New York: New Directions, 1959.

Foucault, Michel. *Discipline and Punish: The Birth of the Prison.* New York: Vintage, 1979 (reprint of New York: Random House, 1977; originally published as *Surveiller et Punir* [Paris: Gallimard, 1975]).

Gaddis, William. *The Recognitions.* [17] New York: Penguin, 1985 (reprint of New York: Harcourt, Brace, 1955).

———

[15]The *Well* — as it is abbreviated — has a really good Star Trek conference too. This private conference is about *sex.* I started messing with computers in junior high when my grades got me out of study hall. Which was good because people used to threaten me if I didn't let them copy my homework. It was on the *Well* that I learned both the address for a mail-order catalogue called *Leather Toys* and how to affix clothespins.

[16]My drinking got really bad in graduate school. In the mid-eighties. I was in love with a woman who was living in Paris and I took the opportunity, at the same time, to get mixed up with a friend in New York. Kate, the second of these women, first played this record for me. The snap of the snare that begins *The Good Earth* has a real tenderness to it, for me. I was playing this record when I was really ashamed of myself and also afterwards when I was hoping for forgiveness.

[17]At the end of my drinking, when I was living in Hoboken, I started writing my first novel, *Garden State.* Later, through a chain of kindnesses, someone managed to slip a copy of it to William Gaddis, the writer I most admired, then and now. Much

Genet, Jean. *The Thief's Journal*. New York: Bantam, 1965
(reprint of New York: Grove, 1964; originally published as
Journal du Voleur [Paris: Gallimard, 1949]).

Gyatso, Tenzin, the 14th Dalai Lama. *Freedom in Exile*. New
York: HarperCollins, 1990.

Hawkes, John.[18] *Second Skin*. New York: New Directions,
1964.

Hawthorne, Nathaniel. *Hawthorne's Short Stories*.[19] Edited with
an introduction by Newton Arvin. New York: Knopf, 1946.

Hogg, James. *The Private Memoirs and Confessions of a Justified
Sinner*. New York: Penguin, 1976.

---

later, long after all of this, I got to know Gaddis's son Matthew a
little bit, and he said that the book had probably gotten covered up
with papers, because that's the way his dad's desk is. But maybe
there was one afternoon when it was on top of a stack.

[18]The last day of class with Jack Hawkes we were standing out on
one of those Victorian porches in Providence — a bunch of us,
because there was always a crowd of people trying to get into
Jack's classes (and they were usually really talented) — firing
corks from champagne bottles out into the street. We got a couple that made it halfway across. Hawkes was mumbling something about how sad it was that so many writers were so afflicted
by drink. In less than a week I was going to graduate.

[19]"Another clergyman in New England, Mr. Joseph Moody, of
York, Maine, who died about eighty years since, made himself
remarkable by the same eccentricity that is here related of the
Reverend Mr. Hooper. In his case, however, the symbol had a
different import. In early life he had accidentally killed a beloved
friend; and from that day till the hour of his own death, he hid his
face from men."

Johnson, Denis. *Angels.* New York: Vintage, 1989 (reprint of New York: Knopf, 1983).

Joyce, James. *Ulysses.* New York: Vintage, 1961.

Jung, C. G. "Individual Dream Symbolism in Relation to Alchemy." In *Collected Works,* Vol. 12, Part II. Translated by R. F. C. Hull. Princeton, N.J.: Princeton Univ. Press (Bollingen Series), 1968.

Kapuscinski, Ryszard. *The Emperor.* New York: Vintage, 1989 (reprint of New York: HBJ), 1983.

Lewis, James. "Index."[20] *Chicago Review* 35 (1 [autumn 1985]): 33–35.

Marcus, Greil. *Lipstick Traces: A Secret History of the Twentieth Century.*[21] Cambridge, Mass.: Harvard Univ. Press, 1989.

Marx, Groucho. *The Groucho Letters: Letters from and to Groucho Marx.*[22] New York: Fireside, 1987.

---

[20]See n. 7, above.

[21]During the period when I was finishing my first novel I had an office job in publishing, from which I was later fired. I judged everything against the books I loved when I was a teenager, *The Crying of Lot 49,* Beckett's *Murphy, One Hundred Years of Solitude,* etc. Besides Lester Bangs (see above), Marcus's *Lipstick Traces* was one of the only recently published books I liked. Another was *Responses: On Paul de Man's Wartime Journalism* (Univ. of Nebraska Press).

[22]In 1987, I institutionalized myself. At that moment, Thurber and Groucho Marx and anthologies of low comedy seemed like the best literature had to offer. I thought I was going to abandon writing — something had to give — but I didn't. I felt better later.

Mitchell, Stephen. *The Gospel According to Jesus.* New York: HarperCollins, 1991.

Pagels, Elaine. *The Gnostic Gospels.*[23] New York: Vintage, 1989 (reprint of New York: Random House, 1979).

Paley, Grace. *Enormous Changes at the Last Minute.* New York: FSG, 1974.

Pärt, Arvo. *Tabula Rasa.*[24] ECM new series 817 (1984).

Peacock, Thomas Love. *Headlong Hall and Gryll Grange.* Oxford: Oxford Univ. Press (The World's Classics), 1987.

Plato. *Great Dialogues of Plato.* Edited and translated by W. H. D. Rouse. New York: Mentor, 1956.

"Polysexuality." *Semiotexte.*[25] 4 (1 [1981]).

Sacks, Oliver. *Awakenings.* 3rd ed. New York: Summit, 1987.

---

[23]"The accusastion that the gnostics invented what they wrote contains some truth: certain gnostics openly acknowledged that they derived their *gnosis* from their own experience. . . . The gnostic Christians . . . assumed that they had gone far beyond the apostles' original teaching."

[24]And Cage's book, *Silence;* and *Music for Airports;* and LaMonte Young's "The Second Dream of the High Tension Line Step Down Transformer from the Four Dreams of China"; and Ezra Pound after St. Elizabeth's, and *Be Here Now* and Mark Rothko.

[25]The back cover of this issue consists of a newspaper photo of a man in a wedding gown slumped over on a toilet, his skin ribbed with gigantic blisters. He's really destroyed, this guy. The photo, supposedly, was from *The Daily News.* And since my grandfather worked for the *News,* the luridness of this horror struck close. This, I learned, was an act of *pleasure.*

Schulz, Bruno. *Sanatorium Under the Sign of the Hourglass.*[26] Translated by Celina Wieniewska. New York: Penguin, 1979.

Sebadoh. *Sebadoh III.*[27] Homestead HMS 168–4, 1991.

Thomas à Kempis. *The Imitation of Christ.* New York: Penguin, 1952.

W., Bill. "Step Seven." In *Twelve Steps and Twelve Traditions.*[28] New York: Alcoholics Anonymous World Services, 1986.

Williams, William Carlos. *The Collected Poems of William Carlos Williams.*[29] Volume II: 1939–1962. Copyright © 1962 by William Carlos Williams. Reprinted by permission of New Directions Publishing.

[26] Angela Carter assigned this book to us in sophomore year. I was taking a lot of quaaludes that spring. One night I stayed up all night on Methadone and wrote a story, cribbed from Bruno Schulz, about a guy who lives in a house that *is actually his grandmother*. Later, when I told Angela that I'd written the story high, she said, "Quaaludes, the aardvark of the drug world."

[27] "All these empty urges must be satisfied."

[28] "The chief activator of our defects has been self-centered fear — primarily fear that we would lose something we already possessed or would fail to get something we demanded."

[29] "Sick as I am / confused in the head / I mean I have / endured this April so far / visiting friends" (p. 428). *Garden State* was published in spring of 1992. I was already pretty far into my second book, *The Ice Storm*. I left Hoboken for good.

Zappa, Frank, Captain Beefheart and the Mothers of Invention. *Bongo Fury.* Barking Pumpkin D4-74220, 1975,[30] 1989.

---

[30]There was a time when I was an adolescent when I didn't feel like I had a dad, even though he didn't live that far away and I saw him on Sundays. This is an admission that won't please him or the rest of my family. The way I see it, though, there has never been a problem between me and my *actual* dad. But dads make the same tentative decisions we sons make. Once my father said to me, "I wonder if you kids would have turned out differently if I had been around to kick some ass." This was during one of those long car rides full of silences. The question didn't even apply to me. He might have been there, he might not have. Didn't matter. I was looking elsewhere for the secrets of ethics and home. I was looking.

ACKNOWLEDGMENTS

Some of these stories make their acknowledgments in passing, but in the cases where they do not: Yaddo, MacDowell, Charlie Smith, John Crutcher, Julia Murphy, Elizabeth Oldman, Judith Schaechter, Donald Antrim, Sandy Huss, Joe Caldwell, Robert Ogden, Jane Shapiro, Jeffrey Eugenides, Daniel Bobker, Mindy Brown, Clare Wellnitz, Laura Barnes, Jeremy Fields, Marian Berger, Bill Henderson, Elissa Schapell, Rob Spillman, Elizabeth Gaffney, George Plimpton, and, especially, Michael Pietsch, Melanie Jackson, my family, Amy Osborn, and Stacey Richter, who loaned me the camera.

THE ICE STORM

Rick Moody

Nixon and 'Nam, pet rocks and shag rugs, wife-swapping and party-hopping. Suburban New England, 1973, and the Hood family are about to wish they'd stayed home.

Acutely acerbic, painfully funny, *The Ice Storm* is an astonishing novel of the decade that taste forgot.

'One of the wittiest books about family life ever written'
Guardian

'A blackly funny and beautifully written novel . . .
[Moody] is clearly a writer to watch'
Sunday Times

'Excellent'
Time Out

Abacus
0 349 11030 1

INFINITE JEST

David Foster Wallace

'Extraordinary . . . an astonishing and vast epic of
contemporary American Culture'
Guardian

Somewhere in the not-so-distant future the residents of
Ennet House, a Boston halfway house for recovering
addicts, and students at the nearby Enfield Tennis
Academy are ensnared in the search for the master copy of
Infinite Jest, a movie said to be so dangerously entertaining
its viewers become entranced and expire in a state of
catatonic bliss . . .

'An exploding star of a novel . . . reading the book is
itself a sort of addiction . . . Wallace writes with
authority, deep feeling and caustic wit' *The Spectator*

'Ambitious, accomplished, deeply humorous, brilliant and
witty and moving. A literary sensation' *Independent*

'A remarkable satire on American entertainment and
addiction . . . Enormously readable and quite ridiculously
entertaining . . . a book of our times'
Daily Telegraph

Abacus
0 349 10877 3

Now you can order superb titles directly from Abacus

☐	The Ice Storm	Rick Moody	£6.99
☐	Infinite Jest	David Foster Wallace	£9.99
☐	Generation X	Douglas Coupland	£6.99
☐	The Big Picture	Douglas Kennedy	£5.99

Please allow for postage and packing: **Free UK delivery**.
Europe; add 25% of retail price; Rest of World; 45% of retail price.

To order any of the above or any other Abacus titles, please call our
credit card orderline or fill in this coupon and send/fax it to:

Abacus, 250 Western Avenue, London, W3 6XZ, UK.
Fax 0181 324 5678   Telephone 0181 324 5517

☐ I enclose a UK bank cheque made payable to Abacus for £ ....

☐ Please charge £.............. to my Access, Visa, Delta, Switch Card No.

☐☐☐☐☐☐☐☐☐☐☐☐☐☐☐☐☐☐☐

Expiry Date ☐☐☐☐   Switch Issue No. ☐☐

NAME (Block letters please) ....

ADDRESS ....

....

....

Postcode ....Telephone ....

Signature ....

Please allow 28 days for delivery within the UK. Offer subject to price and availability.

Please do not send any further mailings from companies carefully selected by Abacus ☐